W9-CBA-575

BAD FRUIT

BAD FRUIT

/ A NOVEL /

BY ELLA KING

ASTRA HOUSE ⋀ NEW YORK

Astra House
A Division of Astra Publishing House
astrahouse.com
Printed in the United States of America

Library of Congress Cataloging-in-Publication Data

Names: King, Ella, 1985- author.
Title: Bad fruit : a novel / by Ella King.
Description: First edition. | New York : Astra House, [2022] | Summary:
  "Bad Fruit is about the difficult, sometimes abusive, relationship
  between a mother and daughter. As the boundaries of mother love are
  crossed, universal themes of family, history, and identity help reveal
  the shattering effects of generational trauma"—Provided by publisher.
Identifiers: LCCN 2022008055 (print) | LCCN 2022008056 (ebook) |
  ISBN 9781662601491 (hardcover) | ISBN 9781662601507 (epub)
Subjects: LCSH: Mothers and daughters—Fiction. | LCGFT: Domestic fiction. |
  Novels.
Classification: LCC PR6111.I544 B33 2022 (print) | LCC PR6111.I544
  (ebook) | DDC 823/.92—dc23/eng/20220301
LC record available at https://lccn.loc.gov/2022008055
LC ebook record available at https://lccn.loc.gov/2022008056

First edition
10 9 8 7 6 5 4 3 2 1

Design by Richard Oriolo
The text is set in Bulmer MTStd.
The titles are set in Bourton Base.

To my grandmother, always

CONTENTS

BAD FRUIT

1 / THE POEMS

MAMA RUSHES AT ME AS soon as I step into the house. She is dressed exactly how she was this morning, pink pencil skirt and a matching suit jacket over a cream shirt with a pussy bow neckline, but her nose is dripping and her eye makeup has fallen, fresh graffiti run with rain. She brandishes Daddy's phone. "Did you know?" Her voice is low, dangerous.

I put on my home face, a blank, stupid thing. "Know what, Mama?"

"About the poems."

"What poems?"

"He's been sending her poems." She jabs the mobile in the direction of the living room. "Hundreds of them!"

"What do you mean? Sending *who* poems?" I say, even though I know exactly what she's talking about. Daddy's been sending poetry to my brother's ex-wife, Francie, for the past three months. Not hundreds, like Mama says, around thirty and nothing very exciting, just the usual famous lines, a bit of Frost, a bit of Keats.

"Francie!" Mama's eyes narrow, her nostrils flare. She's panting with the exertion of the fight. Or is it excitement? "Go on," she says. "Ask him. Ask him why."

Daddy appears at the living-room door, his eyes fixed on the carpet. Mama shoves me in front of him. "Tell your daughter why."

Daddy doesn't look at me. He's dressed shabbily. As a consultant forensic pathologist, he's unwittingly spread shabbiness throughout the department so that, over time, ruffled hair and creased shirts have become badges of minds on higher things—ligature marks, a bone from the North Sea, abdominal hemorrhage from blunt force trauma. Today is no exception; one wing of Daddy's shirt collar is tucked into his jumper, the other sticks out like a puppy's ear, but there are signs in his appearance that trip the alarm. His socked feet are surrounded by pathology journals unimaginatively used as ammunition, his jumper is plucked up and there are three diagonal marks across his jaw—has she scratched him? Daddy puts his fists in his hair, blond strands static against his skin. "Lily doesn't need to be involved."

"You're not covering this up, Charlie. Everyone is going to know, everyone. Tell her why."

"I . . . I felt sorry for her. Jacob treated her so badly, and she's doing such a good job with the twins that I thought someone should admire her, you know?" His green eyes flick up at me, pleading. For what? For understanding?

"He won't admit it in front of you, but he's in love with her. Your father is in love with his daughter-in-law. And you know what, Lily? Let me tell you something, about men, about your father. Do you know what they do with messages from women? They MAS-TUR-BATE over them."

Behind Mama's rage, there's triumph, her lips quiver with it, she almost smiles. She presses her victory home. "How would you like Francie to be your stepmother? Leo and Albie can be your brothers. Right, Charlie? That's your dream, to marry Francie?"

"I've never thought about that."

"Well, she's available. Because she broke up with your son!"

I see an in—Mama is flagging, struggling to think of new taunts and humiliations. If I catch her on this ebb, there's a chance of some letup this evening. Otherwise, she'll maraud about the house until something else stokes her rage.

I wipe her tearstained face. "Poor Mama," I say gently.

She throws herself on my shoulder and weeps. I stroke her hair, my fingers threading through the lengths. At fifty-four, Mama's black hair is now hard and brittle, dulled with dust motes. I hold her so close I can see the strands pushing out of her scalp.

The sobbing slows, and I untangle her and turn her toward the stairs. "Why don't you have a bath, Mama? It'll be good for your joints. I'll bring you some dinner."

"And some juice," she murmurs. "Make sure it's the kind I like. Make sure." She presses her fingers into my forearm, hard. If she could, she would imprint what she wants right into my skin.

THE KIND OF juice Mama likes is juice past its use-by date. She likes the fizz in it, the sour tang. I would have been fine with this if she kept it to herself. But Mama can't be alone in anything, and with the juice, someone has to taste it to make sure it hovers in that sliver of perfection between expired and putrid. Each night, I stare into the plughole, my chrome oracle, and ask the same question—is it better to like expired juice or not? Some days, I wish I liked it, just to make up for the amount of gagging I do. On days when I'm stronger, I'm pleased I don't. My body, succumbed to this madness for so long, has drawn a line in the sand.

To reduce my nightly swills at the kitchen sink, I experimented extensively with the juice. I was quite methodical about it, scribbling down with scientific precision what Mama considered her perfect drink to be. Orange juice—two days. Blood orange juice—three days. Grape juice—a surprising five days after its use-by date. Once I established this, I tried freezing it. But defrosting was a problem; it never defrosted to the right temperature—too warm or too icy. Mama would take one sip, look at me as if I'd betrayed her, and throw it down the sink.

Then I discovered a bigger problem. Even with juice the right number of days off, there was no guarantee Mama would be happy with it unless I tasted it. She always seemed to know if I hadn't. I wondered if she could smell the absence of acid on my breath when I gave her the untasted glass, or if there was just something about me hating it that made it taste better.

So here I am again, standing at the fridge door, my tongue clinging to the roof of my mouth. Blood orange juice, three days off. I try it, gag, and spit it down the plughole. Perfect.

Mama's bedroom suffers from an excess of femininity. An enormous king-size bed with lavender sateen pillows claims the center, magnified by mirrored wardrobes. To the right of the bed, there's a peach velvet window seat, to its left is Mama's en suite bathroom in a bright, sorbet pink. The window seat is covered with teddy bears of all sizes, squeezed together so tightly they bounce off the velvet. The wardrobes, four of them, overflow with pink and purple bags, belts, shoes, clothes.

Mama is on her bed in her underwear, silk shirt pooling on the floor. She's hugging Sapphire, a giant brown bear with a blue bow. Scars ribbon her arms, not self-harm (she'd hurt someone else over hurting herself) but from a car accident when she was a child. She squeezes the bear. The scars twist.

"I'm so humiliated. He's humiliated me."

I set down the juice and swallow my frustration. What would her clients think if they saw her now—burying her nose into a teddy's fur, repositioning its arms? Would they request another partner at Regent's Park Wealth Management, withdraw the hundreds of thousands of pounds they've asked her to invest? Or would it make no difference at all?

I try to inch Sapphire from her, but she resists, sinking down onto her side and pulling a quilt over her head. It's her favorite, an antique. Vermilion peonies have been embroidered on taupe silk and in between the flowers are phoenixes with navy feathers. "Forbidden stitches," the antique dealer had told her, his eyes landing momentarily on me. "Little girls went blind sewing this." Mama bought it on the spot.

"Why would he do this?"

"It's just poetry." I rub her shoulder through the quilt. "Maybe he was trying to cheer her up."

Mama doesn't buy it. "He did the same thing to me in the beginning, pretending to be interested in what I was interested in. That's how he pulls women in. Everyone thinks he's so nice, but he's heartless. Why else does someone become a pathologist?"

These rants about Daddy aren't new. He's cold, he's heartless, he's dead inside, if he'd been a "real doctor" he'd make more money, he travels too much, he's been called away, to a crime scene, to the police station, to court.

"No one's on my side. Everyone's on his side, all the time."

"I'm on your side."

"You get on so well with him." One eye glares at me from under the quilt. "You read together on the sofa in the evenings."

My mouth goes dry. I'm used to this sifting of loyalties, the leading questions, but Mama has a terrifying ability to extrapolate fully formed theories from the tiniest act. I slip my thumbnail between two rows of tiny, round stitches. "We just read. We don't talk. Not like you and I do."

"OK." She emerges from the quilt and holds my face in her hands. "Because you're my favorite, Lily. You and I are the same."

"I know, Mama. That's why I'm here. Looking after you."

"You *do* love me, don't you, Lily?"

"Yes, Mama." And because I'm exhausted and I know it will work, I say, "And Sapphire loves you too, and all the teddy bears love you. That's all you need."

She beams, a child hearing the end of a fairy tale. She sips the juice and sighs with relief. "You always make me feel better, do you know that?"

I nail a smile to my face.

I SETTLE MAMA down with a TV dinner and break away to the attic. Mama wanted me to move into Julia's room after she left for university, but I didn't want to. That side of the house faced the back garden—the slow, windy footpath under the fruit trees, the derelict shed, and beyond that, the dell, where in the evenings, the roar of boys drinking carried across the lawn. So I put Mama off, observing that a better use of Julia's room would be storage for Mama's extra clothes. The room filled quickly, and I remained happily alone at the top of the house.

I can still hear the noises of the house in the attic—the static hum of the television, the clink of cutlery against plate—but the relief of being away from my family, above them, is so intense it almost hurts. Even so, I need more. I pad over to the northeast section of the attic, prize up the three floorboards, and climb inside.

The attic contains things I'm supposed to like, an armoire of pink and purple clothes, a dressing table filled with makeup and hair dye, a French bed with baby-pink sateen sheets, but really, nothing I care about is visible, nothing that would hurt if it was taken away. I'm not there.

Here is where I keep me, in this hole under the floorboards. I made this space after I moved to the attic when I was eight; it took weeks to find a cardboard box that would fit perfectly. I painted the sides a deep indigo, but now you can barely see the blue under my prodigious graffiti. Sophisticated, recent me likes to scribble bits of poetry, but layered underneath are ten years' worth of other things—vendettas and vows, memories and childish doodles, postcards and photos.

I switch on the fairy lights and wait for my heartbeat to slow at the sight of my bomb-shelter spoils. Here are all the books Daddy ever bought me, £20 notes pressed into their covers. Here is my etymology dictionary and a silver, sparkly hair tie. Here is my jar of Japanese paper stars and my drift glass collection, next to the hand mirror from Julia.

I hold up the mirror, push my face against the glass. My reflection is as expected: dark brown eyes, black hair, skin shiny from cooking.

Usually, I linger over this Chinese version of me, trace her eyes, her hair, ask her, *What have you done today, Mama's girl, what have you done?* But I'm not in the mood for exquisite self-harm. I reach for my pack of wipes, scrub off the yellow-undertoned makeup, sweep out the tinted contact lenses, and look again. White skin. One hazel eye. One brown. My hair is still that cheap black, but when I examine my hairline, the brown is already pushing through.

I sit back, relieved. Despite everything Mama has done to bring out the Chinese in me, I remain resolutely myself, her whitest child.

I'm not the same as her.

It's my eyes that calm me more than my skin or hair, the mismatched pair dissolving the tight pit in my stomach. What my father called *heterochromia iridis.* What Julia called my freak eyes. And Mama? She called them *ang moh gui* eyes, white devil eyes, eyes that in Singapore, I would have been drowned for. My life then, a favor bestowed by a mother who loves too much.

Yet here they are, beneath the thinnest circle of brown plastic, reminding me that just once in my life, I'd like to do something worthy of drowning.

Mama calls up to me. "Lily?"

In my fist, the lenses curl.

"Lily? More juice." She asks so sweetly, it could be a song.

2 / TARTS

'M ON A SWING IN a forest of silver birches. There's slack in the rope
so I kick my legs out on the way up, just like Jacob taught me, rolling
my body back through the ascent. Wind lashes against my calves. I
think it's going to rain, but I don't care—I want to go higher. Back and
forth, back and forth, I gather momentum until at the highest point,
I'm soaring, I can do anything, touch anything—the curled bark, the
crushed-mussel shell sky. But when I open my eyes, only the sky is
real, a square of mauve framed by the roof window. I stretch my arms
over my head and sit up. Just once, I'd like it to be the other way round.
That the swing and the forest are real, and this is the dream.

The morning light is soft against the French armoire, the makeup
table, the foot of the Parisian double bed. None of the furniture is
mine. It's Julia's, bartered from Mama in exchange for good grades,
good behavior. Julia gave them to me when she left for university; she
likes to give me things when she leaves me behind.

I'd always shared a room with Julia until I caught a bug that made
me so ill, she complained: "I can't sleep, it's affecting my schoolwork.
She needs to move out." I was eight, she was eleven and had just started
her first year of senior school. Mama agreed. The whole family came
together to help me move to the attic. Mama gave me some money for
paint; Daddy sanded down the floorboards; Jacob and Julia helped
scrub and clean. No one wanted to sort through the inheritances of
paintings and encyclopedias, the racks of old clothes and boxes, so I
asked Jacob to push them into the sloped recesses, hide them under

black cloth. When it was finished, Mama congratulated my decorating skills, but now I wonder if my talent was really for disguise. Sleight of hand, tricking the eye, drawing this into shadows, shifting that into the light—those were my gifts until no one saw the strangeness of living on the outskirts of my family's possessions, of floating in a French boudoir in the middle of a souk.

Mama's alarm sounds from downstairs. I click into action. My mind flips through possible outfits while I'm in the bathroom and when I'm back in the attic, I know what I'll wear, Mama's team colors— jeans and something pink. Jacob's old university sweatshirt, my favorite thing when I'm absolutely alone, beckons to me from Julia's armoire. I shut the door on it and pull on a pink shirt. Today isn't a day I can wear sweatshirts and leggings. I must be perfect.

I know exactly who to be when Mama gets like this. Fights with Daddy are rare—this one about the poems is as serious as it gets—but Mama fighting is not. She loves to fight, she gets paid to fight, she fights with Julia all the time. I thought it would stop when Julia left for university, but Mama is still paying her rent and tuition fees and likes to wield it over her. With my brother, Jacob, it's different. They don't fight because he lets her say what she wants, she calls him every day to "catch up," otherwise known as berating him for every instance in his day where he's failed, every opportunity he's squandered.

I'm putting on my makeup when I hear the attic stairs, then a knock—Daddy? I swallow my surprise; he hasn't been to the attic in years. The garden has long been abandoned to him but inside the house, his territory measures a half-meter radius around his easy chair where he sleeps, eats, reads, walled off from the rest of the living room by waist-high columns of the *Journal of Forensic Sciences* and *The American Journal of Forensic Medicine and Pathology*. Those won't survive the next few days. Incursions have already been made: the scattered journals I saw yesterday, rubble from Mama's shelling, her evening strikes.

"Hi." Threads from the bottom of his brown gardening trousers trail over his socks, and his hands flutter around him as if they're lost. "Listen, Lily, I'm sorry about all of that. I mean yesterday."

"For the poems?"

He nods.

I shrug. Mama knows about the poems, but she doesn't know about the porn. If she'd kept tabs on Daddy's little collection, she could have chronicled his obsession in pixelated print. It was always Asian—he was faithful to Mama like that, but five years ago, the images shifted from plump women with blooming pubic hair to thinner, shaved twenty-year-olds, their vaginas prized open like oysters. Then, one month ago, a new image appeared in the wipe-downable plastic wallet of Daddy's ring binder. A photo of Francie in a green bikini, my two-year-old nephews eliminated into cutouts.

"And for the fight with your mother," he adds quickly.

This is interesting. Daddy has never acknowledged that there's anything wrong between him and Mama. For a second, I consider reaching across the Mama between us and talking to him, just to feel what it would be like to be on another side, for there to be another side. I would say I understand. I would tell him to leave her. But Mama's timing is impeccable. Water gurgles in the pipes beneath us. Daddy blinks. I shake my head. It's too late for new allegiances, and he is too fledgling an ally.

"Lily, I—" he starts.

"You don't have to explain."

"Lily—"

"I'll see you downstairs."

"I wanted to say—"

"—I don't want to talk to you about this, Daddy. Not without Mama." It comes out a hiss.

His face crumples in on itself. For a moment, I think he might cry.

I change tack and play nice. "It's just that you haven't got long. You've got half an hour at most before she starts again."

His eyes flick from the tube of foundation to my bare face and then he looks away, ashamed, as if he's seen me without clothes on. I dig my nails into my palms. *What?* I want to ask. *You know about this.* He squints at me as if to locate the daughter he wants in the daughter I am, but we both know she's not there. I turn my back to him and put on my Mama-face.

THE ORIENTAL SUPERMARKET in Greenwich looks, from the outside, like a dodgy used-car outfit. Set in the middle of a concrete car park, it's surrounded by a high metal fence strung with spikes that, instead of guarding secondhand cars, protects lines of sticky-wheeled trolleys and delivery lorries emblazoned in lucky calligraphy red. The only sign that it's Asian are the two giant golden cats flanking the sliding doors, their paws mechanically beckoning us in. We step into the supermarket and are blasted by a wave of air-conditioning—freezing, stale, smelling like dried goods. Mama, hypersensitive to temperature changes, zips up her pink hoodie.

We're shopping for food for my eighteenth birthday dinner. Mama likes to cook at least one Asian dish for our birthdays, although I don't let her do it alone; she's actually a pretty bad cook. We each have our theories about the birthday cooking. Jacob says it's the one day of the year Mama shows she loves us. Julia says it's to torture us. I don't think it's about us at all. Birthdays are an opportunity for Mama to prove she's a perfect Asian mother, despite her utter failure to keep house any other day of the year.

The timing, however, is dangerous. The dinner will be less about how great Mama is, and more about the poems. She's already told me she's going to find out "if that little whore's been plotting against me. Who knew what."

I told Julia about Daddy and Francie over two months ago. It was the change in evening sounds that alerted me—the tapping of keys from Daddy's laptop instead of the flick of pages. I braced myself, hacking into his account, prepared for a dating website, even an escort agency, but not for "top 100 poems," "top 100 love poems," "poems about love and passion," "100 favourite love poems of Britain." It took two minutes to determine he'd sent the poems to Francie, another five to convene Julia on a video call. The decision to do nothing was unanimous. We comforted ourselves with conflicting platitudes—*it's nothing, it'll burn out*—never daring to consider the fallout if Jacob found out, if Mama did. Who knew what? We've both known. We're both guilty.

Daddy insisted on driving us to the supermarket despite Mama's protests. "For Lily. Let's go together for her." I tried to ward him off, but he refused to meet my eyes, climbing into the car and turning on the ignition before Mama and I were out of the front door. His new play is to act as if everything is back to normal, better even, as if after an evening of Mama's wrath, he's learned to be a considerate husband, a loving father. He's the same in the supermarket, nodding to the K-pop blasting through the loudspeakers, lagging behind us to consider this jar or that packet, brazenly putting items in the trolley. Every time Mama hears an item clang against the trolley bars, she clamps her teeth together.

She's chosen to make pineapple tarts for my birthday, but she isn't shopping for ingredients. She drifts through the supermarket, landing on anything that takes her fancy—an enormous bunch of rambutans, a tin of white rabbit candies, frozen pork buns. In the snack aisle, she goes wild, throwing in Japanese rice crackers, sheets of roasted seaweed, mini fried prawn rolls. The dried squid is a new low, sheaves of desiccated orange rolled into tight cylinders and heavily sugared. Mama rips open a packet with her teeth and pops three into her mouth. The smell of the sweet fish mingled with her crunching turns my stomach. I ask if I should fetch the ingredients for the tarts. She nods. The aisles are suddenly broad and open, invitations to elsewhere. I check my watch to make sure I'm not away for too long; I could get lost in this kind of freedom. I wonder how much time I have.

Turns out, one minute and thirty-two seconds. A scream peals through the supermarket. My rucksack slams into my back as I run toward it. Mama and Daddy haven't moved from the snack aisle but, in less than two minutes, there are already marked differences: the aisle is two deep with open-mouthed shoppers; the spine of a Kit Kat chocolate multipack is scrunched under the front wheel of the trolley; black bean sauce glugs from the shell of a jar. Mama stands with her legs hip-width apart, bouncing slightly, holding a glass bottle of cola wrenched from a cardboard four-pack. She rotates her shoulder, extends her arm back, and pitches. The bottle cuts an arc through the air before shattering at Daddy's feet, the top skittering across the floor, the contents spuming up and drenching his gardening trousers. "You think you can tell me what to do? What to eat? Why don't you go to your whore? Take your shopping with you!"

A shop assistant approaches Mama, pleading for her in Mandarin to stop. Mama rounds on her. "You know what he's doing? He's masturbating over his daughter-in-law. My son's ex-wife!" The shop assistant confesses that she doesn't speak English, so Mama sums up my father's transgressions in one, unmistakable phrase. "*Hum sup gui*, horny devil!" For effect, she grabs a tin of tomatoes from the trolley and jerks her hips backward and forward over it. She is enjoying the supplicative hands of the shop assistant, the appalled stares of onlookers, until a click distracts her from her canned phallus—some jackass has taken a photo. Mama blinks. This is my moment.

"Mama!" I shout to shock her. I wait until her gaze turns from Daddy to me, and then I launch myself at her, hugging her tightly, one arm flung around her middle, the other across her back. She drops the tin of tomatoes. Her heart thunders against my ribs, a pair with my own, both storming in their separate cages and then quieting together, but I don't let her go. I turn to look back at Daddy, clutching the shelf. "Go. Don't take the car." He nods, and then he's gone. The crowd, more interested in displays of insanity than its management, dissipates with him.

"He tried to stop me," she says, her lower lip trembling, "from eating before the tills."

"He shouldn't have done that, Mama."

"I was hungry. I was going to pay for it."

"That's fine, Mama."

"As if he's better than me. He's not! He's not!" She shovels strands of damp hair away from her face.

"No, Mama. He's not. You can eat whatever you want." Her body is slack against mine, so I release her, but her breath is still ragged. "What would make you feel better? More squid? A cracker?' I open a packet of rice crackers and hold up a caramel-colored circle so the glaze catches the strip light—a cheap trick but it works. She crams it into her mouth. The slab of her arm judders. I'm responsible for those arms, for the roll that overhangs her leggings, for the thickened underside of her neck. I imagine all the food and drink I've plied her with lined up in front of me—trollies of snacks, barrels of spoilt juice— and I know I'm a bad person, that there is something coiled and rotten in me, because I don't regret a single cracker. I would buy this peace over and over.

Her focus shifts to me after five crackers, eyes roving to my hands. "What happened to the ingredients for the tarts?"

Careful now, careful. I didn't get any ingredients; I didn't even pick up a basket. I just stared at the baking products until I heard Mama. I put on my innocent/stupid face. "I dropped them when I came for you. When I heard you scream."

"You came for me?"

"I came for you, Mama. I'll always come for you."

The tears come then and I'm thankful, she's much more manageable sad. I hold her in my arms. When we come apart, she touches the side of my arm. "You're freezing. This supermarket is always so cold. Wear this." She pulls the hoodie off the trolley seat and opens it over my shoulders, like a cloak. It smells like her, masculine scents of leather, musk, and sandalwood. I bury my nose into the shoulder. Mama used to wear this beautiful navy coat with a shearling lining in the winter; sometimes, she'd open it and let me into the fur.

"What about you?" I ask. "You'll be cold."

She slips her arm into mine. "You're my daughter. There's no question."

I sink into Mama's hood as we walk to the till. She bought the hoodie from a yoga boutique in the village, pretending to the shop assistant she'd started classes, asking for tips. I nodded along even though it was one of her pointless lies—she's never exercised in her life. The only time I've seen Mama engaged in any kind of sport was today when she took aim at my father. Holding that bottle of cola, she had the absolute focus of an athlete with a discus, a shot put. A javelin.

AUTUMN TERM AT Oxford University doesn't start until the beginning of October, eight weeks away. Eight weeks of apologizing to store managers for fights I didn't start, of avoiding the pitying stares of shop assistants, of enduring car journeys like this one, Mama's drama purring above the sound of the engine. I close my eyes and imagine myself crossing at the lights in front of us, glancing through the windshield at a Chinese woman reclipping her hair and a girl pressing her fingers to her lips. They are no one to me. No one but strangers.

In the kitchen, Mama starts mixing the ingredients for pineapple tarts before I can measure them out, hacking chunks of butter, pouring in flour and icing sugar. Raw egg slides down the outside of the mixing bowl and pools on the counter. Mama slops it back and takes up the whisk. "When I was a little girl, I didn't use electric mixers or cookie cutters. There was no premade jam." She catches me checking the recipe on my phone and snatches it away. "I knew the recipe by heart. I made the jam myself. It showed you were from a good family. My father said the matchmaker was outside listening for the sounds of cooking in the kitchen—chopping, pounding spices, gossip. He said if I didn't learn to cook, I would never find a good husband." She inhales. "Tell me, was he right?"

"Why don't we pretend to be real *nyonyas,* Peranakan girls?" Playing *nyonyas* is one of Mama's favorite games. She's Chinese Peranakan, an ethnic group originating from the rumbles of Chinese traders and indigenous Malays, with its own distinctive creole, ceramics, and food. Mama's frittered away whole weekends telling me stories from her childhood while we recreate elaborate Peranakan desserts—*kueh lapis, tu tu kueh, sugee* butter cookies. Even these pineapple tarts can kill hours. Without cookie cutters, each flower and dough lattice needs to be individually shaped, trebling the preparation time. Time she isn't at Daddy's throat. "We don't need cookie cutters," I say brightly. "We can do it all ourselves."

"Takes too long. If we were going to do it properly, we should have started days ago." She throws herself into a chair after kneading the dough and massages her palms.

I climb onto the kitchen counter to get the box of cookie cutters. On top of the cabinets is Mama's *tingkat* collection—rows of jewel-bright tiffin carriers, the tiers fastened together with catches on either side of the handles. Most have four layers—the top for curry or sauce, the bottom for rice, the middle for vegetables and meat. Mama buys them for hundreds of pounds from Singaporean antique dealers every year, preferring the ones with positive affirmations, *slamat pakkey*, happy using, *slamat angkat*, happy carrying, *slamat makan*, happy eating.

"Bring that one down, we can put the tarts in it," Mama says, and I know which one she means. It's the porcelain *tingkat*, three tiers with a snowy white background and Delft blue flowers, the handle and catches pure gold. It belonged to my great-grandmother, one of the few things that wasn't sold after her parents died in the car accident. She says it's worth thousands.

"Careful!" she gasps as the ceramic lid scrapes across the top layer. The sudden metal in her voice startles me; I flinch.

She snatches the *tingkat* from me before my feet are on the floor, hugging it to her chest before separating the layers. The faraway look in her eyes reminds me to deploy a familiar tactic. She's lost in some memory of her emerald shophouse, her wealthy family. If I can keep her there, we might be able to make it through this afternoon without mentioning Daddy once. "What was it like cooking in your kitchen? I bet it wasn't like ours. I remember when we went to see your emerald house, it was beautiful."

Mama runs the cloth along the handle of the *tingkat* and smiles. "In my house, the kitchen was just beyond the courtyard. It wasn't closed between four walls like this," and even at seventeen, I'm caught up in her alchemy again, her strange power to vanish the red metro tiles and black stools and to conjure up something else. "It was open on one side, straight onto the skywell. In monsoon season, the skywell held the rain and cooled the house, but in the dry season, the jeweler would set up his trestle table in the courtyard and show us what he could make."

I want to shut my eyes and lie down, but I force myself to focus. This landscape, devastatingly lavish, is riddled with mines—how loving my grandfather was compared to Daddy, how wealthy her family was compared to ours. I sprinkle more flour onto the rolling pin and keep her focused. "What was the kitchen like?"

"Much nicer than the one in the blue house." We visit the emerald house in Singapore every year. We can't look inside, it's privately owned, but we always visit the other Peranakan shophouse painted ultramarine that's open to the public. "Ours had many more things. Meat safes hanging from hooks to keep meat fresh, *lesong batu*, mortar and pestle for pounding *belachan*, shrimp paste, *batu boh*, granite mills to grind rice into rice flour. We even had an ice-cream maker." She inspects her work against the light.

"An ice-cream maker?" Mama hasn't mentioned she had an ice-cream maker before. "How did it work?"

She glances up from the *tingkat*. "Why haven't you made any flowers?"

I push a cookie cutter into the dough but when I pop out a flower, the petals crumble—something's wrong with Mama's recipe. I want to add another egg but her eyes track me. I cobble the pieces together and keep her talking. "Tell me about the *tingkats*."

Mama starts drying the layers. "My grandmother's collection. She had a whole cabinet full, many more porcelain ones like this one." She pauses and takes off her glasses. "I wish I'd kept more of them, not sold so many. I'm always looking for those *tingkats*. What if I see them and don't recognize them?"

I brush the flour off my hands and put an arm around her. "You will. You can't feel guilty about selling them. You had no choice; you were all alone." Mama was my age when her family was in a car accident. She broke her leg. Her parents died.

"I still feel alone."

At work, they call her "The Pink Bitch," because she's impossible, combative, a calculating careerist; she's exactly the same at home. But rarely, perhaps only with me, she cracks open and someone very different peers through: an aging woman on the edge of self-sabotage, waiting for someone to pull her back. And I do. I take her hand. "You're not alone. You've got me."

"I'm not a traditional *nyonya*. I didn't do what my father wanted me to do. I should've married a man who could take care of me, instead of me looking after him. I shouldn't have spent so much time away from home. Maybe it's my fault, what your father did—"

"—Stop it." I squeeze her wrists. "It's not true."

She sinks heavily into my shoulder, her chin pressing into my clavicle, but I don't edge her off even though it hurts. I let her stare out into the garden. It's the beginning of August. Sweet peas bloom under pear and apple trees, but no flower or fruit is enough to stifle the shadows thrown by the sprawling oaks of the dell beyond. Closer to the house, a garden swing rusts under a tarp, and just beyond the garden gate is the shed. I called it our oubliette, from the French *oublier*, "to forget," our family's forgotten dungeon, because it was overrun with ivy, the dingy window a hatch. This summer, Daddy's started putting my bike in the shed to protect it from the storms, even though I tell him not to. Now, the door is unlatched, and it swings open like the innards of a beast—Daddy's gardening tools, the deck chairs darkly visible, and then an image flickers in my mind, not frightening in itself, although I'm frightened.

Milk spreading between toes.

My heart is racing, my lungs powerless to fill or dispel air. I break away from Mama, plaster myself against the kitchen wall.

Her hand is against my forehead, her voice comes to me from a distance. "Are you OK? What's wrong?"

"I can't breathe."

She runs a tap, puts a wet dishcloth over my forehead. Water drips over my shoulders. I shut my eyes, press my hand to my heart.

3 / BIRTHDAY

BIRTHDAYS ARE LIKE CHRISTMAS, ALL family and hugs and disaster lapping at the presents. The table is elaborately set for dinner—cut crystal glasses, cyan Peranakan plates, silver cutlery carved with phoenixes. Mama said I wasn't to lift a finger on my birthday, especially after feeling unwell, but Daddy didn't know where anything was, so when she went upstairs to get dressed, I laid everything out exactly as she liked. Daddy caught me folding the napkins, face like a demolished building. I put a finger to my lips.

Mama blames Daddy for my "dizzy spell." "Too worried about me, too worried about your father," she said rubbing circles over my back as we waited for me to catch my breath. "You mustn't do that. Mama's going to sort it out." She sent me to bed, which helped; I did feel better. But not well enough for this dinner.

Mama's pièce de résistance is the seating plan. The dining table seats six, but she's asked her friend, Jonathan, to play Watson to her Holmes, so there are nine of us—Daddy, Francie, the twins Leo and Albie, and Jacob on one side, and Mama, Jonathan, Julia, and me on the other. The squeeze plays in Mama's favor, intensifying the silence between Daddy and Jacob and the squabbling between the twins, which wears Francie so thin, she appeals, unsuccessfully, to Jacob for help. Daddy, Julia, or I would usually step in, but not today. None of us move.

Francie's outfit doesn't help. She's wearing an off-shoulder black top and gold tassel earrings that flatter her collar bones but snarl around her hair so that she is in a constant state of perfecting her appearance, which, of course, draws attention to it. Mama took one look at her and asked if she wouldn't mind sitting in the extra chair, a deck chair Daddy dragged in from the shed. Francie agreed without the slightest hint of being set up. The result is that to Mama, Jonathan, Julia, and me on the other side of the table, Francie looks deliberately, decoratively naked. Mama was always going to play judge and jury. But it shouldn't be this easy.

She starts before birthday cake and pineapple tarts. Leo is stuffing peas down Albie's trousers, and Albie, smaller, less boisterous, is on the brink of tears. "I think Leo's finished his dinner, don't you? Jonathan, help Leo down." The command, designed to humiliate Francie, doesn't have the desired effect. As soon as Jonathan lifts Leo out of his high chair, Francie sighs with relief. She places a hand on Jonathan's arm and mouths a "thank you." Mama glares at the impression of Francie's fingers on Jonathan's shirt and ratchets it up a notch: "I always thought Jonathan would make the best husband, the best father."

Jonathan blushes. He's Mama's "best friend"; they met while she was studying for her master's. Since then, he's come to every family event—birthdays, Christmases, New Years, and never says a word, just grins and does exactly what Mama tells him to. Mama says he's her type, a more "obedient" version of Daddy—single, introverted, too shy for girlfriends, well paid from writing code. Whether Mama is actually sleeping with him is a matter of constant debate. Jacob thinks he isn't with Mama for her scintillating conversation. I think he's asexual, completely uninterested in Mama or anyone else. Julia agrees that Jonathan isn't a viable option, but not because he's asexual, because he's gay.

"Always so considerate, so loyal, don't you think, Francie?" Mama swirls spoilt juice in her glass as if she's circling prey. She's overdressed for a family dinner in a black *sarong kebaya* and *intan* diamond flower earrings. The fact that she's wearing black is enough to make me dizzy with panic, but she's also swapped her pink lipstick for a dark red that tears against her foundation like a slashed throat. "Fuck, Lil," whispered Julia when she saw Mama. "She's worse than I thought."

"Did you tell Jacob about the poems?" I whispered back. I told Julia that Mama had found out, and she was supposed to break the news to him.

She nodded.

"Did he tell Francie?"

Julia glanced at Francie smiling at Mama. "Doesn't look like it. Ready for a storm?"

But Francie isn't schooled in forecasting Mama's weather. From the minute their shotgun wedding was announced, we shielded her from how bad Mama could get, inventing excuses for why she can't come to the boys' events, diverting her from seeing the boys when she was in one of her moods. So it is, in part, our fault that Francie is distracted by Albie pulling at her earrings and Leo ramming his lorry against the table legs. She hasn't realized the threat until she looks up and sees Mama staring: "Sorry, May, did you say something?" She purses her lips.

Mama punishes her just for that, for the pretty twist of her mouth. "Let's play a game, shall we? Just a little bit of fun."

Is it "game" or "fun" that blares the sirens? Perhaps it's "a little bit" because what's coming is not little but a deluge, a flash flood—blink and you'll drown. Daddy sits upright. Jacob clenches his jaw. Julia looks up from her phone. I grip the dining table as if it's a life raft, but it's just wreckage, a plank of a ship before it explodes.

"A question for the girls. Hypothetically, who would you marry out of Charlie, Jacob, and Jonathan?"

"Our cue to leave!" announces Daddy. "Jacob and I will get the cake."

Jacob shakes his head. Never the white knight, he saves his sons but not his ex-wife. "Actually, I need to check on something for work. The twins can help you." They file out. The dining room door closes.

"Come on, Francie, you first," says Mama, smiling.

Slowly, it dawns on Francie that she has been abandoned. She stares after the forms of Albie and Leo, willing them to come back. "I don't really know, May."

"Interesting," says Mama, cocking her head. "So you won't say." She slides me a knowing glance. This moment, the point of Francie's resistance, will occupy her for days.

"It's just not . . ." Francie starts, her earrings agitated birds rustling against her collarbones ". . . an appropriate question."

"What do you have to hide?"

"What?"

"It's just a game. Just for fun. Why won't you play? Lily and Julia would play, no problem. Lily, you go first. Francie can be such a spoilsport."

I keep my eyes fixed on my knuckles, the rips in my cuticles. "Jonathan, of course. He'd make such a good husband." Jonathan emits a high-pitched squeak.

"Why do you think Jonathan would be such a good husband?" says Julia.

She's beautiful, my sister. Jacob looks the most like Mama, the most Chinese, and I look most like Daddy, but Julia is an arresting combination of both. Tall and slender, she has Daddy's pale skin and pointed nose with Mama's dark features. Even now, dressed in her old, school sweatpants, lazily separating last night's smudged eyelashes with her index finger, my sister could turn heads, but beauty is not a good thing in our house. In more ways than one, Julia's had it worse than any of us, and it makes her unpredictable, brittle, likely to snap. She raises her glass, a toast to me, to Mama, I can't tell, except I know what Julia we're about to see. The Molotov cocktail Julia. The improvised incendiary weapon.

"Don't get me wrong, Lil, I agree with you. I just think it deserves more . . . explanation," she drawls. She swallows three inches of liquid and slams her glass down. It's almost certainly gin. "He can certainly provide, make a secure home."

"That's true," says Mama, approvingly.

Jonathan is sitting slightly back from the table. Julia drags her chair in line with his. She loops her arm companionably through his. "And then there's his looks."

Mama's smile wipes from her face. "Stop it."

She doesn't. She leans towards Jonathan and kisses his cheek. Jonathan squeaks.

"Julia!" erupts Mama. She stands up and slams her hand against the dining table. The cutlery jumps. "Why are you such a whore?"

Julia's eyes are flicked blades. "Oh, I don't know, Mama. Like mother, like daughter, I suppose." She steps her fingers slowly, deliberately along Jonathan's leg. Mama starts screaming while Jonathan defends his territory, hairless hands pattering against my sister's moves. Julia rears back, laughing. "I knew it. No reaction. Here, Lil, have a birthday kiss, see if you can get a rise." She shoves my head and Jonathan's together. My skull meets his jaw. "Perhaps not a good trade-up, Francie. Or is it Mama that wants to know?" She smiles sweetly at Mama, who levers back the dining room table and climbs over Jonathan to reach her. "I get confused with all our little games."

The force of Mama's slap sends Julia off the chair. In the midst of Mama's insults ("Worthless, nothing, whore, everything you have is mine, you hear me, everything you have is mine"), Julia fixes her lipstick but not her smirk.

"Happy birthday to you, happy birthday to you—" sing Daddy and the boys. They freeze at the sight of the upturned chair, Julia on the floor, Mama looming over her. Francie pulls the twins out of the room. I escape to the attic.

JULIA'S COMING; I hear her on the stairs. I pretend to be tidying my room.

She steps inside, her eyes sweeping over her furniture, the cobwebbed beams, the bare lightbulb. "I forgot what this place is like," she says in a hushed, reverent whisper. She strokes her dressing table with one finger and then draws back quickly, as if touching it, loving it again, might bind her to us like a curse. She opens her armoire and flicks through the clothes, pulling out an old pair of jeans, a T-shirt.

I wrench them out of her hands.

Julia laughs, chipped nail-polished fingers pressing against her heart. "Let it out, Lil, it's about time you grew a backbone. What do you want to do, call me a whore, slap me around too? Here, have this side." She twirls her hair back into a makeshift bun so that her jawline is exposed. Under her skin, her veins pulse. "The other side's a little red, I'm afraid."

The jerk of her chin deflates me. She's always been a good sister: she got me dressed, cuddled me, read me stories, except when it comes to one thing—our mother. When Mama gets to Julia, a trigger pulls in her brain and in that split second, she'd shoot Jacob or me as long as the bullet hits Mama too. The last couple of months, she's only become worse, all our conversations are sparring matches where she is attacking and I'm defending. A headache falls over me like a shroud. I slump on the bed. "How many times do I have to tell you? Don't involve me in your games."

"All right, all right, it got a little out of hand." She sits next to me. "Mama's too easy to fuck with, especially with all this Daddy–Francie shit. And Jonathan. Dangling him in front of everyone as if he's Daddy's competition. I couldn't resist." She stretches her arms out like a cat and lies down. "She's really pissing me off."

"You mean with your flat?" Mama sublet Julia's flat over the summer because Julia refused to go on holiday with her.

She nods. Her eyes are closed. I put the back of my hand on her cheek. When we shared a room, we used to do this to each other, practice tenderness. Now, the heat of the slap emanates from her skin, and she winces. "You're not a whore, Jules." Out of everything that's happened this evening, that's bothered her the most.

"Hmm . . ." She bites her lip.

"She shouldn't have done that."

"There's lots of things she shouldn't have done."

"Just tell her what she wants to hear. It's not worth it—" I lie next to her "—her doing this to you."

A smile breaks across her face and I remember that aside from being a total train wreck, Julia is the most fun out of anyone in this family. "It kind of was. I just wanted to know once and for all if he's gay."

"Just because someone isn't attracted to you doesn't mean they're gay!"

Then we're both laughing, everything shrugging off us like scales, until a knock sounds at the door. It's Jacob. "Chrissy's here."

She scrambles up. "I've got to go."

"But you only just got here." I thought it wouldn't be that bad this summer, even with the poems, because Julia would be home with me. I didn't expect to be alone. I watch her sling her handbag over her arm. "Did Mama throw you out?"

"Something like that. Doesn't matter, I'm staying with Chrissy until the sublet ends." She refuses to meet my eyes and then I know she never planned to return for the summer. She staged the scene downstairs, set a trap within a trap, but why is it me who's snared? I stare at their heels—Julia's smooth skin, Jacob's striped socks, the growing distance between us. "Wait. Mama's really bad now."

My brother slows down. My sister keeps going.

"She scratched Daddy."

That makes them turn. Because we all know the rules. Slapping Julia's one thing. Scratching Daddy is another thing entirely.

"She's lost it," says Jacob, rubbing his forehead with the back of his hand.

Julia is silent. She appraises me over the expanse of her rug. She's making a calculation, a complicated arithmetic. "You don't have to stay here. Come with me," she says. Her words are kind, but the set of her face is a challenge.

I twist the end of my sleeve around itself. "I can't leave her. Not when she's like this. I just don't want to do it alone. Can you stay? Please?"

Jacob caves, he would stay if I asked him, but he's the most fragile of us, it's not him I need. He puts his hand on Julia's arm, pleading with her on my behalf, but she won't relent. She shakes him off and speaks very slowly, very deliberately, "Either you come with me, or you stay here with her."

Courage, courage, I say to myself, but what does that mean? *Cor* is "heart" but what is *rage*? Perhaps it's what it sounds like, a fury, a madness. Am I heart mad to go or heart mad to stay? I shake my head and watch them leave, disappearing down the steps and then vanishing altogether.

I CLIMB INTO the hole. No one will come. I'm the comforter, not the comforted, and just this once, on my birthday, I'm excused. I listen to my family through the floorboards, matching the sounds that float up from downstairs with the pictures in my head: the door slamming as Julia leaves; the rising and falling tones of Jacob mollifying Mama, the staccato of Mama's rage. Nothing from Jonathan, Francie, or the boys—they must have left. Daddy's voice is absent, but he's in other sounds: the beep of the dishwasher, the click of the kitchen door as he carries the deck chair out. I imagine being right up against the chair's mottled frame, eyelashes catching against the wood, and then, suddenly, fragments flash across my brain.

> *Splinters of glass.*
> *Milk spreading between toes.*

My palms are sweating. I scramble out of the hole and yank open the skylight, gulping down the warm summer air, count *five, four, three, two, one*, over and over until my eyes focus on the slanted rooftops, the absolute dark of the park. What was that? Why am I so frightened?

4 / NELSON'S COAT

MAMA DOESN'T MENTION MY BIRTHDAY the next morning, but what Julia did is in the press of her lips, the way she shoves her arms into her suit jacket, the list she messages me the moment she shuts the front door: 1 Shop for travel insurance; 2 Renew the parking permit; 3 Tidy wardrobes.

The list isn't unusual, I don't mind helping Mama in the holidays, but item 3 signals a deep turmoil, the message of which is clear: the wildness in one area of her life must be atoned by order in another.

I rush through the chores and finish by one. I could have taken a whole day sorting her wardrobes—languorously folding her underwear into thirds, dipping in and out of podcasts—but after last night, I need to get out. The house feels too still, too threatening. Outside, Daddy has moved my bike from the shed to the front. I jump on and head to Greenwich Park.

At the gate, I tie my bike up and scan for a man, the practice calming me. It's a pleasant twenty-four degrees Celsius on an August afternoon, so the grass is teeming with them, students mostly from Greenwich University cracking open beers, lying out topless, listening to music through enormous headphones—there are even two male ballet dancers pirouetting in the shade. But I don't want any of those. He must be walking. He mustn't have children. Ideally, he should be in his thirties, but I've chosen one in his twenties before. On one rule, I'm inflexible: he must be alone.

There, to the right. He's dark-haired, broad-shouldered, a smattering of freckles across his nose. He's on a parallel path trodden into the grass that follows the eastern wall, a route you wouldn't take unless you knew the park well. He isn't on his phone. He watches for his dog who he's let off the lead—a dappled cocker that darts into bushes and emerges with a stick, a tennis ball, an empty carton of juice. I track him from the main avenue.

He's kind, he praises his dog no matter what it brings him, and he's a soft touch; every time it returns, he draws a treat out from his pocket. He'd make a good dad. Near Vanbrugh Castle, he lets an elderly couple shuffle in front of him before finding his route again. He wears a forest green T-shirt that clings to the lower nubs of his spine. I want to touch him there.

I give him a profession—architect. I see him at a drawing table crouched over a sketchpad, his fingers stained in charcoal as he translates onto the page joists and beams, the skyscrapers of his mind. He's on his lunch break. He brings the dog to work.

I glimpse the museum through the trees—it's time. I step off the main avenue, cross the grass and follow behind him, closing the gap between us—four meters, two, then one. I slip on my headphones, get out my phone, stare at the screen, then crash into his shoulder. In the collision, I touch his back, feel the slight rise of his buttock.

"Sorry, are you all right?"

I rub the side of my head, adjust my rucksack.

"I'm so sorry," he repeats, "I didn't see you there." The dog doubles back and wags its tail.

I pull my headphones out of my ears. "No worries. It's my fault, I wasn't paying attention."

He smiles. I smile back.

Where the path intersects with the main avenue, he follows it down to the playground and I hang a left to the museum. His lips pucker into a whistle. There he goes. My one touch of the day.

THE EXHILARATION FADES quickly; by the time I'm down the hill, I'm consumed by the flashes and fragments of, I don't even know what they are—memories?

Splinters of glass.

Milk spreading between toes.

I've brought a library book today, *The Wonders of Language*, my etymology dictionary, and a picnic blanket; I imagined an afternoon of reading in the park, but it's impossible, the rattled feeling scraping against the brightness of the day. I head to the museum.

The National Maritime Museum is my library, each gallery a borrowable collection of emotions: Battle for Jutland for courage; Atlantic Worlds for justice; Maritime London for a sense of nostalgia. I've been here all summer. There was a photography exhibition a few weeks ago called *The Great British Seaside* that reminded me so keenly of going to the Thames beaches with Julia and Jacob—the freezing licks of the river, the acid sting of vinegar on my fish and chips—I bit the inside of my cheek, blood surprising my mouth.

Today, I know exactly which gallery I need—Nelson's Nation & Navy on Level 2. The lift is giddy with children on their last few weeks of summer and when the doors slide open at Level 1, they surge forward. A grandmother calls out to one of them, "Slow down, my beauty, slow down," and I'm absorbed for a moment with pairing woman to child. It's a girl, five perhaps. She acknowledges her grandmother with a grin but doesn't stop, racing flat out onto the Great Map, chin up, hair flying behind her. The grandmother smiles at me, as if to say, "What can I do?" I press the Close button three times.

The gallery is empty, a dimly lit secret cupped over the chaos of the children's areas. Here, among the paintings of naval battles under fired skies, the cool, black steel of cannonballs and mortars, I immerse myself in war to wage it against myself. *Pull yourself together*, I whisper to shut out the dread stillness that came over my brother and sister when I told them about how Mama scratched Daddy. I press my lips so close to the display cabinet of cutlasses, I can see them moving in the reflection. *You can do this. You can get through this summer.*

I come back to Nelson's Navy & Nation for the next few days; my strength, drawn from the relics of naval war, is too fragile for any other place. I sit meters away from Nelson's Battle of Trafalgar coat, the hole on the left shoulder a shot of courage. Bigger things have happened than fragmented thoughts and Mama's rages; rigging has been destroyed; ports have been blockaded; control of the Caribbean has been lost, won. If Nelson can get shot in the shoulder, I can do this. I try to forget that the wound was fatal.

On Wednesday afternoon, I go to the toilets, the clean ones in the East Wing that don't make you grateful for fresh air. At the sink, I get a text from Daddy. It's a photo of the deck chair Francie used, leaning against the house with the message, "Please put away." Striped once, the colors have bled into each other and while the navy has lasted, the white is a fungal green. And then the images come to me again.

> *Splinters of glass.*
> *Milk spreading between toes.*
> *A woman crumpling against a chair.*

I retch into the sink, my heart smashing in my chest. The taps are still on, soapsuds swirling around the plughole. Overhead, there's an announcement about a talk starting. I cover my ears, crawl into a stall, breathe. What's going on? I don't remember any of this, no broken glass or spreading milk, no woman crumpling against a chair. I wait for the panic to subside, for the images to fade to black.

THE SMELL OF browning mince hits me when I get home. Daddy is at the stove; he's home early making an effort. Red wine, mushrooms, and peppers are out on the counter, there's even posh cheddar from the supermarket deli counter, still wrapped in wax paper.

"Bolognese."

As children, we'd have cheered at that announcement after weeks of microwave meals and now he searches my expression for the same reaction. He doesn't find it. To make it up to him, I sit at the table and chop garlic. It's quiet with Daddy, just the blade against the cloves, the thud of his spatula separating lumps of mince. I would usually find it restful cooking with him, but I'm reeling today, the silence prickling with all the things I cannot say.

I'm ill, Daddy.

Something's wrong.

Mama's car pulls into the drive and his shoulders slope, his jabbing movements growing rapid. I abandon the garlic. He understands. Being in the kitchen is traitorous.

It's warm, but even in the summer, Mama insists on wearing her silk shirts without rolling up her sleeves. When she cups her hand under my chin, I smell the damp scent of her sweat.

"Did you do the list?"

"All done."

"Good girl." She gestures towards the kitchen. "What's he doing?"

"Making Bolognese."

She wrinkles her nose.

The wrinkle remains while Daddy serves up. He ladles a generous portion onto a bed of spaghetti. Mama looks at it as if it's raw.

I eat quickly, shoving enormous forkfuls into my mouth, swallowing without chewing. These situations develop quickly. Food can be thrown, swept into the bin, hurled out of the kitchen door, meals for foxes and mice while we go hungry. The scholarship girls would laugh at how quickly I could clear a plate.

Mama dips two millimeters of her fork into the sauce and lays it on the tip of her tongue. "This has cheese in it."

Daddy shakes his head furiously. Mama's always had a sensitive stomach; she has rules about what she can't bear to eat—milk, butter, cheese. He chews for longer than is wise. "Cheese is on the side."

Mama inspects the side plate of grated cheese, as if she can determine by looking at it if a single shaving has ended up in her sauce. She turns to me. "Is there cheese in this sauce?"

I shovel into my mouth what will be my last forkful. My stomach growls. "I'm not sure."

"I can taste it." She pushes her plate away and folds her arms. "What are you trying to do, Charlie?"

Daddy, also sensing the end of his dinner, puts down his fork.

"You know about my stomach. Isn't what you've done enough?"

"There's no cheese in the sauce," he says slowly.

My heart pounds; Daddy isn't used to dealing with Mama. He hasn't tracked her facial expressions when she fights with Julia, the twists in her arguments, the jumps in her logic; he would take himself to the mortuary, to the garden, or shut the living-room door and read his journals.

I try to intervene. "Mama, it's a mistake, maybe a little got in. Let me make you something else . . ."

But she's too far gone. Her eyes blaze. "You're trying to poison me, aren't you?" she hisses at him. "You and Francie are in this together!" She scrapes her chair back from the table. The sound vibrates through my jaw. "I'll find out, you know. I'll find out everything!" She runs into the living room and tears down the towers of medical journals Daddy has spent years building. I watch her rend journals in two and then claw at my father, and think of the word "ransack," from the Old Norse *rannsaka*, meaning "to pillage, to plunder" after storming and capturing a town. There is nothing to do but let her fly.

5 / LADY FINGERS

THERE WAS NO LIST THE next morning, just a simple request: "Can you make dinner instead of him?" The press of her thumb into my palm stayed long after the front door shut. If I try my hardest, I can make this better. I have to.

Yesterday, after the fight, I found Daddy sitting on the toilet lid, the last of the evening rays falling on him through the window in the alcove. He was tracing the long scratches, the double crescent of a bite mark, speaking, not to himself exactly, but as if he was talking into a Dictaphone: "Central bruising of soft tissue caused by compression. Inter-canine distance approximately three centimeters. Refer to forensic odontologist." It occurred to me by the way he analyzed each mark that this wasn't the first time he'd looked at his body like this. Something had happened to him, before Mama, before he'd found his calling. The identification of his injuries made him feel safe.

He hid his arms when I came in, folded them against his chest. "Let me," I said, and he gave in, surrendering his cuts and scrapes to me like a child. I knew how to disinfect his wounds, press plasters over the bigger gashes; I'd watched him enough times. He didn't flinch. This morning, he wore a long-sleeve shirt even though London is gearing up for a heatwave.

I pour over Peranakan cookbooks Mama bought on one of our annual trips to Singapore, trying to find a recipe she'd like. I've never made main meals before, only desserts and snacks, so the ingredients are unfamiliar; I have to look up each one. Candlenuts look like oversized hazelnuts but have an oil content so high, you can set them on fire. *Asam gelugar* is the fruit of a Malaysian rainforest tree, sour, for soups and curries. *Buah keluak* I remember from the *nonya* restaurant Mama took me to, a black nut from the mangrove swamps of Indonesia that is deadly without curing. I can't buy any of these in southeast London.

Luckily, Mama is a magpie, collecting many things from our annual trips to Singapore that she never uses, and when I empty out the cupboards, I find two mainstays of Peranakan cooking—orange shrimp dried to tiny spirals, and an unopened packet of Indonesian *belachan*, shrimp paste that emits an overpowering, fermented smell.

Don't overreach. Something simple.

I settle on *sambal bendeh*, a fiery salad. Mama has been trying to lose weight forever, she'd appreciate the absence of meat, and she loves spice. All I need is okra, chilies, and limes.

I take the bus to Lewisham High Street. Beyond the picture-perfect slopes of the heath, a few minutes from the coffee shops and music conservatoire, the pastel-colored captain's houses slide into modern newbuilds "inspired by Regency architecture" before dropping away into terraced houses and then the graffitied building of the old telephone exchange. Now, we're in Lewisham proper, the mash of fried chicken shops, African hair salons, and launderettes. Next to an Indian grocer is a beautiful carved Hindu temple.

I get off the bus and slip among the shoppers with reusable bags under their arms or dragging wheeled shopping baskets. I blend in better here than in Blackheath Girls' School or Greenwich's terraced streets, another girl, race indistinct, heading for the market.

Mama calls the market "Parisian" but there are no baguettes, no freshly baked croissants or fine-milled lavender soap, just fake watches, SIM cards, meat rotting in the heat, and fruit and veg at cutthroat prices—£1.50 for a kilo of onions, cabbages for 50p, a huge bunch of carrots for £1. Mama once dragged five kilos of lychee from here on a Saturday afternoon after the market closed. We ate them for days and still didn't finish the sack before their textured rinds turned wet and bruised.

In a stall outside one of the halal butchers, I buy the okra and chilies from a woman in a hijab. Julia messages me while I'm paying. "Got something for you. Meet me in Gabrielle's?"

We haven't spoken since my birthday even though Chrissy only lives in Blackheath. We're playing a game; I'm punishing her for abandoning me, she's letting me, and while it seems like I've won, the relief her message brings is unsettling. I take my change and drive my heel into the liquid pouring into the drain. It's blood. Almost indistinguishable from rainwater.

GABRIELLE'S IS JULIA'S favorite café in the village, ironic because the reason it's so popular are the shelves of French sourdough, the glazed sausage rolls, the tiny pistachio cakes dripping with rose icing, none of which Julia eats. In this way, Julia and Mama are the same, wanting things not for themselves but because other people do. Finding a table is a Darwinian feat she relishes—she ambushes families at the slightest rustle of a jacket, scans the crowds for that final swallow of coffee. She pushes her sunglasses to the top of her head and glares at a table of fourteen-year-olds who haven't finished. They leave within seconds. She beckons me over.

"Got one." She waits for me to congratulate her.

I say nothing. Why should I give everyone what they want?

Julia rolls her eyes and takes out her sketchbook. She's always sketched, this is one of hundreds of black sketchbooks she's kept since she was a child: shells; museum objects; the Thames. Since she started medical school, she draws people, what they are on the outside—postures, planes of faces, knuckles—and then what they really are—cartilage, muscle, bone.

She looks strange to me, outlining the triangle of a sacrum, the broad spread of a pelvis; it takes a minute before I understand why—there's very little skin on display. She's wearing an oversize chambray shirt, and around her throat she's wound a thin, leopard-print scarf. She's still stylish, she's spent at least five minutes tucking the shirt into her jeans, but where are her crop tops, her skintight T-shirts, her miniskirts?

We chat about neutral subjects—Chrissy, the twins. A man stares at her openly from the pastry counter, how charming, a beautiful girl sketching. Julia lifts her eyes at him, encouragingly. As he approaches, she flips over her pad to display lobes of a brain, the fronded spray of the cerebellum. He spills his coffee. We burst out laughing. Don't they know? If Julia likes someone, she hides herself completely.

About Mama, Daddy, my birthday, we don't speak. She jabs at the brown paper bag with her pencil. "Lady fingers?"

"The correct term is 'okra.'"

She snorts. "What's Daddy ever made with okra? Don't tell me, she's got Daddy making Peranakan food."

I wait a few beats until she realizes it's me who's cooking, daring her to ask me what's changed, what's happened, but she's too clever for that. She bends her head and labels her drawing in careful print—sacrum, coccyx, ilium. She pretends to Mama that she's revising, but she's not. She does in art what I do with etymology, analyzing breaking things down into comprehensible parts. Only then do we know what to feel.

"Drinks are here." She snaps her sketchbook shut and peers into my hot chocolate when the waitress sets it down. I wanted it iced but the machine has blown with all the requests for iced coffees. "That's a whole day's worth of calories."

"I don't care about calories."

She searches my hairline, my contact-lensed eyes, my makeup, the candy stripe T-shirt I'm wearing, the rucksack I clutch on my lap. I refuse to squirm. "Forgot to give you this last Sunday." The edge in her voice is gone. She draws out a makeup bag from her tote.

I set the contents out on the table—foundation, powder, concealer. "They're your shade. They match your skin tone. Your actual skin tone. I thought I was going to be around to help you try it on this summer but, you know."

I lift the bottle to the light and then hold it against the skin of my wrist. It's pale beige, without yellow undertones. I shove it back into the bag. "I don't need this. I don't want trouble."

She reaches across the table so suddenly, I think she might hit me, but instead, she puts her hand over mine and squeezes. "You're eighteen, Lil. It's time."

"Time for what?"

"Time for this to stop. Your face, your eyes, the juice, now the cooking? You're about to go to Oxford. You need to stand up for yourself."

I shrug her off, try to sit tall, even though this rough wisdom from my sister makes my eyes sting. "I am. I will."

She cocks her head to the side, pulls her pendant taut at her neck. "Will you? Or will you not know how?"

I lift my mug to my lips. The chocolate scalds me beautifully.

MAMA'S KEY IS in the door at six, and I rush to take her bags. While she showers, I pour her a glass of spoilt juice and set it on the table while I finish making dinner (she likes it room temperature). Daddy messages that he's been called by the coroner. I don't believe him, but I'm relieved he's not here; on evenings when he's away, we eat on trays in front of the TV. We like the same thing, Mama and I—nineties movies with Demi Moore and Julia Roberts, or reality TV (Mama is a huge fan of Kris Kardashian), but recently we've discovered true crime—gold-digging, devastatingly handsome psychos who pretend they're cardiologists. Mama crunches popcorn kernels between her teeth when she can't take the suspense.

She comes down, her hair hanging over her shoulders in wet twists and sinks into the sofa, reaching out to stroke the neck of a huge Peranakan urn, as though it's a pet. I was with her when she bought it, my limited Mandarin unable to keep up with the numbers flying between Mama and the antique dealer. At the time, I could see the appeal, the cerulean background, the pink phoenix. But thousands of miles away, the colors seem lurid together, the etchings a child's drawing.

I turn on the TV and set the tray of white rice, topped with *sambal bendi* on her lap.

"What's this?"

"Okra with *sambal belacan*," I say, suddenly shy. "I found the *belacan* in the kitchen and thought it would be nice to try something different."

She lifts a forkful into her mouth and a thousand doubts race through my mind—can she taste that I haven't used calamansi limes, is there too much chili—but she smiles, and they melt away. "I didn't know you could cook like this!"

"Does it taste like it did when you were a child?"

She shakes her head at me in appreciation. "Exactly the same! I haven't tasted this in years!" She puts down her fork and kisses me on the cheek. "My little *nonya*, my favorite girl, my best girl," and I want to snatch those words from the air, imprison them in a jar.

"How was your day?"

Mama drags her fork through the rice. "Pierre is trying to bring in a new partner—this Russian who's friends with his wife."

"Is that so bad?"

"Yes, it's bad. It's another partner eating into the profits. What if he never brings in any of his own clients? It could take him years to develop his own business."

"Can Pierre do that?"

"He can do whatever he wants. Don't you know that? Men always do."

I press the Pause button. "Listen to me. You're the best at Regent's Park Wealth Management. You bring in the most revenue. You're going to get through this. I believe in you."

"You're the only person who does," she says quietly, and I let out a silent prayer that Pierre doesn't hire the new partner; RPWM is one of the only environments where Mama is rewarded for being the shark she is. I watch her bite the okra, the starburst of seeds. Julia was right. These are lady fingers. Sliced open fingers. Sliced open hearts.

> *Two halves of an onion.*
> *Splinters of glass.*
> *Milk spreading between toes.*
> *A woman crumpling against a chair.*

"Are you going to press Play?"

I hold my hand over my mouth, gagging on okra, the smell of *belacan* suddenly putrid. I shove my tray onto the sofa. "I need to lie down. I don't feel good."

HAND OVER HAND, I pull myself upstairs until I'm in the attic. Close the door, lock it, climb into the hole. I'm trembling. Sometimes, just being in the hole is enough to calm me, but not now. I want to be outside smashing into a man—*that* would take the edge off—but there's no way I'll be able to get past Mama.

The walls then. I take a pen, scrawl my favorite quote from Ovid on the cardboard, *perfer et obdura*, be patient and tough, and then the etymology of "obdurate," which I know by heart: mid-fifteenth-century from the Latin *obdurare*, meaning "harden, hold out, persist, endure." My breathing slows, my mind clears, a gift from my father, the certainty that what's happening, no matter how terrifying, can be quantified, measured, solved. I can figure this out.

I force myself to recall what's happened—the flashing images of onions, the broken glass, the milk, a woman crumpling against a chair. I don't remember these things but maybe I've forgotten.

I message Jacob. Julia would call me instantly if I messaged her, ask me what the hell is going on, but Jacob and I do small talk well, linked by a thread of one-line observations and complaints plucked from the fabric of our day—"Man in front of me on the train is watching Peppa Pig," "Albie just said 'patriarchy,'" "What's the name of that Japanese biscuit I like?"

"Do you remember me dropping a glass of milk when I was younger?" I type.

"No, why?" he replies.

"Just a random memory." I can't ask him about the woman without raising more questions.

"Don't think so." There's a pause and then he writes, "TTL, David's here," and I wonder if I'll get the call later, the one where his voice cracks recounting another day when David, his supervisor, shouts at him for replying too slowly or taking too much initiative. He's a trainee at a top law firm, he's done fine in the first six months, but he can't bear confrontation let alone screaming. Now, he's sitting with a man who shouts instead of talks.

I say goodbye to him and close our messages. If I can't remember these images and no one else can, why can I see them? Only one thing can help me. Google.

I open the white oracle of a search bar, stare at the winking cursor while I craft my question: "seeing things that aren't there." Twenty million hits. The first few pages help me eliminate various possibilities instantly: I'm not having nightmares because I'm not asleep, neither am I delusional because delusions have an absurd element, like thinking you're Gandhi or being controlled by robots. I might, however, be hallucinating. The Latin root for "hallucinate" is irresistibly beautiful, *alucinari*, something you would name a Victorian child. But that's where the research ceases to be helpful, forking into a slew of either useless statistics or frightening ones. It takes me hours to come to a very simple conclusion: either I'm crazy or I'm very sick.

Around seventy percent of schizophrenics experience hallucinations. I feel strangely grateful; I'm at least in some kind of company. And there are upsides to schizophrenia—if I'm a hallucinating schizophrenic, I'm not bipolar, a small victory to eliminating psychiatric disorders on a very long list. But the symptoms of schizophrenia don't quite fit; I don't have disorganized speech, disorganized behavior, and I'm not emotionless or lacking an interest in the world.

There are many non-crazy alternatives: Dementia with Lewy bodies; Parkinson's; Charles Bonnet syndrome; Creutzfeldt-Jacob disease; temporal lobe epilepsy; lesions. When I find out that lesions include brain tumors, I climb out of the hole, go to Julia's dressing table and switch on her makeup mirror. It's long past midnight now, the darkness crowding the bright, circle of light, but I position myself so my whole head is in the reflection and walk my fingers over section by section. I imagine it's the size of a cherry tomato hidden in the dark furls of my brain, pulsating with its own daily rhythms. I'm seized with the urge to shave my head, I'd be closer to it then, separated only by millimeters of skin and bone, and then I turn off the mirror and go to bed. I won't let sick make me crazy.

I'd prefer it to be a brain tumor. Hallucinations are a symptom of an advanced stage, so it would be over quicker, a year tops. But schizophrenia frightens me. The worst is not that it's incurable or that I'm destined for a lifetime of depressive episodes. The worst is that I might never leave. Oxford used to be another pirouette in a perfect performance, but now that I might not be able to go, I realize it's more than that. It's somewhere else. Another place.

Morning breaks through the skylight, falling over the eaves, the throng of boxes and clothes. I used to love this time in the attic, the dawn chasing away the dark, the dust turning iridescent. Now I think this is all the beauty that will ever belong to me. Brightening shadows and dust.

I'll make an appointment with the doctor tomorrow. I'll deal with this by myself. I'll go to Oxford. No one needs to know.

6 / DOCTOR

BLACKHEATH SURGERY IS LOCAL, although I haven't been there in years. Daddy never saw the point. "There's very little I can't treat," he'd say, and we adored him fussing over us because it happened so rarely—his enormous palm on our foreheads, the gentle way he spooned strawberry cough syrup into our mouths, laid antibiotics on our tongues. Even when I caught that virus and was off school for months, I never saw a doctor.

Mama disapproved of doctors' surgeries for a different reason—germs. "It's the dirtiest place," she'd say, and suddenly, my imagination was on fire, I could see them, the millions of writhing bacteria and viruses smeared on doorknobs, sneezed on surfaces, tiny missiles honed on us. Now, as I click on the surgery's number, I put the speakerphone on rather than holding it to my ear, even though I know the receptionist isn't sick, that germs cannot travel with sound.

"Blackheath Surgery, Lisa speaking, what's your name and date of birth?"

I put on my poshest, private-school voice. If there's one thing Blackheath Girls' taught me, it's to speak as if I should be here, rather than deserving it with anything as grubby as a scholarship. How you appear is more important than who you are. "Good morning, Lisa." I tell her the information she needs. "Do you have any appointments?"

"Any doctor in particular?"

I can hear the tinkle of glass, she's on the iced coffees. "No, I'd just like an appointment today."

"No appointments until middle of September unless it's an emergency."

"It is an emergency," I say firmly.

"Can I ask you what's wrong?"

I watch myself say the words in the mirror, the dark of my black contacts, my smooth made-up cheeks. "I think I have a brain tumor."

There's a pause on the line, then typing. She's pulling up my records. "You're eighteen."

"Yes."

"What symptoms do you have?"

"Hallucinations."

"I've got an appointment with Doctor Aiden at ten-thirty if that's any good. Can you be here in an hour and a half, dear?"

The "dear" makes me feel very small, very vulnerable. "Yes," I whisper, my private-school voice ebbing away. "Thank you."

THE DOCTOR'S SURGERY is a few minutes' walk from the village, on a main road roaring with buses and lorries. Even with the noise, this is still the most affluent part of Blackheath. The buildings on each side are not so much houses as mansions transported from the antebellum South—wraparound porches, columns, green shutters, gravel driveways. When I drive by with Mama, she'd say, "Waste of money, they should have bought investment flats," but her dismissal signals a deeper turbulence within her and within me. Why didn't our family have enough to purchase investment flats? Why did she interrogate Daddy about any expenditure over £5, and play games with Julia about the rent on her apartment? Surely, she hasn't spent all her earnings on Peranakan antiques and pink clothes.

I didn't tell her that her finances impacted me beyond mere observation. Blackheath Girls' offered four fully paid scholarship places to the brightest girls whose parents couldn't afford to send them. In my year, it was Tatum, Lucy, Constanza, and me. We suited each other well enough. Unlike Slone and the other popular girls, we never spoke about our families, never invited each other over, poverty was a shield that protected all of us, until two years ago when Mama bought me a pair of diamond studs for my sixteenth birthday. She harangued me until I wore them every day over the summer. By the time school came round, I was so used to them, I didn't register I was wearing them on the first day of term. The scholarship girls, however, did.

"Fancy," Lucy said, as we filed back to our form rooms from assembly.

"Birthday present."

"Crystal?" Lucy had always been the most covetous of us, obsessing about what new toy Sloane had, fantasizing about saving up for this brand of jeans, that designer handbag.

"Don't know."

"Cubic zirconia then?"

I shrugged, but I was aware of her eyes lingering on my ears.

She leaned forward to take a closer look and then playfully flicked my earlobe, but in the sharpness of her nail against my skin, I knew she was appraising the stone's weight, she was jealous, she wanted to hurt me. "How can you not know?"

"Cut it out, Luce," Connie said.

Lucy ignored her, upturned her palm. "Take them out, I want to see."

I was vicious before I could stop myself. I slapped her open hand. "Why the fuck would I do that?"

She clasped her hand to her chest, silenced. But Tatum edged forward. "Show them to me."

"Fuck off," I said, unnerved. Tatum was the poorest of us, but also the smartest, not like Constanza—who was a polymath—or Lucy—a virtuoso violinist. Tatum was whip smart, someone who could navigate the world with barely anything. Take her uniform. Her parents couldn't buy the whole set, not even from secondhand sales, so for few months, she subsisted on one pinafore and one shirt. I knew because the shirt had the faintest ring of sweat under the armpit and I saw that ring day after day. Then, she became School Uniform Prefect. I never saw the stained shirt again.

"They're real, aren't they?"

"Why do you care?"

She looked at me with hard brown eyes. Her eczema left a whitish patina on her skin and as she stared me down, she smoothed her cheeks to present her best face for my denouement. "I have a theory about you."

"Nothing better to think about?" The bell rang. Around us, the other girls rushed to get their books out from their lockers, but the four of us were frozen, transfixed on the unfolding scene.

She licked her lips. "Do you know what the income bracket is to qualify for a full scholarship?"

I rolled my eyes, but she was closing in on something, something worth breaching our unspoken rule—we do not pry—and I was losing ground because I didn't know what it was.

"Less than thirty-eight thousand pounds."

"How do you know?" As soon as I said it, I regretted it.

"I had to know." She stabbed her sternum. It made a hollow sound. "My parents can't read English, so I filled out the scholarship forms. But your dad's a doctor and your mum's in finance, you go on holiday to Singapore, you get diamonds for your birthday," and then her tone changed to a sneer, "you wear makeup."

My hand flew to the tideline of makeup at my neck. They'd been talking about me, the shade of my face, the paleness of my neck, what a freak I was, perhaps since they first met me, perhaps always.

"How did you qualify?"

"I don't know," but I suddenly did, as I watched the righteous blaze in Tatum's eyes, the drop of Constanza's gaze, Lucy shifting her feet. Mama had lied on the scholarship forms.

There was no more walking through the park or visits to the museum or summer picnics, not with Tatum and Lucy at least. Constanza tried for a bit, furtive, strained meetings where she made me swear not to tell the others, but these tailed off. I pretended not to care, dissecting meaning in my etymology dictionary, scribbling on the walls of the hole. I wasn't scared of being ratted out. I was scared of something else: that fleeting, dangerous moment when my friends glimpsed something about Mama I didn't know. Still, I never asked Mama why she did it. Why she'd lied about how much money she had.

DOCTOR AIDEN IS Indian, with a pretty plumpness about her. In the warmth, she wears an electric-blue sleeveless dress, no tights, and ballet pumps. She smiles at me from behind black framed glasses. "Have a seat. How can I help?"

I take a plastic chair, careful not to lean back; I want to limit how much of my body touches these contaminated surfaces. The earpieces of a stethoscope hang over the edge of the table. I sit very still to avoid them brushing my knee.

She reads the notes on her computer then looks at me. "You're having hallucinations?"

I nod.

"How many have you had?"

"Four."

"Can you tell me what happens in one?"

"Just images. Onions, a smashed glass of milk." My throat is a rasp. "A woman."

"They don't sound like hallucinations to me. Hallucinations are like seeing spiders climbing up the wall or a figure that isn't there. Do they feel like that?"

I shake my head.

"They sound like flashbacks."

"Flashbacks? But that doesn't make sense. The glass of milk smashing, the woman crumpling, I don't remember these things, I checked with my brother, I'm sure—" As my hands gesture manically, I accidentally touch the stethoscope and jerk away.

"Sometimes," says Dr. Aiden, kindly, "we don't want to believe a flashback is ours. Are they upsetting in any way?"

"Not really." I wipe my fingertips on my leggings and regret it immediately, imagining the germs burrowing through the material onto my thigh.

"How do they make you feel?"

"Can I have some hand sanitizer please?" I point to the dispenser behind her.

She hands it to me.

"A bit panicky I guess." I squirt out a handful and rub it on my leggings, making sure to cover a circumference wider than where I'd wiped my hands.

"Has anything happened recently? Any changes at home or at school?"

"No. I'm on summer holidays before uni."

I do my hands next, the palms, the backs, between the fingers. When I look up, she's watching me in a way I don't like, as if she's trying to piece something together, and I wonder if there's something unfathomably wrong with me that medicine and science are powerless to solve. "If they aren't distressing and nothing's happened to you, there's not much we can do. Are you in pain in any way? Any trouble sleeping, difficulty concentrating? No depression or anxiety? Do you feel isolated or withdrawn?"

It's a dizzying array of symptoms. I say something just to feel curable. "I've been a little tired."

Dr. Aiden visibly brightens. "Ah. Let's get you a blood test, check your iron levels and thyroid. We'll give you a call if anything's out of the ordinary."

She prints out a blood test form. When she holds it out to me, she leans close. "If the flashbacks get worse, come back and see me. What you say here is completely private. This is a safe space."

I jump up. The stethoscope falls off the table. By the time she retrieves it, I'm out the door.

THE WAITING ROOM for the blood tests is the same for appointments so there are no seats left, it's packed. Patients are fanning themselves with medical leaflets, and windows have been flung open to let in a breeze that doesn't blow. I squeeze sanitizer onto my hands, trying to ignore a child at a grubby activity cube winding the gears as fast as he can. Mama would never let me play with toys laid out at the dentist or in a child-friendly café, she'd tell me stories to distract me from all those primary colors. With Julia, it was different. Mama would pin Julia's arms behind her back to stop her: "It's full of germs, do you want to get sick?" But the tighter she held her, the more Julia struggled, and when she broke free, a fever would take hold of her; she touched everything—board books with their chewed corners, prams with gray-faced dolls. Once, she even ran her tongue along the frame of a tambourine. Mama dragged her out kicking and screaming.

The nurse assembles a tray of tools after she calls my number—tourniquet, needle, plaster, test tubes, then asks for my arm. I give her my left and turn away. Julia was always fascinated at the needle disappearing into the skin, the dark draw of blood, but not me. Why look at what's hurting you?

In the seat across from me, another nurse is checking the details of a girl dressed in expensive gym gear with thick blonde hair in a low, side ponytail. She trails the strands languidly between her thumb and index finger, shakes out her fringe, and then I know who she is, I went to primary school with her—Charlotte Warren.

She has retained the same horsiness in her face that she had as a child, and watching her, I come to the same conclusion as I did when I was younger—she's a stupid girl. It didn't matter though. At nine, I wasn't friends with her because of her intelligence. I was friends with her because of her hair. She wore it in a thick braid flung over her shoulders, or in a French plait that drew in the honeyed strands from the top. I was obsessed with it—how did it stay in, how had she done it? Julia could braid, but the end result was always bumpy and messy, never that effortless rope.

Eventually, she told me that her mother spent fifteen minutes every day doing her hair. It was an after-breakfast ritual, she'd bring down her box of accessories and sit perfectly still, while her mother wove in devotion and fastened it in place with a silver, sparkly hair tie. I was done with her when I heard that. I ripped off her hair tie and called her a baby until she cried, pure joy jolting through me at making her ashamed of what I coveted.

Is it strange to know at nine who it was safe to be friends with and who it wasn't? The girls with shiny braids and lunchboxes of crudités and hummus, whose daddies threw them up into the air, whose mothers would ask why you were wearing makeup, they weren't safe. They would invite you to their houses for sleepovers and would expect an invitation in return. These girls would want our parents to be friends. No.

The nurse snaps off the tourniquet and asks me to press a cotton ball over the puncture. I watch her name the test tubes.

Charlotte catches up with me as the doors of the surgery swing open. She puts her hand on my arm and smiles. "I'm sorry, do I know you?"

I look into her clear, blue eyes. What is it like to be that naive, that simple? All that hair-brushing has made her soft. Know me? She could never know me. I peel her manicured fingers off my arm, watch her smile vanish. "I don't think so."

7 / PARTY

MAMA SAYS THERE'S A BIRD tapping at her window, but when I check, it's not there. She called me down from the attic to get rid of it, her shouts razing my thoughts until I can think of nothing beyond, *Why is it raining, run my bath, deal with that bird.* Now I can hear it too.

"Can you get me a towel?" she calls, sitting up from the bath. She's on her period, there's meat in the air, so I brace myself not to smell but also not to look. I know an object by its edges now, I only need to see a corner to recognize a sodden sanitary towel unfurling against sheets of toilet paper, or two unswallowed Tylenol tablets.

"Did you get rid of the bird?" she asks, drying herself.

"I couldn't find it."

Wrapping a towel around herself, she steps toward the window, peers timidly left and right. She hates birds. It's why she'll never walk on the heath, because of the swans and moorhens and ducks. She screamed once when a gaggle of Canada geese flew overhead, threw her arms over her head and rocked. I had to call Daddy to pick her up in the car.

She seems to return to herself after confirming the bird isn't there, sitting on the bed and rubbing in body lotion. "You've forgotten, haven't you? The engagement party? I spoke to Jonathan yesterday. Your sister really frightened him. Worthless whore, behaving like that, everything she has is mine, everything she has I gave her, I paid for her medical school, I paid for her apartment. She better not let me down this evening."

Mama has been looking forward to Felipe Christofidou's engagement party for months. Felipe is the founder of one of London's largest hedge funds, and Mama is convinced that attending his party is hitting the financial advisor jackpot. But we've only been invited because of his daughter, Chrissy, Julia's best friend, and after Julia and Mama's fight at my birthday, Mama thinks Julia will ask Chrissy to pull the invite, or worse, embarrass her in front of all those rich venture capitalists.

She examines her face in the mirror above her bedside table before unscrewing the most expensive skincare item she owns, a tiny pot of Korean whitening cream. She places five dots on her face, rubs it in sparingly. "Has she said anything to you?"

"No, Mama."

She turns around and puts her palm to my forehead. Her face glistens. "You're warm." Mama is always a little paranoid when she thinks I might be ill, a legacy of the virus I had as a child. "Are you feeling OK?"

I nearly say "no," I hate parties, the stilted conversation, the suffocating feeling of pretending to have fun. I'd rather hunker down in the hole and research flashbacks. But Mama needs me, Daddy needs me, there's no choice. "Just a little warm."

"OK." She strokes the shape of my chin. "I almost forgot. With all that silliness on Sunday, I didn't give you your birthday present." She reaches under her bedside table for a red, silk jewelry pouch embroidered with gold dragons. I sit on the bed, unzip it. It is an emerald ring surrounded by tiny diamonds. Another piece of jewelry worth a chunk of unpaid school fees. "Do you like it?" she asks anxiously.

When Mama and I go shopping, I play this game. I give myself a choice between two things and ask myself if she weren't here, what would I choose? An opal wallet or blue? Black boots or brown? But my instincts are elusive. If choosing is a muscle, mine has atrophied from disuse and although I keep practicing, I don't think I'll ever be able to do it. You have to picture yourself when you choose an outfit or a piece of jewelry, imagine yourself wearing this or that, but when I think of myself, I see only my made-up face and pink jumpers, me in Mama's image, and then I don't want to think anymore.

I slip the ring on. "I love it, thank you."

"Only the best for my daughter." She kisses me on the cheek. "I'm so proud of you, do you know that? You were always the smartest, the best. My baby girl, going to Oxford."

I hug her, inhale the scent of her skin. This is the Mama Julia and Jacob never see, the Mama that is just mine, the Mama who looks after me. She strokes my hair, and then I feel her stiffen. "Lily, your roots. The brown's showing."

"Sorry, Mama, I've run out of dye." How could I be so stupid? This evening more than any other, Mama needs me not just to *be* her perfect daughter but to *look* her perfect daughter. She blinks rapidly and I wonder which incident she's thinking about—in London, when the late class monitor wouldn't release me because she didn't think Mama was my mother, or in Singapore, when fruit-stall owners would lift my hair to catch the brown in sunlight or tilt my chin up to get a closer look at my single hazel eye: "So white, barely any Chinese." Her solution was simple. Change my hair, my skin color, my eyes. No one would question whose daughter I was.

I cover my hairline with my hands, hating myself for ruining the moment, hoping I can bring her back, but it's too late, she's slipped off the bed and has opened her wardrobe. "Help me get ready."

She's proud of the blouse she's planning to wear this evening, purchased after months of trawling through Selfridges and Liberty's, the boutiques of New Bond Street. Rose-gold sequins cover a bustier shape stiff enough to conceal her burgeoning stomach, and the sleeves are sheer, gauzing over her scarred arms and flattering each wrist with a triplet of pearls. I retrieve Mama's Spanx from her drawers— mammoth nude knickers and a black strapless bodysuit that extends into cycling shorts. I hold them up to her. "Higher power panties or full body?"

"What do you think?" She appraises herself in the mirrored wardrobe door, tracing the scars on her arms, stroking their shiny surfaces, and then moves to put her bra on. She sucks her abdomen in, the light catching the crisscrossed stretch marks.

"Higher power. You don't need more than that."

She falters after she puts them on, the enormity of the panties ridiculous. "Do you think Francie wears Spanx?"

"I know she does, Mama. Full body. Every day." She smiles, and I'm exultant thinking this will last, this will hold. But then the bird pecks, and she startles and I remember. Any magic I have is glass-slippered, half a fairy godmother's, less. It's a daughter's. It's already gone.

TWO HALVES OF an onion. *Splinters of glass. Milk spreading between toes. The woman.* The images kept catching me off guard while I helped Mama get ready, startling me when I slid a diamanté pin in her hair, fastened the clasp of her necklace. Now, on my own in the attic, they eddy and surge, a washing cycle without end. Why am I seeing these things?

Think, think, think. Doctor Aiden said they were flashbacks. And even though I don't remember these events, I know I hold the answer. My eyes fall on the dust sheets covering my family's possessions, everything I've camouflaged against the walls. I fling off the material and start searching.

My boxes are crammed with report cards, records of achievements, exercise books. I flick through each of them, pass my eyes over my eleven-year-old flair for language, my intellectual curiosity (although there is a mention of my "unconventional appearance"). What the teachers never understood was that I wasn't like the other scholarship girls, I didn't have talent. What I had was a physical revulsion to a problem, the chaotic mess of it. Once that took hold of me, I was obsessed with carving a path through it, that snarling, overgrown forest, slashing it down, trampling it into place.

I find a diary I made when I was seven. It was a school project and I pore over it, hoping to find a reference to a smashed glass of milk, but there is nothing except entries about movies I'd seen at the cinema (complete with ticket stubs) and park games I'd played with Jacob and Julia. I pause over an entry of Daddy taking us out for milkshakes and burgers. I'd forgotten that. Where was Mama?

"What are you doing?" Julia leans against the doorway rubbing the side of her nose, her bag slung over her shoulder. She is stunning in a full-length silver lamé maxi dress, long-sleeved, the sharp shoulders, the dramatic jewelry toughening up the ruffles of the skirt. "This place is a bomb site."

"Sorry," I say, and then hate myself for apologizing. I slip my diary back into a box. Currents of dust billow through the room.

She heads toward the dressing table, hauls her bag up against the mirror. "Can I get ready here? My room is filled with Mama's stuff."

"I thought you were staying at Chrissy's."

"Mama thought it would be nice if we arrived as a family."

"And you agreed?"

"Sure."

There's a dynamic between my sister and my mother I could plot on a graph. It lasts about a month. Mama will cajole, threaten, bribe Julia into being the kind of daughter she wants. Julia will go along with it. Mama will ask Julia for something she will not give. Julia will snap. Mama will punish her. Julia will retaliate. Mama will buy her off.

That's what happened this summer. Mama asked Julia if she wanted to go on holiday with her. Julia freaked out and went to Greece with Chrissy. Mama sublet Julia's flat while she was gone. Julia came on to Jonathan. The way Julia is shaking her foundation identifies exactly where we are in the cycle—at its most dangerous point, just before Mama buys her off.

"What's she said this time?"

Julia buffs the liquid across her skin angrily. "She won't let me move back into my flat, unless I behave."

"Can't you stay with Chrissy?"

Her fingers don't stop moving but her reflection is lifeless. "Do you know what it's like always asking your friend for something? To be the one taking, taking, taking? It's embarrassing." She thumbs her dress and I know she's borrowed it from Chrissy. "It's—" she breaks off, not because she can't think of the right word but because she can't bear to say it. "Humiliating" from the Latin, *humiliare*, "to humble," from *humilis*, "lowly," from *humus*, "earth." To be brought low. To be brought to the ground.

I sit on the floor next to her. She strokes my hair for a second and then carries on with her makeup, her tremble palpable through her skin. I lean my head against her thigh. I'd do anything to make her feel better, but I don't know what that is.

"Whad'up, guys?" Jacob arrives in a tux, twirling around, throwing shapes with a brittle confidence that isn't his, borrowed from a drink or a pill, some pick-me-up to make our family outing more bearable. "Ready to see those vulture capitalists?"

Julia stands up abruptly. "Have you been drinking?"

He rolls his eyes at her. "Oh come on. I'm going to a party with my Dad, who's in love with my ex-wife. I need a little help."

"You can't drink with your antidepressants. You'll feel worse."

He takes four minibar vodkas out from the inside of his jacket and shakes them like castanets. "Lighten up, Jules. It's a party!"

Julia snatches them from him. "Everyone just needs to behave."

THE CAR MAKES everything worse, the steel hulk a carnival mirror distorting ordinary objects. The driver's seat is a throne Daddy isn't entitled to assume. He hesitates before putting the key into the ignition, jangling them at Mama in case she wants to drive. The back seats are a time warp. We pull out of the drive and slip into younger versions of ourselves—hyperalert, skittish, vigilant. How have we let this happen? I clutch my rucksack and glance at my brother and sister to check if it's just me. It isn't. Jacob's knee bounces manically up and down. Julia claws back her panic the only way she knows how: she goes on the offensive.

"Felipe is going all out on this engagement party," she says as Daddy brakes at the crossing. "Definitely check out the champagne, it's nine hundred pounds a bottle. Chrissy says the whole evening is costing him at least two hundred thousand pounds. Can you imagine spending that much on one party?"

She's punishing Mama for holding hostage the rent on her flat, daring her to pay it—*This is what your clients do, the people with real money. They don't barter with their daughters. They don't make them beg.*

Mama ignores her. She presses the wand of her lip gloss deep into her cupid's bow until a single clear drop appears.

"It's almost the cost of my flat."

I drive my elbow into Julia's arm. I will spend the entire evening on high alert as it is, I don't want to be on call for a disaster. She ignores me and re-pins a loose strand of hair. "The cost of your mortgage."

Stop, I mouth to her.

She doesn't. "Do you ever feel like we're invited to these events, but we never really belong? Doesn't matter what we look like, what we wear. We're worthless to them. Nothing."

Mama snaps her compact mirror shut and a silence falls over the car because we all know: with those words, Julia has sealed the fate of the evening. Under her sequined bustier, her Korean makeup, her Jimmy Choos, Mama's worst fear has been unleashed, and with it, an unpredictable, whipping jealousy. *Bring low, bring to the ground.* How dangerous it is to play our humiliation games.

THE ENGAGEMENT PARTY is at one of the few locations in London large enough to hold 250 people with outdoor space for fireworks—the Christofidou mansion on Blackheath's private estate. Everywhere, there are wildflowers. An arch of foxgloves frames the front door, and as we step into the hall, goldenrod, sweet williams, and cornflowers stream down from the central chandelier so that the light is a midsummer gold, pink, blue. In front of us, hollyhocks and daisies trail over a staircase that can only be described as palatial.

Mama gasps. I know what she's thinking. The hallway alone is bigger than our entire downstairs and even if we had this space, what would we do with it? We certainly wouldn't adorn the walls with actual art, or display a sculpture we didn't understand, or lay down an impossibly thick Persian rug. It is suddenly preposterous that we're even here.

Mama deflates by my side. I take her hand quickly and squeeze. *Don't think about this anymore. Do what you've come to do.*

Hours later, I'm in the center of the ballroom trying to keep everyone in view, but it's like playing chess with traitorous pieces. Daddy, who Mama usually lets duck out of these events, has been dispatched to fetch drinks, but he's using the bar queue as a pretext to scroll through BBC News. Jacob keeps disappearing into the garden. Each time he emerges, his cheeks are more flushed and he grows more unsteady on his feet. Julia, at least, is behaving impeccably. She swipes Jacob's drinks from him, and otherwise joins Chrissy flirting with black-tied bankers, the pair cutting striking figures in their matching metallic, floor-length dresses.

But my eyes are always on Mama. She moves from the waiter serving champagne to touch a man's elbow, a business acquaintance. The cluster of people surrounding him expands to include her and she is suddenly animated, saying something that makes them all throw their heads back and roar with laughter. A heavy woman in a blue dress catches her eye, and she extricates herself from the cluster and heads toward her.

I've been watching her all evening, putting on her different faces. I wait for the slip, the chink in her extraordinary performance. Maybe it's me. Maybe I'm wrong to think that after what Julia said in the car, Mama can't last among the streams of flowers, the snow-white table-cloths, the impeccably dressed women.

I'm not wrong.

There.

She's at one of a dozen tables laden with champagne flutes, fool-ishly unmanned. Instead of reaching for a glass, she picks up two open champagne bottles, swaying slightly—she's tipsy. She looks behind her. When she thinks no one's watching, she empties the £900 cham-pagne out onto the marble floor. A bubbling tide rushes from the white-clothed table and she steps away, gathering up swathes of her rose-gold skirt.

I don't need to watch anymore. The flare has been sent, the sig-nal is clear—Mama needs me now. I head over to her. Across the ballroom, Julia catches my gaze. She points at Mama as if I haven't seen her, but her open expectation, the way she gestures at me to take Mama away, makes me mutinous. She's done it again, trapped Mama, trapped me, *Mama's girl, Mama's doll*, why should I do this? I turn on my heels, grabbing a flute of champagne from a waiter, weaving in between the other guests, not caring where I'm going except I want to be away from my mother and sister. In front of me, the bar glitters with frosted highballs and apothecary-colored bottles. The glass sets my teeth on edge. If Mama shatters here, there will be so many fragments.

Beyond the bar, a curtain flickers over a doorway cordoned off by a velvet rope. I peer through. It's a stairwell, cool and dark. I edge past the rope, pull the curtain behind me, and celebrate my victory with a sip. Warmth spreads through my chest.

"There's a door here if you want to make a quick exit."

The voice makes me jump.

A man steps from the shade of the curtain into a triangle of light. His shirt has wilted, and his sleeves are rolled to the elbow. The end of a bow tie hangs from his trouser pocket, and his dinner jacket is slung over his forearm.

He feels for a handle, twists. A corridor opens out in front of us, throwing light into the stairwell. Guests pass in and out of vision, a woman tottering on stilettos, an elderly woman wreathed in pearls. "If you go down there, past the library, you'll be at the entrance hall. You know your way out from there, right?"

I bristle. He is exactly the kind of man I'd stalk on the heath—a banker or a lawyer with the lazy handsomeness of the cool girls' boyfriends—but now that one is really talking to me, I don't like the knowing way he opens the door with one hand. "Why do you think I need a quick exit?"

He blinks. "My mistake." He lets the door close. "I just assume there are people like me in every party, making quick exits, hiding behind curtains."

"Who are you hiding from?"

"My mother. Black dress, choker." He parts the curtain and points to a slim woman in her late fifties with a constellation of diamonds at the base of her throat. It's the woman of the evening, Felipe's fiancée.

"Your mother is Stephanie Quinn?" I read about Stephanie online—she's the head of diamonds in one of the London auction houses, Sotheby's or Christie's.

The man winces. "Quinn was my father's name. My mother returns to Quinn between husbands."

"Why?"

He raises his eyebrows, and it strikes me that even though I'd stalk this man for a momentary press against his chest, I don't know how to position my body, the right tone, the right questions. "Security, I guess." He holds his whiskey up to the light and tilts it so it flashes from amber to shadow. "And you? Who are you hiding from?"

"My mother. Rose-gold sequins, matching skirt." I point her out. She's stopped in front of Jacob. He is with a girl now, whose plunging neckline reveals a spray of freckles he can't tear his eyes from. Mama is scolding him, tugging at his arms, which are wrapped around the girl's waist. The girl giggles. Her dress lifts higher up her thighs. But looking out is a mistake—Julia spots me. She detaches herself from Chrissy and heads to inform Mama.

"Shit." Drinking is inexcusable; it's something Julia does, not me. I search for somewhere to put the champagne, but there is nowhere, only the marble floor. The man studies me and then, in one fluid movement, switches my flute with his drink. I stare at the liquid, confused.

Mama flings back the curtain. She's about to tell me she's had enough of this party until she sees the glass in my hand. She snatches it from me and sniffs. Her features reconfigure at its contents, and at the man who presents himself from behind me. "You're Lewis! Felipe's stepson-to-be!" She thrusts her breasts at him like a handshake.

"I'm May, Lily's mother. Did she tell you she's going to Oxford? To read Law." She tells the story of how she got into Oxford on a scholarship but couldn't go because of the accident.

"You went to Oxford, didn't you? And now you're a professor?"

He nods.

"Fascinating, absolutely fascinating. I wonder if you could give Lily some pointers. Some tips. Maybe lessons? So she can get a head start?"

Trust Mama to secure as many freebies as she can. A trained accountant, there's a spreadsheet in her eyes.

The man is silent for a moment, no doubt thinking how he can politely decline. Mama breathes in sharply, preparing another line of attack. But, to both our surprise, he says, "Of course, it would be my pleasure."

"Wonderful!" She is about to carry on when she sees Jacob reaching inside the girl's dress. There's a flash of nipple. "Will you excuse me? I must speak to Felipe. Lily will get your details." She shoots me a look and hands me the highball.

I smell the drink when she's gone. It's not whisky at all. It's apple juice. "Thank you for this."

"Don't worry about it." He takes out a business card and writes on the back.

"You really don't have to," I say.

Beyond the curtain, the countdown for fireworks is in full swing. *Five. Four. Three. Two. One.* Then, as the celebration breaks out, cheering and corks and the rush of champagne, he presses it into my hand. "Lily, was it?"

I read out what he's written: *Lewis Quinn, The Polar Explorer House, 39 Eliot Vale.*

"Come and talk to me sometime. After two p.m. is good."

"What would we talk about?"

"Anything. Anything at all."

MAMA IS FURIOUS with Jacob on the way home, even though he's long since left in a taxi. "Did you see him at the party, getting drunk? He can really pick them. One whore after the other." The narrative weaves in Daddy too. "The two of you, picking the same slut, it's disgusting." Daddy pretends Mama isn't speaking about him.

Mama's had three drinks—the engagement cocktail, a passion fruit Bellini, and a glass of champagne. She sways in her bedroom as she pulls off her silk skirt, her sequins, her Spanx, the alcohol running quick and warm in her. She's asleep when I return with the makeup remover. I take it off gently and stroke her cheek.

I go downstairs for some water. Daddy's light in the living room is already turned off. In the kitchen, I lay the business card on the counter. *Lewis Quinn.* I fetch a glass with one hand, google him with the other. He's a lecturer in philosophy of religion, no relevance to law, but that doesn't matter, Mama will think I should see him anyway. I scroll through his list of publications while reaching for the water jug in the fridge. He's only published three papers; he's young for a lecturer, early thirties. The jug catches on the lip of a bowl, an unfinished microwave meal of prawn noodles, which tips over itself and smashes. And just like that, another flashback slices into my thoughts.

The bowl of soup smashed against the checked floor, but her father didn't care, flinging things out of the fridge—two halves of an onion, a white cabbage.

"So, our milk's not good enough for you."

"It is, Baba, it is!" cried the girl.

He weighed a bowl of minced garlic in his hand and then let it fall. Sylvia, the parrot, squawked in her cage. Someone screamed.

"You should have drunk it when your mother asked you to."

"I'll drink it now!" She reached for the glass of milk, but he knocked it out of her hand. The glass splintered. Milk spread between her toes.

"Too late for that!"

The girl's mother tried to come between them, but he shoved her. She crumpled against the chair.

"I found it," he said in a terrible singsong voice. He took out a carton of orange juice. "See how smart your father is. Orange juice has calcium in it, just like milk." He uncapped the carton and held it out to the girl.

It was a trick, but she couldn't figure it out until she tasted it—the juice was sour. She spat it out.

He grabbed her hair, twisted it around his fist. She smelled whiskey on his breath. "Drink it." He nudged her mother with his foot. "Watch her. I want her finished by the time I get changed."

Her mother pulled herself up against the kitchen table and stumbled over to the girl. She pulled her onto her lap. "I'll drink it, he won't know."

"He will," said the girl. She didn't look at the mess on the floor or her mother crying. She shut her eyes and drank.

My mouth fills with saliva, and then I'm doubled over, heaving into the mess of leftover noodles. But I cannot purge myself of the Mama's girl inside me, or my own tongue punishing me with the hundreds of times I've tasted her spoilt juice.

They're not my flashbacks.

They're someone else's.

Someone who likes spoilt juice.

Mama.

I want to rip out my tongue.

I want a blade.

I hunch my body into a tight ball, tuck my knees and head within the taut circle of my arms. I'm a dying star held together by a handclasp. An explosion undetonated by a single prayer. Inside my mouth, my tongue sings.

8 / THE POLAR EXPLORER HOUSE

WAKE.
   Eat.
Disappear.
Eat.
Sleep.

Eating slips. When Mama and Daddy aren't here, I forget.

Sleeping slips. There's a heatwave. While the rest of London celebrates Mediterranean weather—evening ball games, drive-through cinemas, garden barbecues that go on late into the night, I keep jolting awake, dreaming of spoilt juice, gagging on baby-pink sateen.

Disappear. Mama is in Santorini. She announced she was going away with Jonathan the day after Felipe's engagement party, consuming me so completely with what she was going to pack that it was easy to uncouple the woman from the child at the fridge. But without her lists or Peranakan cooking, the house seems dead. I'm afraid to be alone.

So when Daddy leaves for work, it's not enough for me to walk to Greenwich Park or the heath. I pedal like a child, rucksack slamming into my back until I reach the slope overlooking the boating lake or the benches on the triangles of grass in front of the village. These are the moments I feel most safe, surrounded by the clamor of families and tourists. The air we're breathing is the same, warmed by sunlight, not electrostatic with threat.

Even here, the flashbacks hunt me. Mama's, of course—the woman crumpling against a wall, milk spreading—but also my own. The curl of my fingers around the glass when I tasted the juice for the first time. The look on Mama's face as I swallowed. When Julia found out, she flung the open carton into the sink, juice fizzing over the ceramic, spraying her new school uniform. She was eleven. I was eight.

Mama's girl, Mama's doll.

Is that why this is happening to me, why Mama's memories are now mine? Because I make her spoilt juice, because I let her dress me in pink? "You and I are the same," Mama always says.

Blink and I'm in Mama's kitchen. There is a low purr of fear in me made worse by the sounds of crying, the cold liquid between my toes. Then, hands dig into my armpits, dragging me, which makes me wild and savage. I'm not Mama, not a child. I'm Lily. I thrash and kick, my legs hare-like and powerful, and then I'm free, about to round on my assailant, but he catches me, grabbing my shoulder. I scream.

"Lily?"

My eyes fly open. I'm disorientated for a moment and then the white spots in my vision fade and I measure out this time, this space. I'm on the heath. I can see the Hare & Billet pond in front of me and people spilling out of the old coaching inn pub to my right, but they are all sideways—I'm lying on a bench. My mouth hangs open. I clamp it shut. I'm fine, fine, fine, everything is fine. Except it's not. Because standing in front of me is a man in a navy T-shirt and khaki shorts. He waves, a hesitant, awkward gesture, and I wonder if he touched my shoulder or if that was just my dream. I sit up.

"We met at the engagement party, remember? I'm Lewis. I gave you my card."

The man turns to a boy, maybe ten or eleven, who is sitting cross-legged on the grass. In front of him are playing cards laid out in two rows. "Is it all right if we call it a day, Noah? Play again tomorrow?" The boy looks from Lewis to me and nods. He pushes the cards into a pile and walks into one of the houses behind us.

"Are you all right?"

I shield my eyes to make out his face, but it's in shadow and the effort of searching for his features is exhausting. I drop my hand.

"You were having a nightmare."

I touch the side of my face. I can feel the imprint of my book on my cheek, and at the corner of my mouth, there's a crust of saliva. I close my eyes. Pinpricks of red, blue, and green appear. I watch them converge, dissipate.

"Can I walk you home? I just want to make sure you're OK."

Home, home, I want to go home, but not my home, some dream of home where I will cry and my mother will come.

"I've said the wrong thing, haven't I?" He stoops down to pick up the playing cards. "Listen, I live just over there; do you want to come in, get some water?"

I shake my head. Why does he want to help, what does he want? I grip the edge of the bench to stand up, but my pulse races and I stumble. Under my T-shirt, I'm drenched in sweat.

"Have you been here all day?"

I don't know, I don't know.

"Drunk enough? It's the hottest day of the year."

Eating slips. Drinking slips.

He holds out his hand. For a second, it's the only thing I can see, my entire world, his outstretched palm. I take it.

THE POLAR EXPLORER HOUSE is immaculate. From the outside, it's like all the other pristine town houses on this stretch of the heath—three stories of floor-to-ceiling windows; Juliet balconies filled with hydrangeas; a small, manicured front garden. Inside, the house is so white I feel impure. The walls are pale, the floor is marble, and from the third floor, a window floods the hall with skylight. The only thing that isn't white is a chestnut staircase that rises up like the luminous spine of a conch. My cheeks burn under my makeup. I want to check it, put some more on, but I'm afraid of my reflection in this house.

The room the man leads me to, though, is the opposite of immaculate. Books are crammed into every space of the walls, stacked in towers, spilling over coffee tables, marked and tabbed in what can only be a complex system of primary-colored Post-its. It's a library chaotic with passion, a room surrendered to some obsession, and that obsession is a whirlwind that has blown the pages wide open.

"Lily? Did you hear what I said?" He is exactly as I remember—early thirties, dark brown hair, except two-day stubble blooms on his jaw, and rimless glasses frame his eyes. He sets down my rucksack and book. "Are you all right?"

I laugh, then stop, because I sound like a hyena. Lewis flinches and then carries on tidying, bundling things under the desk, transferring books from the sofa onto the rug. He gestures for me to sit down. I edge myself between two enormous volumes and try not to think or act crazy.

"Let me get you a drink."

I check the time on my phone—four in the afternoon. My alarm is set for five. This is the alarm that tethers me to my obligations; without it, I don't trust myself to get home before Daddy. What does he think I do while he's at work? Perhaps he doesn't think of me at all. Why should he? I'm exactly who he thinks I am. *Mama's girl. Mama's doll.*

My hands start to shake. When Lewis comes, I knot them behind my back.

"I was going to fetch some water and then I thought this would be better." He hands me a neon blue sports drink the color of those slushies Daddy used to buy us at the cinema when Mama was away. He'd let Julia order, she'd ask for three giant boxes of popcorn, hot dogs, nachos, and slushies, but Daddy never seemed to mind. He'd buy it all.

"You're trembling."

"Sorry." I drop the bottle, open my rucksack, and put on Jacob's sweatshirt, zipping it up to my chin, but that doesn't hide my chattering teeth.

"You don't need to say sorry," says Lewis quietly. He rubs his jaw and picks up the bottle, pressing it into my hand. I think of all the rules I'm breaking—don't talk to strangers, don't accept anything from them, never go into their house, and half of me thinks, *run*, but the other half is curious about what this man is doing with me, what I am doing with him. I put the bottle to my lips and swallow.

He opens the library windows, and when he judges it isn't sufficiently cool, he fetches a fan from another room, sweeping away the books on a side table so he can position it in front of me. The sound of the blades cutting through the closeness is calming. I peel off Jacob's sweatshirt, my skin is hungry for the cool air, but the thought of Lewis seeing my tideline of makeup is unbearable. I clutch the sweatshirt against my neck.

He settles down in a leather armchair opposite me, the first time he's sat down since I arrived. He takes out the playing cards from his pocket and thumbs them from one hand to the other, occasionally dropping a card on his lap. The flick of cards is hypnotic.

"What are you doing?"

"Noah, my neighbor, always slips some extra cards in from another pack. Look." He splays five kings in his hand, two are diamonds. "I bet there are more."

"The boy?"

Lewis chuckles. "Don't let him fool you. That boy is an expert card player—and a cheat."

"Why do you play with him?"

He shrugs. "His dad's gone; his mum works a lot. He spends a lot of the summer with his nanny."

"What game were you playing?"

"Slam." He looks up from the cards. "Do you want to try?"

I turn off the fan and sink to the floor. He cuts the deck two ways and lays out five piles of cards in front of him.

"Wait a minute, this is Spit." It was all the rage in primary school. Danielle Olins was the best in our class, a petite girl whose pretty freckles and shiny black hair belied her aggression at cards. I was second best, so we were constantly pitted against each other, our whole class gathering around us at breaktime. The last time I played was with her. I'd won a few rounds, and she started throwing her cards down messily so I couldn't see the last card, couldn't make a move. When she slammed down her final card, I slammed my hand down on hers, dug my nails into her freckled skin. "Stop cheating," I hissed. She screamed. That was it for Spit.

Lewis's eyes brighten. "An expert." He hands me the other half of the deck and then sits back and smirks.

The mockery, the challenge, are part of the game itself, but my strategy is always to focus on the cards. I lay the first card down and then I know my body is back under control in a way it hasn't been for days, blue sugar coursing through my bloodstream. I let my fingers take over. The cards fly down.

He looks up at me from behind his glasses. "Should I be worried?"

I smile at him. "Let's find out."

First three rounds, I lose. Lewis is quick, but I know I could be quicker, the connections between my mind and body are slow and rusty—I hesitate when I shouldn't, my fingers are clumsy, my left hand is sluggish. But in the fourth round, the stars align. Lewis lays down a ten, I have only royals left. Throwing down one card after the other, there is panic and elation and, just before I slam down my last card, a moment of velocity where nothing else matters.

Lewis blinks at me. "Where did you learn to play?"

"The streets of Blackheath."

He throws his head back and laughs, a laugh that fills the whole library. "I want a rematch."

"You're on."

We play again. I pretend to be checking my phone, but I really press Record. His power to make Mama's flashbacks seem very distant stuns me and, although I know my phone will only pick up the sounds of shuffling cards, the silly banter, the urge to capture this is irresistible.

"Why is this place called the Polar Explorer House?" I ask. It's my turn to deal. Through the bay window, two boys and their father take turns shooting a football into a portable net. The ball careens off in one direction and the boys chase after it, the warm breeze carrying their shouts into the library.

"Sir James Ross, polar explorer, lived here. He discovered the North Magnetic Pole."

"I didn't realize that was a place."

"Nor did I before I found out about him. He also discovered some kind of animal when he was in Antarctica, a walrus or a seal, something that lived on the ice."

"Is it yours?"

"It's my family home. Back when my parents bought it, it was worth next to nothing. Thirty years later . . . well, I don't think I could ever earn enough to afford it."

I split the deck, give him half, setting up quickly so I'll have a few seconds to look at him. He would be handsome apart from his nose, which is too long for his face, and there is a rabbity quickness to him that makes me feel a step behind.

My alarm blares. I jab manically at my phone and stand up. "I've got to go. Thank you for the drink."

Something crosses his face, disappointment perhaps, masked quickly. He picks up my etymology dictionary and *The Wonders of Language*, scanning the back cover. "Any good?"

"Very."

"You like linguistics?"

I shrug.

He walks me to the door, unclicks the latch, and then blinks before asking, "Do you want to play again sometime? During the summer, I do some gardening in the morning at The Queen's Orchard—we could play after."

Is this how relationships with older men begin, with kindness and cards? "Where is it?"

"At the bottom of Greenwich Park, just beyond the playground. It's closed to the public, but I volunteer most afternoons." He clears his throat, and I notice a slight tremor in his hand. "There are some other people around, but they won't bother you. Just ask for me at the gate."

He pulls the door open. Outside, the father has folded up the goal post and the trio are making their way home, the football tucked under the arm of the older boy, the younger one dancing around his father's ankles. Behind them, the traffic is building across the heath, the sky deepening to fig, and I think if I could stay, not even in the library or the house but here in this doorway, I'd be all right. Instead, I step out into the evening.

9 / DUMPLING

THE FIRST SUMMER AFTER JULIA left for university, Jacob started asking me to meet him for lunch—not every week, once a fortnight that might slip to once a month. He didn't explain why, but I guessed he thought I'd feel low alone, sluggish after watching episode after episode of reality TV with Mama, my life narrowed to a clutch of characters. His law firm, Hunter & Howell, is a five-minute walk from Spitalfields, so we started meeting up there when he became a trainee, in the old market where the food stalls are.

Jacob is eating his usual, *xiǎolóngbāo*, soup dumplings, one of Mama's favorites. I'd eat them too, but I'm afraid of the pinched parcels of pork broth, of anything Mama might like—I don't want to trigger a flashback. As my brother eats, I keep my eyes on the floor.

"You all right, Lil?" asks Jacob.

I nod.

"You're acting really strange."

"Sorry." I put my head in my hands, glimpse the market through my fingers: a Brazilian couple eating pulled-pork sandwiches; the queue of people at a curry stall; a pigeon pecking at crumbs. The heatwave confuses the business executives from the nearby office blocks, who repurpose their outfits: tights have been peeled off; suit jackets discarded; aviators located and pushed onto noses.

"What's wrong?" he asks. "Is it Mama? Is she getting worse?"

I wait for him to finish his last mouthful of dumplings. "Do you think Mama and I are the same?"

"The same?"

"I mean similar. Do you think we're similar?"

His left shirt sleeve has unfurled. He rolls it back up and stretches his arms out to feel the last few minutes of heat on his skin before returning to the office. "Why are you asking?"

"I look like her, I wear the makeup, I dress in pink, I drink spoilt orange juice—" My voice is high, I feel as if I might cry.

He rubs my shoulder. "None of that's true. You're wearing makeup *to look like her*, you make spoilt juice *for her*, you don't even like pink, do you?"

"I don't know."

"You do all that stuff to . . ." he searches for the right word, doesn't find one. "But it's not you. You know that, right?"

"I think maybe what I've been doing isn't very good. What if when you act too long like someone, you start thinking like them?"

"Lil, what are you talking about?"

I nearly blurt out about the flashbacks, but the tautness of his forearm as he grips his napkin stops me. However crazy they make me feel, I can't tell him. His body, coil-sprung to help me, is also the body that's failing him. He had a breakdown a year ago after Francie divorced him, he started crying and couldn't stop. Now he's on antidepressants, which work wonders, but he still can't cope with the twins, with loud noises, with the demands of his job.

"Are you worried about going to Oxford? Jules said she talked to you about it."

I grimace. I hate that they discuss me. "She thinks I need to . . . stop doing things before I go. You know, for Mama."

He puts his arm around me. I sink into the strength of him, my big brother, the one man whose affection I don't have to engineer. "Well, you're going, ready or not. You can be whoever you want to be. Leave all this behind. You don't have to be—" he breaks off, he's never repeated Julia's taunt, *Mama's girl, Mama's doll*, but I know that's what he's thinking. "You can be yourself."

Apart from Mama, who is that? Is it the me in that two-by-one-meter hole? I imagine the walls of cardboard rising up, breaking the floorboards of the attic, the quotes, the poems, the bright blue beneath expanding to fill my university room.

We wind through the crowds to a coffee stall. Jacob orders two iced lattes. "Dad called me the other day."

"Really?" I'm constantly surprised that other relationships exist outside the nexus of Mama—Daddy and Julia, Daddy and Jacob.

"We talked about the whole thing with the poems. He's pretty ashamed about all of it, apologized . . ." He makes a hand gesture, as if he's cutting through to the main point. "The important thing is, I don't think he's in love with her. The poems . . . I think he was just bored."

"Does it matter why he did it?"

Jacob stirs his latte, the milk turning the coffee pale, and we start to walk to his office. "It kind of does. I've been thinking . . . when I get better, come off the pills . . . I want to try again with Francie. Make us a family."

I stare at him, incredulous. Francie divorced him because he would disappear for days when they first had the twins. "He's not ready for fatherhood," she'd said, but it isn't fatherhood he can't abide, but the noise. He was like this as a child. Whenever Mama started shouting at Julia or screamed at him for not getting an A, he'd leave instantly, go out if he could, or pull a duvet around his ears, retreat into a numb, blank space. "Jay, the twins are always going to be loud, they're boys."

A hardness settles over his face, he rubs his ears, as if he can hear them shrieking now. "I'm doing better."

Is that true? This summer, Jacob persuaded Francie to start dropping the boys off with him, an hour here and there, when she wants to go to the gym or for a run. In short bursts, it's fine, Jacob watches movies with them, plays games. But every time one of them starts to cry, he calls Julia and me, making us swear never to tell Francie.

We reach his office. He nods to a few colleagues. "What do you think?"

I think no, Jacob, no. Francie's going to find out you can't cope. And even if she doesn't, she isn't going to want to marry back into our family, not after those poems, not after Mama's through with her. I watch his gaze trail to the revolving doors; his supervisor is heading back into work. "You should go. You don't want to be late back."

I watch him disappear into an elevator and then startle, glimpsing Mama in the reflection of the polished glass—how is she back, what's wrong, what has she heard? I lift my hand to wave at her. The reflection does the same. It's not Mama. It's me. I hightail it to the tube.

10 / ORCHARD

THE WALL AROUND THE QUEEN'S Orchard is the same as the wall around the park. Moss covers ancient red and purple bricks that bulge under centuries of weight, and from the cracks, weeds bloom, their stalks curved toward the sun. I snap off a dandelion, hear Jacob's voice in my head, *Make a wish*. Julia always refused, crushing the seeds between her fingers so that they fell out in clumps, but Jacob and I would do it together, wish and wish, send seeds flying. Now, I can't think what to wish for. The flower quivers. I blow.

"You know each dandelion has two hundred and fifty seeds, right?" Lewis walks toward me from the other side of the gate. I've been outside for a while, undecided about going in. What does he want from me? Why would a lecturer in his thirties play cards with an eighteen-year-old? He smiles at me from under his New York Yankees baseball cap. I drop the stalk and try not to grin.

He flips the latch, holds open the gate. "Let me show you something."

I see lavender first, blooming along one side of the wall, so alive with bees that in the sunlight, they seem not so much flowers as an experience of color. Arches of apples separate raised beds and, as I follow Lewis, a childish joy flickers through me when I catch sight of what's growing in them: sprouting webs of courgettes; ears of corn in silks; butternut squashes tailing into flower. I glimpse something black, part the leaves. Aubergines hang from their vines, illuminating their canopies with their dark light.

"Look," says Lewis, stretching his arms out, and then I see it. The orchard is flooded with thousands of winged seedlings, drifting over the roses, coming to rest in the freshly watered beds.

I hold out my hand. Seeds glance off my palm. "They're beautiful."

"They are, aren't they? But they'll take over the orchard if you let them. I'm weeding dandelions under the fruit trees—you can help if you want." He clears his throat, speaks softly. "Or if you're tired, there are benches around the orchard."

I blink. I want to be different today, self-possessed, ponytailed, and when I play this person, I instantly forget the other me, fold her away like a set of clothes. But now, with Lewis, she's squeezing through, and I wonder if that's really why I'm here, not because I want to play cards, but for this single, transgressive moment when I feel all my lacerated pieces. "I'm fine. I want to help."

SEED HEADS CATCH on my leggings, grass prickles my ankles. There's a volunteer ahead of us in a small, untamed meadow, the others, five or six, are back at the raised beds. Lewis greets each one we pass, but mostly everyone keeps to themselves. The only human sounds are raking, digging, the steady roll of wheelbarrows.

"How often do you volunteer here?" I ask.

"Just in the holidays," he says, nodding toward the vegetable beds. "Some of the volunteers stay for a few weeks, but the regulars I've known for years. When you come out of homelessness, planting a seed is powerful."

I stare at him, the sun on the back of his navy T-shirt, the sheen of sweat on his neck. He is wearing cargo shorts, his calves have caught the sun, and the stripe of skin between his T-shirt and hairline is the same color—warmed copper. "You don't mean you, do you? You haven't been homeless?"

He nods. We stop under an apple tree, and he sets out the tools.

"But you live in that incredible house."

He lifts up the dandelion leaves with one hand and then finds the root with the tip of his trowel. "You think people who live in beautiful houses can't be homeless? Anyone can fall off the edge."

"How old were you?"

"Fifteen."

"You ran away?"

He nods.

"Why?"

He inhales suddenly.

"Sorry, sorry, I'm an idiot, I never know the right thing to say . . ." but he isn't Mama, I don't know if an apology will work. I tear a blade of grass, wind it around my second finger, which purples.

"Don't do that."

"What?"

"Say sorry as though you're frightened. I'm not going to hurt you. Don't do that either." He gestures to my hand.

I release the grass. My finger returns to flesh.

He passes his hand across his face. "It's me, not you. I haven't spoken about it in a while."

Is it then that I really see him? Not a man in a tuxedo or the owner of The Polar Explorer House, but under an apple tree in the aftermath of confession. One arm is folded over his stomach as if he's expecting a blow, and in his irises, there are shards of orange. I'm not the only person who looks out and sees burning.

I don't ask him any more questions, I don't need to. I drop to my knees and start to weed.

WE GARDEN FOR hours, not talking very much. It's hard work in the heat, my T-shirt is damp against my back, but we take breaks from digging, snipping off the blowballs of dandelions or dividing the weeds into parts: stems for composting; roots and leaves for volunteers to make tea and salads; anything left is sent to rabbits at a nearby farm. Nothing is wasted.

When we're finished, he leads me to the compost bins at the top of the orchard. "Compost" from the Latin *componere*, to put together. I throw in the stems. Underneath armfuls of ivy, some rotten beets, the soil is dark and fluffy.

"Anything we harvest, we put over there." Lewis points to a small greenhouse. Crates of shallots and onions are stacked around its edges, bay leaves and lavender are drying on trays. I take up a stem, inhale its scent.

"Take it."

"Really?"

"You can take anything from the orchard. We'll have French beans and figs in the next few days. I'll get you a flower pot to take things home."

I follow him to the shed, but at the threshold, a smell stops me— rotting wood and rust that brings a metallic taste in my mouth, and then Mama's past that I thought I'd escaped from in this orchard, flickers into motion.

After the girl came back from her uncle's, she stood outside her house, taking in the chicken wire fence, the rusted metal hinge, the buckets catching water from the leaking gutter. Her mother had put the washing out to dry, and it dripped on the three plastic chairs, the line of sandals. Not once had the girl thought of these things; she never judged them to be good or bad. But now after her uncle's, she knew. They were poor. This was ugly.

Uncle Henry's house was a bright emerald, on a street where all the houses were colored. Around each window were tiles, matching green with pink flowers in the center. There were teak benches inlaid with mother-of-pearl instead of plastic chairs, and there were no leaking gutters, no washing on display. Sandals had been whisked away by two maids and returned when it was time to leave.

The girl's mother met her at the door. She looked more like a maid than one of the family. There were sweat patches under her arms, her skin was tanned, and she never wore jewelry, except that plain, purple jade ring. The girl thought: Baba was right not to let her come to Uncle's.

"How was it?" asked her mother.

It was the most beautiful house the girl had ever seen, but she knew she couldn't say. "It was OK. Nothing special."

"Were they nice to you?" asked her mother, folding the apron against her stomach.

The girl nodded. She didn't say that her aunt had taken one look at her dress and led her upstairs, how she knotted her daughter's old sarong at her waist and slipped a kebaya of pink flowers over her head. The girl had wanted it so badly, she almost cried.

"What did you eat?"

"Chicken curry," she replied quickly, except it wasn't like anything she'd ever tasted. Her cousin had laughed when she asked what it was. "Ayam buah keluak! You don't know what buah keluak is?" She shook her head and her cousin waved over the maid, who brought out a jar of black seeds that looked like shriveled mushrooms. "That's buah keluak. You'll die if you eat it before it's cooked," said her cousin. The girl spooned the sauce straight into her mouth to show her she wasn't afraid. Her father saw and smiled.

"What else?" asked her mother.

"They had these tiny cakes, kuehs they called them—"

"You went to your uncle's house and ate cake?" Her mother's voice was suddenly shrill, the apron in her hands wrung to rope. "How many times have I told you? You never eat cakes! You eat meat! Cakes are cheap—flour, milk, eggs . . ." She counted the ingredients out on her fingers. The apron dropped to the floor, ". . . but meat, meat! When the Japanese come, meat will disappear like that."

The girl hugged her very tightly, "Mama, the Japanese aren't coming anymore. The war is over."

She said it again and again until her mother's lips moved, until they were saying it together: "The war is over, the war is over, the war is over."

"Lily?" says Lewis.

I back away from the shed, stumble into the sunlight.

"Here, have some water." He thrusts a bottle at me.

I take three swallows, put my head between my knees. I'm soaked in sweat.

"Breathe, breathe; you're all right, Lily, you're going to be all right."

He says it over and over and I listen to him, the rhythm of his voice, that promise. The terror of the flashback ebbs away. I slide down against a tree trunk. Bark snarls my T-shirt.

He sits down next to me. "Are you all right?"

I shake my head, and it seems like the bravest thing I've ever done.

"What just happened?"

"You wouldn't believe me."

"Try me."

The tree makes it easy to say. I'm under the boughs in apple green light, not the person frantic to be believed; she's out there, in the open meadow. "I'm having these flashbacks. But they're not mine. They're my mother's."

Under his baseball cap, Lewis's expression is unreadable. He balances his chin on his knees, his left foot is tapping lightly. "How is that possible?"

"I don't know."

"When did it start?"

"The day before my birthday. A week before the engagement party."

"And you've just had another one?"

I nod.

"How do you know they're your mother's?"

It comes out in a rush, the image of Mama's father forcing her to drink the spoilt juice, how I make it for her too, and then I'm acutely aware that his left foot is still.

"Does she ask you to make it?"

I strip the bark off a twig. "Sometimes. Sometimes, I know she likes it, so I just make it for her. That's how I know the flashbacks are hers."

The silence between us is a choir, and then I unspool, imagining what he must think. I snap the stick into pieces. "I know I sound crazy, but I'm telling the truth."

He stops me with his hands, holding them out in surrender. "I believe you."

"Why? It doesn't make any sense."

"No, it doesn't. But I don't think you're lying."

I push a piece of twig deep into the soil. The earth is a dusty light brown. "Why is this happening to me? How can I stop it?"

He lifts his head to me. Under his cap, his eyes are starbursts of blue. "I don't know. But we'll figure it out."

11 / THE SAIL BOAT

*U*NCLE HENRY'S HOUSE WAS A *bright emerald.* The line rolls around my mind all the way home, weaving its way through the stories Mama told me, snaking in and out of my own memories, an inverse alchemy turning gold to dross.

The house was in all her stories. She said she was born there, it belonged to her father's family for generations, that was why she'd been devastated when she had to sell it after the car accident. She described the mother-of-pearl inlaid benches, her grandmother's *tingkat* collection, the kitchen of the emerald house was why we sought out Peranakan food like it was a drug—the taste of *otak otak,* fish cake grilled in banana leaves, the deep spice of *bak kut teh,* pork rib broth. We'd visited the house so many times, pulled up year after year on that incredible road in Joo Chiat, the humidity overwhelming as we stepped out of the cab. "There," Mama would say, pointing through the gate, "that's where I lived." I thought she was proud of where she'd lived but now, I think those visits must have been something else, for something else, and then my memory fractures.

Why has she lied?

I don't go to the hole. I head to Mama's bedroom and take it apart, easing clothes out of wardrobes and drawers, checking inside each bag and pocket. I pull out everything from under her bed, leaf through her old jewelry case, peer into old packaging for a hairdryer, a jewelry cleaner. There's nothing about her childhood. No mementos or photos, no letters or cards.

I check the attic. It's sweltering, and this, mixed with the disappointment of finding nothing makes me rough pushing aside Julia's junk—mud-encrusted tennis shoes, a hockey stick, posters of boybands and feminist slogans. I fling it all across the attic, the thwack of her hockey stick on the floorboards quelling something dark and inarticulate. A tin of her old charcoal sticks springs open, I crush each one to dust. My hands come away with shadow.

Eventually, I come to Mama's belongings, four suitcases filled with old coats, shoulder-padded jackets, and leather trousers, but they aren't what I'm looking for. Here's something, a folder with her birth certificate and academic records. I pull out her GCE grades—Bs, Cs, even a D. A single A for maths.

Mama told us she'd been the best at school. In the holidays, she'd force Jacob and Julia to practice their maths, railing at them when they didn't understand and, in the run-up to the 11+ exams, she physically tied Julia down to the kitchen stool to make her study. The impression of Mama as a straight-A student has always been so strong, I knew to mimic her effortless academic achievement, but now I glimpse another Mama—shabbier, not a genius, not the best.

She told us she won a scholarship to Oxford, but there is no offer letter, no correspondence from them at all. When I received my acceptance letter, she hugged me. "You're just like me, Lily, just like me." I was so happy I didn't see the clues she'd left all along. If she'd had an offer, it would have been from a specific college, but she never mentioned one. If she couldn't attend because of the car accident, they would have deferred her place.

Beyond that, there is her acceptance letter to the University of Singapore, and university transcripts. Nothing of Mama as a child, nothing to prove she lived in the emerald house or she didn't. Compare this to Daddy's belongings—two folders of his qualifications, and boxes stuffed with his old stamp collection, school reports, photo albums of him and my grandparents.

The wheels of Daddy's car crunch gravel on the drive.

I bound downstairs, meet him as he unlocks the door, his photo albums under my arm. "Where's Mama's stuff?"

He puts down his satchel. He's wearing a short-sleeve shirt in a light yellow, one of Mama's purchases for him, on sale because it is the exact shade of curdled cream. He blinks at me. His eyelashes are so blonde, they're almost white.

I hold out his childhood photo albums. "These are yours, right?"

He opens one slowly, his features brightening. "I haven't seen these in years!" He thumbs at someone's features.

"But where are hers? Why doesn't she have any?"

Daddy shields his eyes from the shafts of sunset to look at me. "Are you OK?" he says.

I press my fingers over the sockets of my eyeballs.

"Let's eat out this evening. Your choice. Anywhere you like." He smiles at me the way he'd smile at Leo or Albie, like whatever is wrong, he can fix. I wish I believed him.

HE GETS US a table at The Sail Boat, a restaurant overlooking the Thames that I've never been to before. We don't go out together, just him and I, although I've gone to dinner with Mama hundreds of times alone. It's an interesting choice for him, more suave. The banquettes are turquoise velvet, and overhead are dozens of copper pendant lights. He speaks to the maître d', a spry man with gelled-back hair, who greets him like a friend and leads us to a table beside French doors open to the river.

The sun has set, the deep lapis of the Thames is studded with the office lights of Canary Wharf, but it isn't the view that astonishes me, it's my father. He's in his element. He orders a medium-rare eight-ounce sirloin steak, a bottle of sparkling water, and a Peroni without looking at the menu. I didn't even know he drinks; he never touches a drop at home. He asks me if I want to share his onion rings, because "they're good here." I slide my eyes down the menu to check the prices.

It's the kind of place that doesn't bother with pennies, his steak is a straight £27, the onion rings, £8. Mama's going to freak out.

"Daddy," I ask, choosing the cheapest thing on the menu—a green salad. "How are you paying for this?" Mama checks his credit card religiously, calling him up to justify his expenditure. A meal like this would raise more than a red flag.

He takes a long drag of beer. "No need to worry."

"This is going to set her off." Mama's obsession with Daddy hasn't abated while she's away. She makes me report on his activities before I go to bed—what time he came home, what he's eaten, whether he's been in touch with the boys or Francie—and I do, faithfully copying and pasting last night's report and editing it with enough changes to look freshly written. Her responses flood in overnight—questions, clarifications, commentary on anything she finds suspicious, so that each morning, a storm of her thoughts engulfs me before I'm even out of bed. "She's on the warpath. You and I going to dinner, she'll find out."

He flaps open his napkin and lays it on his lap. "I have a private income."

"From where?"

"I do a bit here and there. Consultancy for historical cases, interviews, that kind of thing." Julia told me to always filch £20 notes off Daddy because he never realizes, he always has loads. Now I know why. He's been covering his tracks, a different income stream, a different bank account, cash-only transactions, and then I don't recognize him. Of course I don't. My only gauge on him is the person he is at home, my only impressions, Mama's—"worthless," "nothing," "lazy," but now I see he is none of those things. He's successful. He's a consultant. He has a life beyond Mama, one he's clearly enjoying. My father I can't imagine having an affair with Francie. This man, I absolutely could.

The onion rings arrive in a basket. He pushes them between us. The coating between my teeth is crisp; he's right, they are good. I wait till the steak arrives before speaking to him. The lies come to me easy. "I'm doing something for Mama, a surprise for when she gets back, so I was looking for photos of her from when she was little. There are albums of you as a child and Uncle Bobby, and ones of us," I speak as if we're all assembled in front of him—Jacob, Julia and me—"but none of Mama. Are they somewhere else?"

He shakes his head.

"What do you mean?"

He dips a fry into the black peppercorn sauce and shrugs. "She doesn't have any. She lost those things in the fire."

"The fire?"

He waves his fork at me. "You know, the fire that killed her parents."

"You mean the car accident. Her parents died in a car accident." He looks at me strangely. "She broke her arm, remember?"

"She broke her arm jumping out of the window when her house was on fire."

My head swims. "She definitely told me she'd been in a car accident."

Daddy slides a shred of rocket onto his fork and smiles at me, as if he's indulging a junior pathologist who's identified the wrong cause of death. "The scars on her arms are consistent with fire." He dips a chip into ketchup. "Have I ever told you about my first case?"

I shake my head, annoyed at the distraction.

"It was a five-year-old girl. Her grandmother had a heart attack and knocked over a heater, which started a fire." He gestures across his front. "Tiny body, third- and fourth-degree burns on the head, neck, and upper chest areas, soot in her upper airways. They found her under the bed; that's pretty common. Children will hide from a fire rather than run. So when your mother told me she'd jumped from that burning house, I thought, this woman is the girl that got away. Even as a child, she was smart enough, quick enough to run."

The girl who hid, the girl who ran, a car accident, a fire, which of these is Mama? She is a Russian doll, so many layers that I don't know if I'll ever reach the last one. I stir my water. Bubbles cling to the striped straw.

Ask me, ask me what's wrong, I will Daddy.

But he doesn't. I'm not loud enough for him, not a small, charred girl or a bludgeoned cheekbone or unusual fibers clenched between a jaw, and then my voice is suddenly loud. "She told me her parents died in a car accident, I remember, I'm not making it up. That's not all. I found her school transcripts. She hardly got any As, just one for maths. I don't think she even got that scholarship to Oxford!"

Daddy carefully puts his fork down. "Listen, I know your mother has always had high expectations of you all. You, out of the three, always seemed to meet them, no problem. You're so similar to her."

"Don't say that."

He wipes a smear of ketchup from his lips. "Maybe I should have said this before. I've thought about it, but there was never a good time. But you shouldn't push yourself like you've been doing. Now you've got into Oxford, you've done it, you've achieved something, you don't have to get As. What your mother got or didn't, doesn't matter. You don't need to compete with her."

His words ricochet through my brain, the left-field psychoanalysis, so wrong, so right, finding its mark. Compete? Mama is the only one who competes.

"Dessert? Strawberry ice cream?"

I stare at him dully. I liked strawberry ice cream when I was seven.

"You can try the ice cream here, but there's a new place that opened a few months ago, I took Francie and the boys there. After you finish, we'll go."

He pays with cash, his wallet so heavy, it swings open.

Later, when he's asleep, I steal five crisp £20 notes from him, far more than the weekly £20 I'd normally take. He'll never suspect me, not his strawberry ice-cream eating, seven-year-old daughter. Even if he does, who would he tell?

12 / DANDELION

A FLURRY OF MAMA'S MESSAGES greets me in the morning.

07:25: Anytg happen lqst n8t?

I grip the phone. Mama is so dangerous because she has an instinct for when things are off. True, her gift isn't specific, she suspects Daddy is visiting Francie, but it's enough to unsettle me about going to The Sail Boat. I have to be careful.

07:27: Keep yr eye on him.
07:27: U tell me if he goes to that whore's place.

"Whore?" The only person Mama calls "whore" is Julia, and I wonder whether the holiday was a good idea after all because it hasn't curbed her paranoia, it's given her time to weave a more outlandish narrative: Francie is to blame. Although why, I don't understand.

I sit up and prepare my report to Mama, recounting an eventless dinner, rejecting that he has visited Mama's new enemy, vowing allegiance, loyalty, love to a woman I'm not certain I know.

I'M SO EXHAUSTED from composing replies to Mama, I don't stalk a man when I reach the park. I want a quick rush, the force of a body against mine. In the park, I see one walking toward me, white T-shirt, black jeans, tortoiseshell Ray-Bans. I crash into him.

Almost instantly, I know I've made a mistake. He smells like a teenager, no complex aftershave, just locker-room deodorant over damp clothes, and up close, he isn't wearing black jeans at all but sweatpants that are bobbling, and no socks.

"You're in a rush." He is smiling, but something is missing from his eyes. He grabs my arms. "Speak English?"

A tattoo rises from the neck of his T-shirt, the tail of a snake.

"Kon'ichiwa."

A fleck of his spit lands on my chin. I think, good, little Mama's girl deserves this—spit on her, grab her, speak racist shit—but it is my skin that hurts under his fingertips.

"Fuck, I love Japanese girls."

My stomach flips. There is a place in this man that is wild. But I have a wild place too. I wrench my arms away and scratch his face, three clean marks just like Mama made on Daddy.

"Bitch!" he shrieks and stumbles back. People freeze, some edging forward, others uncertain. "Calm down, calm down," he says to them. "*She* bumped me." He pushes past, swearing.

"Are you all right?" an elderly woman asks. Her husband peers at me from behind her shoulder.

I don't answer.

PETE, THE HEAD gardener, lets me into the orchard. He tells me Lewis isn't here yet and asks if I'm all right to carry on weeding. I nod, don't trust myself to speak. Everything is out of control—Daddy, Mama, the man, my claws.

Under the apple trees, hundreds of dandelions bloom. I imagine unseen things—the sharp crackle of growth, larvae tunneling through fruit, the quiet menace of roots reaching into the soil, and the need to rip them out is overpowering, an unslaked thirst. I fall on one, tearing at the plant, scrabbling at the earth until I find the stem, chase it deeper, pull.

Lewis arrives quietly behind me. He hands me a trowel. "It's easier with a blade."

I plunge it into the soil.

By the end of the afternoon, I'm exhausted and elated, filling five buckets of dandelions. I sort them into their parts, hesitating at one I can't bear to dismantle—a dandelion with a magnificently gnarled taproot. It's something from a fairy tale, a witch's finger beckoning all beasts to itself. I want it as a museum piece, to turn it over in the hole and savor its hideousness. I shove it into my rucksack.

"Keeping that one?" says Lewis.

I nod. "For my room."

"Let me find you something better. How much sun does your room have?"

"None." He blinks and I realize it sounds like I live in a dungeon. "I mean, I want something that grows in the shade. What grows in the dark?"

"Let me check with Pete; he'll know."

My right hand is stiff from digging, my little finger aches. I rub the curve between my joints. The pain flares.

"Do you have time for some cards?"

I half shrug, half nod. We haven't spoken since we've been in the orchard, slipping into the rhythm of the work, but now I'm shy with him, the only witness to my anger. It's twenty-six degrees. Lewis wants to get something iced, so we walk to the café at the museum. At the entrance, I pause. Through the windows, I see a group of students spread over four or five tables, their arms draped over each other's shoulders. In front of me, two girls smile coyly into selfies. In moments like this, I glimpse the meagerness of my own connections. The students clapping each other on the back, the pair of girls are connected to hundreds of people in complex webs I'd never understand. "Can we stay out here?"

"Sure." He reaches into his pocket and hands me his deck of cards. "Shuffle. I'll get us something to stave off this heat."

I pull out a seat, flick through a newspaper someone's left behind. The heatwave dominates the headlines: trains breaking down on their tracks; rumors of a hosepipe ban; torrential rain to come. In Singapore, the weather would never make the news, and then I remember standing outside a Hainanese bakery on the east coast when the rain switched to deluge, the banana trees, the road suddenly invisible. I'd never seen anything like that, hadn't understood until that moment what it meant when the sky opened. Mama stood next me, handing me my breakfast—*kaya*, coconut jam, toast and *kopi*, a thick black coffee sweetened with condensed milk that I'd become addicted to. "What did you do when it was like this?" I'd asked her.

"Nothing," she'd said. "Waited for it to stop," and then I'm crying at Greenwich in the heat, at Singapore in monsoon, at my mother speaking about a childhood I don't know is real.

"I got you an iced latte," Lewis says, setting down a tray.

"Thanks." I brush my tears away quickly.

He slips me a napkin. Behind it, I close my eyes.

"Are you OK?"

"The flashbacks make me question everything—all the stories Mama told me, all the things Mama and I did together. I don't know what they mean anymore." I ball up the napkin.

He cuts the deck, the cards flicking against his hands as he shuffles. "You're close, your mother and you?"

"So close. We're best friends, we're the same—" My hand flies over my mouth. "She confides in me, she always has. But the flashbacks undermine all of that. The Mama in them isn't someone I know."

We start playing, not competitively, but slowly, Lewis mirroring my pace. "I know a little about what that's like," he says, "thinking you know someone. There was a scandal before my father killed himself . . . a girl accused him of hurting her. I still don't know if it's true." His face is impassive.

"Does it drive you crazy, not knowing?"

"It did, for years, and I found a lot of answers. But there came a point when I had to accept I would never really know."

I tell him about the emerald house, the transcripts, the accident, and the fire. "Each time I look, there are more questions."

"I could check if she got a scholarship to Oxford if you want. I'll call the admissions office."

"You don't mind?"

"Won't take me any time at all." He has a flush of royals—jack, queen, king, ace. I have a queen, which could block his ace if I'm quick enough, but I don't put it down. He takes the round. "And there might be a way of working out if your mother lived in the emerald house. Do you know the address?"

"It's in Joo Chiat, there's a row of them. I don't know exactly what number it is, but I could probably find out."

"If you have the address, you could do a land registry search, most countries have one. That will show you current and historical owners. If your mother's parents are on the list, maybe she isn't lying."

I watch him pull at the neck of his T-shirt, an attempt to get the air moving, and an awful mistrust yawns in me. Why is he doing this? What's in it for him?

Do you know what men do, Lily? They MAS-TUR-BATE.

Men do whatever they want, don't you know that, Lily?

Kon'ichiwa.

I put my coffee down. "I'm not going to fuck you if that's why you're doing all this. And don't think I'm some philosophy paper you can write up—the girl with her mother's flashbacks. I'll deny everything."

He levels his navy eyes at me. "Is that what you think? I'm grooming you or exploiting you?"

I stare right back. Every minute of my life is people saying, "I love you," "I promise," and it never means anything except that they want something. "I'm not naive. Why are you helping me?"

Lewis takes off his cap, drags his hand through his hair. He stares at the rise of the hill, the green leaching to straw. "No one would talk to me about the scandal even after my father died, not my mother or any of my family. He was just gone, and there was this silence." He draws his palm across the air between us. "It took me years to figure out what had happened. I remember promising if I got through this and I saw someone struggling, I wouldn't let them go it alone."

Inside me, walls collapse, ramparts crumble, not under airstrikes or gunfire but surrendering before an old, forgotten power—a child's vow. "Is that why you ran away?"

He nods. "I felt alone. I didn't feel like I belonged."

After the café closes, I pretend to leave Lewis at the Greenwich gates and then double back, follow him up the avenue of horse chestnuts and over the heath until he disappears inside The Polar Explorer House. I would stay outside his house all night if I could, the dry grass underfoot, the sun beating against my back. I want this feeling, the feeling of a friend, the feeling of not being alone. I get my phone out and take photos—the shadow cast by the library curtain, the lion handle on the front door, close-ups of the yellowed grass. Capture it, hold it forever.

13 / SWIMSUIT

DID I THINK I COULD have a nice afternoon like that without pay-back? Impossible. My family will extract their pound of flesh, and there is no one to prevent the shedding of my blood. As I unlock the door, the stillness makes my heart pound. I don't go inside. I drop to the doormat, my legs stretched out into the porch. Half in, half out, I check my phone.

Mama has been manageable during her holiday, photos of her startling white villa pepper her interrogations about Daddy. But now, I have five missed calls and three messages in that irritating patois she reserves only for texts.

> 16:44: 2 missed calls.
> 16:45: U not picking up.
> 16:46: Where r u? Why u not answering?
> 16:51: 3 missed calls.
> 16:56: Call me.

Then I'm consumed by Mama again, my mind flickering down familiar paths. Are these statements or accusations, commands or threats? Does the full stop signal more trouble or less? I check my other messages. The bomb is buried in the "Family" WhatsApp group, detonated at 16:02. Mama has sent a photo of herself in a baby pink swimsuit. It's clever really, accentuating her best features—the cutouts at the waist baring triangles of skin, the plunging halter top cutting across her cleavage. She could just about pull off the one-piece, but not the pose. She is holding her hands above her head, her mouth curved into a pout, her eyes closed in ecstasy. I hold my breath as I scroll through the messages.

Mama: 16:02: Wish you were here.

Jacob at 16:04: Are you having a nice time?

Mama at 16:05: yah. need a BREAK. so beautiful.

Jacob at 16:07: You look happy.

Mama at 16:09: I am.

Julia at 16:12: You look ridiculous. Put your tits away, no one wants to see that.

Julia at 16:13: Except Jonathan. Does he love it?

This is normal, nothing unexpected—Jacob—diplomatic, Julia—incendiary—but my hand trembles when I read Julia's messages to me.

16:15: Have you seen this shit? Haha.

16:40: So Mum called Dad and shouted at him for twenty minutes. Dad told me to stop replying because I'm making this worse.

16:41: She's such a bitch.

16:42: Are you there?

I don't reply. She's a hound with Mama, scenting blood, circling for the kill. Maybe Mama didn't tie her to a chair to make her study for her 11+ exams. Maybe she just tied her up for a little bit of peace.

I message Mama, apologizing for missing her messages and calls, telling her I'm here if she wants to talk, telling her that I lost my phone and have only just found it.

She doesn't reply. The minutes grow. The hopeful half of me tells me *she's asleep*, but the cynical half says *she's angry with you*.

Daddy pulls into the drive. He switches off the engine, opens the door, but he doesn't come out. Then I realize why Mama isn't messaging me. She is screaming at him down the phone, her anger blunted by bad reception. I stand up slowly so I can see him. He's leaning against the headrest, his forearm flung over his eyes. I listen for a few minutes and then push the door shut.

When he finally comes into the house, he makes a dinner he'd make the twins—fish fingers, boiled potatoes, peas. We'd never eat this if Mama was here. Daddy would heat up gourmet microwave meals, but he's distracted, opening one drawer and then forgetting what he's searching for. He holds a glass under the tap. Water overflows down the sides. I turn the tap off and lead him to the table.

He slouches over his plate, cutting into the fish fingers. After a few mouthfuls, he puts his cutlery down. His voice is hoarse. "Do you think she's coming back?"

"Did she say she wasn't?"

"She says she's happy in Santorini with him."

He looks toward the fridge and blinks. I can't reconcile my father crushed in front of me with the stranger and his private income; there are as many versions of Daddy as there are of Mama. I tell myself not to get involved, not to say anything, but the way he's lost himself in the middle distance exposes such a private hurt that I can't help myself.

"Would that be such a bad thing? If she went to live with Jonathan, you wouldn't have to hide going to The Sail Boat or drinking Peronis, you could go where you wanted, spend what you wanted. How she's been with you lately . . ." I think of the scratches on his face, the bite mark on his arm, the pitch of her shouts from the car, all that without even knowing about the porn or his secret bank account. "It might be better for everyone that way."

Daddy's chin is on his chest, his shirt is stained with ketchup. "How could it be better? She's my wife. She's your mother."

"Daddy—"

"—I love her!" he roars, and it's the most shocking thing I've ever heard, more profane than the most explicit swear word, more obscene than the sickest secret, and in that instant, I understand why my father is in my mother's thrall. The burned girl he couldn't save, her soaring highs and devastating lows make him feel things that someone who slices open cadavers and examines strangled throats doesn't feel. Even his subterfuge is devoted to her, achieved only because of her control. He doesn't want to be free. Subjugation is very close to love.

I put my arm awkwardly around his back, but he doesn't emerge, so I do with him what I do with Mama; I tell him what he wants to hear, doesn't matter if it's the very thing he should dread. "She's coming back."

He beats away tears with his fists. "Really? How do you know?"

"I know," I say, because I do. He's right where she wants him.

LATER THAT EVENING, I join Daddy in the living room. We used to read together all the time before Mama and the poems; Daddy flipping through his medical journals, me with a novel. It started off as a kind of homework club. Jacob and I didn't have desks in our rooms so Jacob took the writing desk in the living room, and I spread my textbooks out on the coffee table. Even Julia joined us sometimes. Perhaps that's why Mama didn't clamp down on it sooner, the shroud of schoolwork protected us. "I'm overqualified," she'd say if Jacob asked her for help, "ask your father." We stayed late into the evening. Mama was a deep sleeper, she needed a good ten hours to function in the morning; as long as she thought we were studying, she didn't really notice we were just reading. But on the rare occasion she walked in on us, she only needed to look at me and I'd follow her out.

Daddy is already lying on the easy chair reading a thriller in striped, blue pajama bottoms and a white T-shirt. The T-shirt makes me wince; moth holes riddle the edge. The standing lamp throws light over his head and torso, accentuating his age, the thinning hair, the sag of his jowls, a hollowness around his eyes.

His eyes widen when he sees me, but neither of us says anything. I sink into my old place at the couch and research the address of the emerald house to enter into the Singapore Land Authority. The road comes up after a few minutes of googling, and then I use Street View to find the number of the house. My heart hammers as I drag my cursor past a blurred photo of a small woman. Is it Mama? Will I find her here?

14 / TANTRUM

I COULDN'T SLEEP LAST NIGHT, worrying about Mama's return home tomorrow. Some things I can predict—that she'll be livid after Julia's message, that she'll have devised some strategy to deal with Daddy—but I don't know if the flashbacks will get worse. What am I going to do if Mama tells stories about her emerald house, her scholarship to Oxford, the car accident? Play along? I stared out the window, a blanket round my shoulders. There were no stars, not in London, but the skyline was studded with other lights—the soft glow of the Millennium Dome, the cable cars festooned over the Thames. The whole world was awake, why should it be any different for me? At 3 a.m., I stopped pretending I might go to bed and headed downstairs to prepare for her arrival, a cursory tidy at first, and then I went inch by inch, color-coding her wardrobe, organizing the crystal hairpins in her jewelry box, folding her socks so that they stood up like soldiers.

Lewis messages me while I'm dusting her windowsill, asks if I can meet him outside the Royal Observatory this afternoon; he has news. I spend half an hour composing the word "yes."

I'm interrupted later by a different message; Jacob on the "Brother & Sisters" group chat: "Can you come over? Boys are here."

A familiar dread seeps in, alarmingly cold. He's sent similar Mayday messages three times this summer when Francie's dropped off the twins, so I know what this means: something's happened with Leo and Albie. I stare at the screen and wait. Julia messages, right on cue: *Pick you up in 10?* She always shows up for Jacob and me. She's volatile and crazy with Mama, but with Jacob and me, she's loyal to a fault.

She arrives in Chrissy's car wearing a kaftan, strange because Julia isn't one for covering up. From a distance, it's easy to think her outfit isn't anything special, but up close, that kaftan, with its rainbow chevrons, is Missoni, the sunglasses carelessly pushed to the top of her head are Prada. She is wearing about a month's worth of rent.

"Bets on what it is this time—a tantrum or a fight?" Her chestnut eyes are almost black.

"A fight."

"Wishful thinking."

"Yeah."

A car pulls out in front of us, making Julia swerve. She sounds the horn for longer than necessary and then smashes her palms on the steering wheel. I see then what her long sleeves can't conceal, the thinness of her wrists, the jut of bone against her watch. "Fuck! How long are we going to keep doing this?"

"What?" I grip the edge of the seat. It's only with Mama and Julia that I get this vertiginous feeling, like I'm at the top of a roller coaster before it clatters down.

"Sorting out Jacob, protecting Leo and Albie."

I stay quiet.

"You know I got into Durham, Bristol, Nottingham. I could have been away from here. But you both keep me back. Look after your fucking selves!"

"I do look after myself."

Julia sneers. "You're worse than Jacob."

"That's crazy. I can actually look after children—"

Julia cuts me off. "Jacob knows why he gets like that with the boys, we talk about it, he's seeing a therapist. But you? What do you know? Only how to placate Mama." Her laugh is mirthless. "You're—"

"Don't say it, Jul—"

"Mama's girl! Mama's doll! Why do you take that rucksack everywhere? Why are you wearing pink and that god-awful makeup?" She swipes at my face. "Mama isn't even in the country!"

"It's just habit!"

"Well fucking break it! When I think about how weird it was that Mama dyed your hair, that you were wearing makeup at eleven, how she came after you every dinnertime saying it would be better if you looked more Chinese, I could kill her!"

Heat rises up my cheeks. "That's not what happened. I was the one who wanted the makeup so I could look like Mama."

Julia doesn't take her eyes off the road, but her body gives way against the seat, a marionette with the strings cut loose. "This is why you're more fucked than Jacob. Because you don't actually remember."

I look out of the window, my hand against my mouth. How can two people in the same house have such different impressions of events? Mama never made me. It was my choice.

We don't speak for the rest of the journey. I put in my headphones and listen to the recording of Lewis and me playing Spit.

JACOB LIVES AT Millennium Village, a glass-fronted, mixed-tenure development on the peninsula. "It's basically a council flat," Mama hissed when he told her about the "help to buy" scheme, despite the smallest apartment costing more than £350,000.

The screaming is audible from outside the building, so we pick up the pace. Julia fumbles for the key, swears, and when the door swings open, we take up our stations—me with the boys, Julia with Jacob. Jacob isn't in the living room, it's just Albie thrashing on the floor and Leo watching TV. I kiss the silk of Leo's hair, ask him if he's OK. He doesn't reply and for a second, I think I'm seeing a young Daddy—impassive, desensitized, destined to seek more dangerous highs. I hold him tightly.

Albie is mid-flow, his mouth open in a scream, back arched and rigid, head thrashing from side to side. He's flung off his dinosaur T-shirt and is scrabbling at his chest. How long has he been like this?

I hold his hands away from himself. His pudgy wrists twist inside my grasp.

"Don't want you!" he screams, his voice hoarse.

"I know, but you're hurting yourself."

"Get Daddy! I want my daddy!"

"Daddy can't come right now."

"Get my daddy now!" The command sets off a drumroll of kicks against an armchair. I keep hold of his hands, do what all the parenting books say—speak in a low, calm voice, tell him I love him while casting around for clues. There are no unwashed plates in the sink, the surfaces are wiped down, but on the small square dining table, a mug has rolled on its side and coffee drips onto a chair. The floor underneath is a mash of plate shards and peanut butter toast.

I think Albie must have done this, and then it dawns on me that this is greater than a two-year-old in a highchair can accomplish. It was Jacob. Albie must have started having a tantrum, and Jacob couldn't stop it. Out of rage, perhaps, or to shock him, Jacob swept their break-fast off the table. A memory comes to me, unbidden—Mama doing the same thing to Julia. "You don't want to eat? Don't eat!" The span of her arm was an eagle's, sweeping not just Julia's breakfast but all of ours off the table.

Beneath me, my nephew's body convulses with rage, his screams a constant "Get my daddy!" I know how he feels, wanting someone who won't come. How can a two-year-old contain that? I can't. "I love you, I love you; it's all right," I whisper to him. "Kick, kick if it makes you feel better." He takes me up on it and beats and pounds and hollers.

THE EXERTION OF the tantrum has drained Albie; he's fallen asleep. I carry him into the stroller. He's a cherub now, the soft pudge of his arms, the slight pout of his lips, but he's clammy, his cheeks puffy. I search the nappy bag Francie's left, pull out some cream. Even before the poems, Mama hated Francie for getting pregnant—"she's ruined him, so easy, open your legs and you've snared a lawyer"—forgetting that it's Francie, not Jacob who's sacrificed the chance of being a lawyer. Her intellectual rigor, her organizational skills are now redeployed to packing all the essentials her sons might need.

"Nap time, Leo," I say, holding out my arms to him. "Into the pushchair."

He comes to me, the first time he acknowledges my presence, burying his head in the nape of my neck. I strap him in, tell him he can watch the end of his show before we go. "Back in a minute. Just checking on Daddy and Auntie Jules."

Outside Jacob's bedroom, I hear Julia comforting Jacob so tenderly, my flint and flesh sister. "You didn't hurt them," I hear her say. "You just wanted Albie to stop."

I push open the door and gag. It's the private smell of used sheets overlaid with something cloying. I nudge a pile of clothes with my foot. A pair of jeans tumbles down, unfurling a pool of vomit. Jacob is sitting in the corner with his duvet over his head, his eyes red like the inside of a mouth. Julia sits next to him.

"Albie's passed out, but Leo's still awake," I say. "I thought I'd take them out for a nap in the stroller. Do you want to come?"

"Did you hear Lil?" Julia says softly. "The boys are fine. Lil says they're fine. We can go out together."

Jacob shakes his head. He did this as a child, pulled his duvet around his ears when he couldn't cope, but he's not child now—he's a father. I recall the blue TV glare reflected in Leo's eyes, the scratches over Albie's ribs, the peanut butter. "You're coming, Jay," I say.

He doesn't move.

"Get up."

"Stop it, Lil," snaps Julia, but I don't.

I open the window behind them. "It stinks in here, it's disgusting, this whole room is disgusting. Now get up." I prod him with my foot. "This isn't going to be how your sons' day with you ends. You are going to get up and we're going out. Your sons need you."

He pulls the duvet tighter round his shoulders.

I fling it off him. Julia gasps. Jacob stands up to reach for it.

I slap him.

The sound fractures the air and I stumble back, astounded not at my own violence but at the breaking of a promise—we'd never hurt each other, we'd always protect each other. Isn't that why we're here?

Julia is shouting, "Stop it, you don't understand!" but she doesn't have to. I fall on his neck.

"Sorry, I'm sorry, I'm so angry. I don't want to be like this, I don't want you to be like this."

"S'all right, Lil, s'all right."

Julia presses into the wrecked trinity of our arms, and I cry, vowing to master the lessons the boys learn at nursery: keep your promises, don't hit, forgive.

"Let's go to the beach," Julia whispers. She is remembering us spending our summers on the banks of the Thames. "All three of us."

"I want them to be with you today," he says. "They'll be safer."

She shakes her head at me, it's no use, and kisses his cheek. I squeeze Jacob's hand on the way out.

In the living room, Leo's show isn't finished so I sit on the floor next to him. Julia lays her head against a sleeping Albie. Together, we watch an episode of the perfect rescue mission where heroes know what to do and drowning people can be saved.

15 / BEACH

FOR ALL MAMA'S BITCHING, THERE are few places in London where a trainee lawyer can live by the Thames. There's no sand, just pebbles and, with the tide receding, the bank has turned to marshland, the river silted and opaque. Even so, there's something about being by the water on a hot day that feels like a holiday despite the skyline of cranes and half-finished developments. The cable cars string out across the river like fairy lights.

Leo falls asleep as soon as we're outside, so we push the stroller along the slipway and lift it onto the pebbles. I pull the shade over the boys while Julia lays out a picnic blanket, and then we do what we always do when we're at the beach, we run our hands along the pebbles, searching. Centuries of the Thames as London's sewer bring drift glass to the shore—broken pieces tumbled underwater until the edges are worn smooth, the surfaces frosted. On this beach, I've found the cornflower shoulder of a poison bottle and a Victorian marble with a swirl of rainbow.

Julia, however, prefers to collect shells, not even beautiful ones—tests of sea urchins, muddy razor clams, gray-painted top shells, mussels. As she talks, she picks out drift glass for me, shells for herself. "You can't just freak out at Jay. You could make things worse. He's getting therapy. He's doing better."

"How was that better?"

"He used to be bad when the boys cried, remember? He can deal with that now. But the fighting and Albie's tantrums are a whole other level." She wipes a smear of mud off her fingers before scraping her hair back into a bun. "It's triggering for him, and when he tries to stop Albie, he thinks he's turning into Mama."

"Maybe he is."

"Never say that, never!"

"There was hot coffee on the chair and broken plates on the floor. They could have been hurt."

She shakes her head. "It's just a phase. Albie will grow out of, it'll get easier. Jay's stressed at work; his supervisor reminds him of Mama."

I pick out for her the kind of shell she'd like, a ridged oyster shell the color of slate. "He was hungover. He shouldn't see the boys when he's like that."

"You say it as if it's so easy—don't do this, get up, stop freaking out."

"Because it is."

"Oh really? Just like that?" She snaps her fingers. "Could you help yourself when you slapped him?"

"That's different."

"It's not different. It's just like you and how you take that rucksack around with you." She steals it off my lap and jumps up. Drift glass and shells spill off the blanket. "Is it so easy for you to leave this at home?"

Blood roars in my ears. "Give that back."

"What's in here anyway?"

"Stop—" but she upturns it, pours it out onto the rug. When she sees my wallet of cash, my *London A–Z*, spare mobile battery, snacks, the energy drains from her. She repacks it carefully and hands it back to me. "I didn't know you were worried about all that, I didn't know—"

"Don't, just don't." I hug it to my chest.

We make our excuses to separate after that. Julia says she wants to check on Jacob, I tell her the boys should have some time on the beach. We're both relieved. My mind ticks over her insinuations every second I'm with her. I want to be away.

When Albie and Leo wake up, they are completely normal, daring each other closer to the water's edge, squealing at the mud squelching in their sandals. If Mama was here, she'd scold them and wash their feet with bottled water, but she's not and it's boiling. I take off my shoes and roll up my jeans. "I'm co-ming!" I growl in my scariest monster voice. The boys shriek and run, scoot toward the water, back to the shore. I grab Leo under his armpits, spin him around. The curve of his smile fills my vision. "Again, again!"

"My turn!" yells Albie, tugging at my jeans, the pitch of his voice a whine. I spin him higher than Leo and faster, his feet flying. I worry about him the most. Leo is self-possessed, blessed with Francie's easy grace, but Albie is fitful and jealous, drawn to proving himself with extraordinary acts of foolishness. One word from Leo, and Albie would swallow a rock or run straight into the water.

When the sun grows too hot, I move us into the shade of the bushes and set out the picnic. They eat quickly and then they're back out to the river, the water soaking their shorts. I stay on the beach, collecting "dinosaur eggs" for the boys, white stones flecked with gray. The tide brings a piece of driftwood to my feet, something Julia would like. I pluck it from the water, rub it dry against my T-shirt. It is almost weightless, a short length gnarled into two branches, pocked with holes, and as I stare at it, the darkness of the holes seems to grow larger, as a flashback breaks in.

The girl's mother checked the apartment number against a scrap of paper, and then knocked. A pretty woman came to the door, dressed in a plain top and patterned skirt. She lit up when she saw the girl's mother. "Jiějie, older sister, is it really you?" The woman threw her arms around the girl's mother. They started crying.

"Come, Mei." The girl's mother coaxed her out from behind her dress. "This is Auntie Liling, my měimei, younger sister."

The girl was shocked. She knew her mother had a younger sister, her mother had told her about the games they'd played in Hangzhou, but she'd never mentioned she was in Singapore.

Her auntie crouched down in front of her and brushed her cheek with her finger. "Bǎobèi, baby." The girl liked her immediately because no one called her bǎobèi and when she smiled, it was her mother's smile. "Come upstairs."

Her mother and her aunt caught up in the kitchen about her aunt's journey to Singapore, how she was settling in, her businessman friend, and then the conversation seemed to tilt toward her mother, and the room changed.

"I wanted to bring you something, to welcome you to Singapore, you're my little sister, my only family, but Jimmy, he . . ." Her mother shook her head and gripped her own forearms. Her eyes were shut to block out the shame of coming empty handed, to shut out what the girl's father was like, but the girl knew her mother was seeing all the things he did to her, could never really shut it out.

Her aunt ushered her mother into the living room, but the girl could hear her mother's suffocated voice carrying over her sobs: "He takes everything I earn, he drinks, and sometimes . . . he does things, bad things . . ."

The girl took Goldie out of her bag. Goldie covered her ears with her paws.

On the way to the bus, her mother stopped suddenly and crouched down to look at the girl straight in the eye. She didn't have to warn the girl not to tell her father about her aunt; the girl already knew to keep it a secret. Instead, she said, "Remember, Mei, how to get to your aunt's, her address, the bus route. You can come here if you need to. It's important." The girl remembered. She still remembers.

"Auntie Li-ey?" Albie is tugging at my leg, Leo behind him. I drop the piece of driftwood and blink as the river consumes it, and then press the boys close to me, gulp down their two-year-old scent—a balm against my panicked body, my grandmother's veiled confession.

It's stifling. I want to call Julia to drive the boys home, but I can't bear seeing her. I call Daddy instead. I tell him the same story I've told the boys—Jacob had to work unexpectedly, but he doesn't interrogate me when he arrives, his focus is only on the twins. He hasn't seen them since my birthday and he inhales them, their ruddy cheeks, their shiny hair. He straps them into their car seats and sings them nursery rhymes.

But as we draw closer to Francie's, the dark side of his love picks up. His fingers drum the steering wheel.

"When we get there, you take the boys in, I'll stay in the car." He falters, unused to issuing instructions, but I hear the moisture in his voice when he says "there" instead of Francie's name. What's that experiment? If you think of something sweet, your mouth waters.

The heath blazes to my left. I want nothing to do with this. "Let me out."

"What?"

I open the car door, dip a trainer toward the rushing road beneath me.

He pulls over.

I get out. "Bye, boys," I call through the open window. "See you later."

"Bye, Auntie Li-ey." The twins wave.

Daddy composes himself. "'Li-*ly*,' boys," I hear him say, "it's 'Auntie Li-ly.'" As the car drives away, I want to tell the twins there are more important things than the consonants of childhood. More important things to lose. More important things that can be taken.

16 / THE ASTRONOMERS' GARDEN

AVOID THE ROYAL OBSERVATORY as a rule. It's too busy, and it always reminds me of a school trip in year eight watching the class cool girl Sloane and her cronies take videos of themselves jumping between hemispheres. Constanza said they looked ridiculous, but we couldn't peel our eyes away from the expert changes in their expressions, how they angled their faces for the camera, the perfect images that flooded social media. To punish them, I swiped Sloane's phone. I wanted to hold it up to the scholarship girls like the grizzled head of Medusa but knew they'd freak out—so I smashed it against the park wall instead, picking the shards off piece by piece.

"Lily?" Lewis's headphones are around his neck. He is wearing a gray T-shirt and navy shorts. "This way." He starts walking, pulling his baseball cap low over his head; it's started raining a little, but not enough to dissipate the heaviness of the air. Around us is a student group with matching T-shirts and rucksacks, couples taking in the view, a pair of joggers checking their watches.

I follow him blindly, assaulted by elbows and umbrella handles, but when we finally stop, it's silent. We're in a garden of curves set against globes and orbs—a red ball on top of the astronomer's house, a great dome above the trees. A lawn, crisped by the heat, is bordered by curved box hedges and dark lavender. Perhaps in any other weather, the banishment of straight lines wouldn't have made the garden extraordinary, but the rain works some alchemy on it so that it appears alive, vibrating, shaking with light.

Lewis leads me to a bench, sits beside me. "All right?"

I don't know whether to shrug or laugh.

"Have you had another one?"

"About half an hour ago, in front of my nephews." Rain studs my eyelashes, turns the lavender to haze. "My grandmother was saying to her sister . . ." panic flutters through me, ". . . she was saying that my grandfather drank, that he did bad things to her."

"What kind of things?"

"I don't know. That was all she said."

Lewis's eyes are narrow behind his glasses.

"It doesn't make sense. Mama's always told me she loved her father. She said he always looked out for her, provided for her. She measures every man against him. He's the ideal."

"Or *an* ideal." He takes off his glasses, wipes the rain with the edge of his T-shirt. "If you were going to recreate your past, the first thing you'd reinvent is the worst person. Does your mother talk about your grandmother or aunt?"

"Never. She talks about the emerald house and her father, but not her mother. I didn't even know she had an aunt. Why?"

He slips his glasses back on his nose. "I wonder if you love someone, you stay faithful to them, even to their memory. Maybe that's why she doesn't involve her mother or her aunt in the fabrication."

Beyond the red brick of the old observatory, one of the domes is opening, the thin split down the center slowly pulling apart to reveal the rig of the telescope, the dark circle of the lens. An astronomer will be looking out tonight, it's eye-end poised for galaxies while I search for a different kind of star.

"I heard back from the admissions office. Your mother was never offered a place at Oxford. There was no scholarship."

I didn't know until he said it, how much I wanted Mama to have told me the truth. In the rain, the grass is slipped blades.

"I'm sorry."

"Tell me something."

"Like what?"

"A story, a thought, anything."

Beside me, Lewis breathes in and out slowly. "When you told me about the flashbacks, I thought of this place. It's called the Astronomers' Garden now, but it used to be called the Home of Time Garden. The Observatory has always measured *chronos* time—"

"From the Greek."

"You know Greek?"

"Latin, but I like etymology."

"You're wasted reading Law, you know that, right?"

I shrug. I don't want to speak to him, I just want to listen. He could say anything, doesn't matter.

"*Chronos* has become time as we know it—hours, minutes, seconds, that constant, measurable march. But in Ancient Greece, there was another type of time—*kairos*. *Kairos* moments are significant moments, moments when the fates change. When I think of your mother's flashbacks, I think they're *kairos* time, incredibly important. Each time you have one, you're one step closer."

"Closer to what?"

"The truth."

"Do you think if I find out the truth, the flashbacks will stop?"

"Possibly. I don't think it can hurt to find out."

"She comes back tomorrow." Rain is soaking through my clothes, the dark patches turning my skin chilly. I turn my hand up to catch the drops, the same hand that slapped my brother. "I feel unreal. Like I'm unraveling and no one's watching. Have you ever felt like that?"

"A few times. When my parents would fight, and then on the streets." He swipes rain off his shorts and stands up. In the observatory, staff are setting up for an event, laying out champagne flutes on white tablecloths, the scene lit by the brassy glow of cogs and dials, the clockfaces of ancient timekeepers. He adjusts his rucksack and says something so quietly I'm unsure I've heard him. It could have been: "You've got me. I'm watching."

I GET THE email from the Singapore Land Authority as I'm crossing my front garden. It confirms a number of things. The emerald house belongs to Rachel Tan and before that, to Henry Tan, or as Mama called him, "Uncle Henry." It was never owned by Mama or her father, Jimmy Tan. Which means the flashbacks are true: Mama's been lying. She never grew up in the emerald house. And then I need Lewis so badly, I want to run all the way to The Polar Explorer House, one glimpse of him will be enough—a curtain being pulled shut, a light being turned on.

Stop.

I've already followed him home this afternoon. Poorer substitutes will have to do.

I find the dandelion I've saved from the orchard a few days ago and plant it in a pot. As I carry it through my treacherous house, I think this twisted root holds the light of flowers, a light I'm bringing in. In the hole, the dandelion beside me, I write Lewis's name and snippets of our conversation on the cardboard walls. *You've got me, I'm watching.*

17 / LOVE LETTERS

MAMA LANDS IN SIX HOURS and I'm making *kueh kapit*. It's a festive biscuit, usually a Chinese New Year snack, but I don't care—it needs to be special to smooth over the fallout from the swimsuit photo, her mood when she gets back, my nerves. I measure out the rice flour and pour in the coconut milk. In Singapore, huge tubs of these wafer-thin biscuits are sold in the shopping malls under Chinese New Year decorations. I remember Mama's face brightening as she clutched one to her chest. "I had these every year when I was a child." Is that true or invented?

Julia walks into the kitchen holding two empty shopping bags, wearing another kaftan, this time, in intricately embroidered cream.

"What are you doing here?"

"Hello to you too." She drops the bags and jumps up onto the counter so she's close to the window. I opened the windows to get a little airflow, but there is none; the rain hasn't broken the weather.

I push down lumps of flour clinging to the sides of the mixing bowl and start to whisk. I never use the electric mixer, it's nice to have something to beat.

Julia's heels bang against the cupboard. She dips her finger in the mixture before I snatch it away. "Making love letters for Mama again?"

"Don't call them that—it's a Westernization." My cheeks burn. "In Malay, they're *kueh kapit*."

"Worried about Mama coming home?"

"Are you?" I nod at the empty bags. "Isn't that why you're here, to take back more of your things?" Julia has acquired an extraordinary amount of clothes in her eighteen years at home, mostly from wheedling Mama over grades. At her peak, the monetary value of an A was £600. She laughed at me for not "benefitting" from my schoolwork. "You're missing out. You can buy anything you want," but I never had her appetite for acquisition. The idea of negotiating with Mama for hard cash was as inconceivable back then as it is now. "How do you think Mama's going to punish you, set your jeans on fire?"

Julia hesitates and then throws her head back, laughing hysterically, her dark hair shaking. I roll my eyes at her, but the knots in my stomach are already loosening.

After she calms down, she draws out a wad of cash from her pocket, smoothing her hair back behind her ears before she fans out the notes. She counts them as though she's dealing cards, parting them expertly with her thumb.

"Where did you get that from?" In the daylight, all I see of her is bone and shadow—the clavicles under her skin, her thin ankles. I order myself to keep whisking.

"Daddy." She points a note at me. "He'll give you money when you're at Oxford too, more if he's feeling guilty, like he is about the whole Francie thing. Catch him when Mama's not there, and he just empties his wallet."

"You knew he had a secret bank account?"

"He's had one for years."

This is becoming rapidly familiar: I'm the only one who doesn't know. Of course Julia knows about my parents' income; all her fights with Mama are about money. "Why doesn't Mama give you enough?"

Julia stuffs the cash back into her pocket. "Because she's a tight-fisted little hoarder. She keeps it all to herself, her clothes, her handbags, her jewelry, always trying to look like someone she isn't. She doesn't care if we actually live in poverty, just how we look, and then when you actually need it, she doles it out only if you act the right way, study the right thing. It's her way of control."

I'm not so sure. Mama has a list of things she wants—a Hermès handbag, a Yves Saint Laurent envelope wallet, Manolo Blahnik pearl boots—but she never checks those items off, not even after a bonus or a birthday. She likes to go to Harrods, to Liberty's, Harvey Nichols, but more to skim her fingers over the designer clothes and bags. When she does purchase something expensive, she agonizes over it for months, checking constantly online like a fluctuating share price, trying to apply seasonal discount codes. Otherwise, she buys mounds of pink and purple imitations on the high street. But she can't have spent all her money on that.

"Why are you asking anyway?"

"It's nothing." I rub oil on the inside of the *kueh kapit* press. It's two iron circles, four inches across, attached together with lengths of metal. On one side is a pattern of rabbits, on the other, a rooster. I spotted it in a supermarket above a metro station in Singapore, an ancient tool lying among the packets of disposable cutlery and gingerbread cutters. "Buy it," Mama had said, "you can't find anything like that in London." Looking at it now, I have the same thought I had then—it would sear a pretty pattern on a cheek, the plates a perfect weight to bring down on a head or a neck.

"Anything happen with the boys after I left?" Julia's feet swing in and out of vision.

"Nope."

She nudges me with her toes. "What's wrong?"

I almost don't say anything. But she's the only person who would half understand and, once Mama comes home, I won't see her as much. I sieve the batter and swallow. "What would you say if I told you Mama never got a scholarship to Oxford?"

Julia snorts. "Who cares?"

"Remember a few years ago when we went to Singapore? It was just you and me. Jacob was at uni."

Julia links her fingers together and stretches her arms out in front of her. "That was boring. Until I made friends with those guys."

I dismiss the image of my seventeen-year-old sister leaving the hotel with a man's hand around her waist. "But before that, do you remember visiting the emerald house?"

"Vaguely." She yawns.

"Did you think it was real?"

"What do you mean?"

"Do you think she really lived there? Did her family wear *sarong kebayas*? Do you think she grew up eating this?" I wave the sieve.

"Honestly, Lil, I stopped listening to Mama a while back."

I spoon batter over the mold. "What if she was lying?"

Julia stares at the packet of rice flour, the empty cans of coconut milk, and then at me holding the mold. "If she's lying, what the fuck are you doing?"

I switch on the stove. The gas roars. "Did you ever wonder why she's the way she is?" I thrust the mold into the flames. "People aren't born like that, so up and down. Maybe something happened to her."

"Don't feel sorry for her."

"I'm not, I just . . . what if she had a really bad childhood?"

Julia rolls her eyes. "How tragic, the fire that killed her family and left her all alone—"

She's told Julia about the fire? Am I the only person she's told about the car accident?

"—who cares? It doesn't matter. She is who she is now." She gives the batter a stir. "She's not some mystery you need to solve. You've got six weeks until uni, and then you're out. Oxford is two and a half hours away."

I eye her warily. How does my sister—who is terrible at geography, who has never shown any interest in my education—know how far Oxford is from Greenwich? She must have checked. "You want me gone?"

"I want you safe."

"Don't be dramatic." The *kueh kapit* crisps in the mold. It's nearly ready. "I am safe. The way she is with you, she isn't with me."

Julia snatches the mold from me. The plates swing dangerously close to my face, and I think everything I imagined has come true—I will have rabbits burned into me—but nothing touches me except a band of heat. She drops the mold in the sink, the metal clattering against the ceramic. Her fists are clenched at her sides. "It's OK, is it? If things happen to me but they don't happen to you?"

"You provoke her."

"That's who she is."

"You make her that way."

"Oh, really? Do you remember her throwing Jacob and me out of the car? Or why you had to make *kueh kapit* the first time?"

I remember. I was thirteen, Julia, sixteen. She'd been driving Mama's car to and from school for weeks. Mama discovered the transgression when she came home early with a cold. She thought the car had been stolen. I messaged Julia while Mama called the police. "Stop her!" Julia replied, so I did, I told Mama a half-truth—that Julia had borrowed it to practice. Half was bad enough. Mama hit her across the jaw when she stepped into the house, screaming, "You're nothing, you're worthless, you whore." I checked the clock each hour—ten, eleven, midnight—but Mama was relentless with the insults, the attacks. That's when I started making batter. My voice shook when I called Mama over to taste my *kueh kapit*.

I push past Julia and lever open the mold. It's a perfect golden circle, the rabbits and rooster visible. Julia puts her hand out for the biscuit. I hold it back. "You know what I'm saying. No more stunts. No more photos." I fold it into quarters to make a fan shape and lay it on her palm.

Julia traces the shape of a rabbit. "It makes me feel better."

"No more!"

"Oh, come on! What did she expect, sending that photo? Everyone to fawn over her and tell her how—"

Then I'm shouting. "I'm still here, Jules, I'm still here!" The words choke my throat. "So don't come in here on the day she's coming home and tell me what you're doing is fine. Because if you push her, all the biscuits in the world are not going to be enough. I'm just trying to—"

"Survive?"

I look away.

"All right, Lil, all right, I won't fuck with her. But you promise me something too. Don't let your guard down. You know she'll come back worse."

I start on a new biscuit.

"Can I do anything?" Then I know she's really sorry because she wouldn't lift a finger otherwise. "Have you made juice?"

"Always."

Julia hugs me. Her arms around my neck are loose and cool. "That bitch," she whispers.

FIVE HOURS TILL Mama lands. I put the final touches to Mama's room, but—surrounded by her things in the sweltering heat—my heart pounds. Julia's right, Mama's going to come back worse; unsupervised, she'll have grown more paranoid. My head is roily fitting Mama's freshly ironed satin sheets, smoothing her Peranakan quilt over the end of her bed. Daddy has fitted a new bulb since she's been away, but the light is too white, she'll wince under it. I swap it for a softer one and then start on the teddies, angling each of their faces so they look out over the bed. I give Sapphire special attention, propping her up against a pillow, retying her bow, pressing the ends so that they sit flat against her tummy.

I can see Daddy in the front garden, he's busy with his own preparations for Mama's return—deadheading the roses. The sounds carry through Mama's open window, the thud of petals, the shears slicing through the still, summer air and I know, instinctively, that I must shut the window if I don't want another flashback, must shut my eyes, but it's too late—I've already seen the blades of the shears, the metal overlaid with a delicate patina of rust.

"Who's that?" the teddy whispered. Goldie and the girl were under the bed covers, having a tea party. The girl tilted Goldie's head this way and that as if she was pricking up her ears.

"Neighbor," replied the girl. "Drunk again."

The girl listened to Baba click his lighter open on the other side of my bedroom door and drag on a cigarette. "Unlock this door!"

"It sounds like a bad man," said Goldie.

He rattled the handle. "Stupid girl! Just like your mother!"

Goldie put her paws to her eyes and started to cry.

The girl cuddled her. "Don't be scared bǎo bǎo, baby. That man? Nothing to do with us. Just a neighbor, drinking too much."

The girl heard him take a swig of whiskey. "Everything you have is mine—the clothes on your back, your teddy!"

"He sounds close," said Goldie.

"He's not. He can't get through the door."

"You're nothing, you hear me, nothing! When I get you, you'll see what I'll do. I'll take off your clothes! I'll push you outside!"

Goldie looked at the girl, her glass eyes uncertain.

"Worthless!"

The teddy hid in the girl's neck.

The girl squeezed her tight. "He'll fall asleep soon, and then Mummy will come home. Come on, don't let him ruin our party." It was hard to keep the sheet over them and hold Goldie, so she lay on her back and used her feet to prop up the blanket. "See, we're

in our special tent. Want some tea?" The girl fumbled for her
plastic teacup, offered it to Goldie's thread mouth.
     "Whore!"

I'm clawing at my chest for a teddy who isn't there, my ears ringing with the sound of a fist against a door, those terrible words. Sapphire has fallen to her side, and then I'm broken, clutching her against me because I understand what she is, who she's supposed to be. She's Goldie upgraded, a plusher, beribboned incarnation, the teddies on the window seat, Goldie multiplied, and then I know why Mama likes the teddies positioned the way she does. They aren't staring at Mama in bed. They're alert for the door—sentinels watching for the moment Mama's drunk father rattles the handles.

Is this why I'm having her flashbacks, so I'd understand her, so I'd pity her? Then it's done, don't show me anymore, I'll be better, do better. How many teddies would it take to make Mama feel safe? Tell me and I will buy them, a thousand times over.

I fetch the plate of *kueh kapit* from downstairs, position Sapphire and the other teddies around it. I brush the fur back from their eyes so that they gleam, round and inviting. I'll redeem the teddy bears' tea party from her childhood, from behind that locked bedroom door, bring it out into the open, a celebration of her return. There's nothing to be afraid of.

18 / AIRPORT

THE TWO GIRLS WITH THE sign look like ballerinas. When the passengers surge through the arrival doors, they spring up as if they're about to go onstage, feet *en pointe*, arms extended, a "Welcome home, Mum" sign above their heads. I register their moves, bank them for later. I can mimic their focus on the swinging door, I can go on my tiptoes scanning the crowds.

Daddy comes back from the tills with a tray—coffee, fries, a chocolate milkshake. He upends the cardboard packet and nods for me to take a few. I decline. The silence between us is brittle, made worse by the hum of air-conditioning, the loudness of other people's chatter. I tune in and out of the conversations around us—dinner plans, baby anecdotes, boyfriend trouble—struck by how easy it seems, how impossible.

"When your mother comes back," says Daddy, dipping his fries into barbecue sauce, "probably best if you stop reading on the sofa."

The shock of it is a knife sliding between my ribs, and suddenly I'm a child again, six, maybe seven, poring over the books Daddy gave me—*Matilda, Little House on the Prairie, Charlotte's Web.* He snuck them to me in secret, slipping me one with the bookshop bag wrapped tight around it, or leaving two for me in my bedroom. I thought he was trying to tell me something, something just for me, maybe he'd say he loved me or that I was special or not to worry about the woman we lived with. It was weeks until I felt the knife. There were no secret messages.

He waggles his finger at me and grins. "And let's not mention The Sail Boat."

I put my hand out to stop him.

"Can you start putting your bicycle away, as well? We're in for a few storms."

"I'm not putting it in the shed."

He takes a fry. "It's going to rust."

"It's fine against the house."

"It's still going to get wet."

"I use it every day."

He cocks his head to the side. "That's not going to stop it from getting wet now, is it?"

"Just leave it!" I shout.

He stares at me, stunned.

I feel the prickle of other people's eyes on me. "I'm going for a walk."

He hands me my milkshake. "Take this with you."

I snatch it from him, sling on my rucksack, push through the restaurant. Why have the last few days turned me into a child? Is this what it would be like with Mama gone?

The pair of girls waiting for their mother are restless now and tired. They've laid the sign on the floor, and close up, I see it's the work of an entire afternoon, decorated with hearts and rainbows, an impressionistic unicorn. They look around eleven and eight, one a brunette, the other, a strawberry blonde. The older girl braids her sister's hair, glancing warily at the doors, scolding her sister to stop fidgeting, to hold this butterfly hairclip, that sparkly hair band. Then, it happens. The girl transforms, her eyes widening, her fingers frozen in her sister's hair and then the braid is forgotten, the sign is forgotten. The girls dart under the railing and sprint to their mother. She is appallingly ordinary, inconspicuous in a gray T-shirt and jeans, clothes Mama would never wear, and she stops her trolley, doesn't matter about the other arrivals, and throws her arms around the girls, kissing them again and again. Over my wrist, pain dawns. I've grabbed it too tightly.

"She's here." Daddy sails past me, his thriller tucked under his arm. I tear my eyes from the girls and follow his crumpled polo, his smoothed back blond hair. Mama is too bright for the beige hues of the airport, in her magenta trousers and a matching straw hat. She's put on lipstick, and I indulge myself in the fantasy that this is romantic, that my father and mother are reuniting after a long time apart, but then Jonathan trudges behind Mama pushing the trolley, his baby-smooth skin reddened by the sun, and Mama doesn't wave or smile when she catches sight of us.

She allows herself to be embraced, Daddy rounding off his hug with two pats on the back. I throw my arms around Mama, an absurd mimic of the other girls, but she doesn't notice. She watches Daddy greet Jonathan with the polite acknowledgment of a butler, which bewilders Jonathan so much he acts like one, lumping his suitcase off the trolley before stuttering an excuse to leave. Mama clucks her tongue, annoyed at her disappearing knight, but she is warrior enough. As Daddy takes over the trolley, Mama's eyes dart behind us. I wait for everything to click into place, and it does. There is an awful easiness to it.

"Where are the boys?" Mama asks.

Daddy gives Mama a dizzying smile. "It was too late to bring them. They wanted to see you though."

A crease deepens between her eyebrows. "They wanted to see me, and you said no?"

Daddy calls the lift, pressing the button twice after it lights up. "It's past their bedtime."

I watch Mama's ribs expand and contract under her white shirt. She is nearly hyperventilating with the idea that the twins have asked for her even though Daddy has certainly invented this exchange. I put my hand on her elbow to steady her, but I lose her in the lift. Untethered, she says above the hum of other people's conversations,

"Why would you stop my grandchildren from seeing me?" Her power falls over the small space. Everyone is thrown into confusion, no one knows whether to look at her or not, to stop talking or continue. They are all in her thrall.

Daddy doesn't reply. He fixes his eyes on the descending floors as if they're a slide of tissue from a suspicious death, a move not without cost because by the time we get out and step into the humidity of the car park, Mama's thoughts have taken a more dangerous turn. "When did you speak to the twins?"

Daddy slows as we approach the car. "Yesterday."

"Why did you see them?"

"I brought them home from Jacob's."

"Where was Jacob?"

"He had to go back to work, he couldn't take them home."

In the car, she clicks her seat belt into place. "So you didn't spend the day with them?"

Daddy searches for the parking ticket in the side pocket. His answers are distracted, unconvincing. "No."

"Did you go up to the flat?" Mama drums her fingers. She isn't wearing her wedding ring. Instead, there is a new bracelet around her wrist, the kind a twelve-year-old would love, silver dolphins chasing hearts.

"No, I just picked them up from outside."

"So you didn't spend the day with Francie?"

"Of course not," says Daddy as he reverses, employing the same silly-little-girl tone he uses with me. Mama's fingers stop tapping.

"And then Jacob had to leave, and you drove the boys home with Lily?"

"Yes." He nods at me while checking the rear window. I shake my head. Why does he think I'm going to cover for him?

"Lily was with you? The whole time you dropped the boys off with Francie?"

I slide my knife in. I've been sharpening, whetting. "I didn't go to Francie's. I got out at the heath."

Mama's voice is a hiss. "You went to Francie's alone?"

Daddy grips the steering wheel. "I wasn't alone, I was with the boys. I had no choice, Lily just got out of the car!"

What's a little evening knife play?

"Is that true?" Mama has craned her neck around. "You let him go by himself?"

It's a good try by Daddy, but not good enough. I'm better at defensive moves, I've had more practice. The tears fall quick and easy. "I didn't want to be there with Daddy and Francie. I didn't want to see that."

Mama turns around, satisfied. She pushes back her dark hair and points a manicured finger at me. The dolphins dive against her wrist. "Look at what you've done to this family. To your daughter. She can't even be in the same car as her father anymore. I knew I should have stayed with Jonathan, just stayed away. Do you love her? Have you slept with her?"

Daddy, so confident in the airport, dulls into monosyllables. In the back seat, I watch the road unfold in front of us, miles of accusations, recriminations, games. We're so far from home.

I CAN'T MAKE out exactly what Mama is screaming about downstairs, but just the ebb and flow of her voice is enough to show me how bad it is. I catch my reflection in the window and wonder what Lewis would think of me now—legs crossed, forehead pressed against the banister, a caricature of imprisonment. I release the railings just in time before Mama flings open the living-room door and climbs the stairs. I hold my arms out to her on the landing. She buries her devastated face into my shoulder. The back of her neck is tanned, she forgot to apply lotion there.

When she pulls away, I wipe her tears with my thumb and shush her the way I would comfort Leo or Albie: "Don't cry anymore. You're OK. Everything is going to be OK."

She balls her hands up into fists and drags her knuckles across the tops of her legs. "No one wants me back, he doesn't, your sister doesn't, the boys don't care about me. The only person that cares is Jonathan."

"I want you back. I've missed you." I'm so hungry for her to see me, I almost bite her. But her fists don't stop pummeling her thighs. I gesture to her bedroom. "Come, look who's here to greet you."

Her face lights up at the scene I've set and then she sits next to the teddies, stroking their heads lightly as if she can't bear to disturb them. "You did all this for me?"

I nod.

"Thank you, thank you." She holds Sapphire to her, inhales her chestnut fur. "What are they doing?"

"Having a tea party. Eating *kueh kapit*. One of your favorites. Here, have one."

She takes up one biscuit, admiring the pattern. "They're beautiful, Lily. Remember when we got some from that stall? When we saw that couple making them?" She's thinking of when we went for one of our walks, the kind we only do in Singapore, just out, no destination. The stall was a lean-to with a long trough filled with white-hot coals, the molds laid over the top. "How many were there?" she asks.

"More than twenty." The couple had been in their seventies, the woman filling the molds from one end and emptying them from another, flicking the biscuits to her husband with expert skill. The man chatted to his wife, then with Mama in rapid Mandarin, his fingers busy folding the biscuits and packing them into tins. He said they only spoke about auspicious things so that the biscuit was golden.

"We watched them make an entire tin, so we knew they were fresh."

"We ate them straight off the coals."

She lifts one to her mouth and bites. "I wish I could go back to that time, before this happened with your father, when I was happy."

Were you happy then, Mama? I don't think you were, not in Singapore at the love-letter stall. But I will help you. I will do everything I can to make you feel better.

"Is there any juice?"

Mama's girl, Mama's doll. I steady myself against the wall. "I'll get you some."

IN THE HOLE, I sit by the dandelion, get out my phone and scroll to "New Recording 5." I change the title hundreds of times a day just to see how it looks—"Lewis—3 August 2020," "Spit," and my personal favorite, "Lewis and me," although I always change it back. I press play at 18 minutes and 25 seconds. To the sound of his laugh, I think of the constellation of his eyes, of laying my hand on his heart.

19 / GREEN JUICE

MAMA IS PUTTING ON HER makeup while expounding on her newest theory—that Francie has "seduced" Daddy. The word "seduced" makes me want to laugh, as if Daddy is a ruined maiden, tricked into surrendering his virginity. No one was more willingly led astray.

"She let him spend so much time with her."

I'm only half listening. It's Mama's first day back at work, and she has a client meeting so I'm hunting for her suit jacket that will be too warm to wear. I've located the matching skirt; the jacket must have fallen off the hanger. If I can't find it quickly, Mama will complain I haven't organized her wardrobes properly.

"Albie said he was there all the time."

Inside the wardrobe, I flinch. In the last few months, Mama has started telling Albie that he's her favorite, and whenever I hear that, a stillness comes over me, like being slowly submerged in freezing water. I say to him, "Careful, Albie, careful," but when he asks me why, I don't know what to say.

"When did you speak to him?"

"This morning on video."

Why would Francie let Albie speak to Mama without her? I find the jacket but stay inside the wardrobe, watching Mama through the hinged edge of the door. "He's only two, Mama. Children will say anything."

Mama's mascara is frozen in her hand. "Albie is completely reliable."

She waits for me to agree, but Albie and Leo are perhaps the only issue I would resist her on. I change the subject. "Found it." I hold the jacket to the light. "There's a mark on the corner, see? A bit of pen. I'll wash it out." I head to the bathroom, so Mama has to call after me; the flood of adrenaline will drown out her thoughts.

"Are you crazy? I've got a meeting in an hour."

"Sorry, Mama. Do you still want to wear it?"

Mama glances at her watch. "It's fine, it's fine, I'll just hide the stain behind the desk."

I smooth the jacket out on her bed.

Mama pouts into the mirror and applies her lipstick. "I'm just going to ask her."

"Who?"

"Francie," she says through puckered lips.

"Ask her what?"

"If she seduced him. I'm meeting her this evening," she says. I stare at the crystal pins in her hair, her makeup shades too pale, as if they will answer this new, dangerous question—why is Mama trying to blame Francie?

"What?" she says layering on the fuchsia. "You think it's a bad idea?"

"Do you really think she's involved?"

Mama neatens her lip line with her ring finger. Her eyes are flint in the mirror. "One hundred percent."

JACOB PICKS UP almost immediately. "Hi."

"Why are you whispering?"

"David's coming back in a sec, what's up?"

My brother, who has fought to get into this law firm, who has been interviewed and tested to prove he deserves his place, is whispering in his pristine glass office. "Can you step out?"

"Hang on." He puts me in his pocket. When he speaks to me again, a coffee machine splutters in the background. "Everything OK?"

"Does Francie know Mama's found out about the poems?"

"Well . . . no. I don't want to bring that up."

"Not even after my birthday? What did she think was happening?"

"She just thought Julia was misbehaving."

"You need to tell her."

"Why?"

"She's meeting Francie this evening." There's no need to say who "she" is.

Jacob inhales.

"There's something else. She's started saying it's Francie's fault. That Francie seduced Daddy."

I hear the tension in his voice, the dawning awareness that Mama's narrative is snaking slowly toward him. "How is this Francie's fault?"

"I don't know. But Francie shouldn't go alone. She could make things worse." I pause. "You need to go with her."

"I can't."

"Are you working?"

"You know I am."

"But it's important!"

In the silence that passes between us, I know what he'll ask and that I'll agree, and I wonder why I called him when I always knew it would end like this. "Can you go? You can handle Mama best."

Mama used to make Jacob and Julia sleep in the downstairs hall for tiny things, leaving something out in their bedrooms, spilling a drink at dinner, but I knew how to get them back. I wouldn't argue with her. I did the opposite. I'd hold her hand and list their crimes, recite word for word how they deserved their punishment. Without anyone to fight, Mama's aggression would ebb away, and after she fell asleep, I'd tiptoe downstairs and tell them that the coast was clear. Will I always feel guilty for being Mama's favorite? For being upstairs when they were down? "OK. But promise me something."

"Anything."

"Tell Francie before this evening."

"All right."

"And Jay, you need to keep it together the next few weeks. There's a lot going on."

"Sure, Lil, sure."

WE'RE AT THE Vine, Mama's favorite restaurant in Blackheath, the tablecloths pristine, the menus embossed with gold. Sloane had her fourteenth birthday lunch here with three of her closest friends; they were at the window seat when I came in with Mama, a basket of truffle arancini and sparkling water on their table. I made a shy half-wave to them. They sniggered. Now, when I come into The Vine, I keep my eyes low.

Francie orders just a green juice—avocado, mint, spinach, and parsley; the mash of green reminding me of the ivy Lewis gave me hours earlier. He'd spoken to Pete about plants that grow in shade and gave me three pots trailing dark, glossy leaves. I stalked him back to The Polar Explorer House for that, and, before leaving for The Vine, I plucked three leaves for luck. Now, I comfort myself with his gift, holding them in the pocket of my jeans.

Mama one-ups Francie by ordering a hot water and then mutters that I should try the blackened cod, which means that's what she really wants, she just doesn't want to look fat in front of Francie. I order it, dreading the stomach upset that follows when Mama eats out—the trips to the toilet, the irrepressible bad mood, and then I remember the flashback about the spoilt juice—her father punished her because she wouldn't drink a glass of milk. But why wouldn't she? Could it be that, all this time, Mama has some kind of undiagnosed milk intolerance? No wonder she likes Peranakan cooking, there's barely any lactose.

"I need the toilet," I say.

Mama glares at me to sit back down; she doesn't want to be left with Francie. I pretend not to understand. When I'm out of sight, I cancel the blackened cod and order a tossed Asian salad from the vegan menu.

Mama and Francie are still not talking when I get back. Mama drums her fingers on the table, watching Francie speak to her friend on the phone.

"They didn't have blackened cod today, so I chose something else," I say as I sit down.

Mama nods distractedly. Francie hangs up and starts telling us anecdotes about the boys. Mama feigns interest. As soon as the salad arrives, she goes straight for the kill. "Did you know he's in love with you?"

Francie freezes. This is what I was afraid of, she's not prepared. Mama's never really attacked her like she does Julia or Jacob, not directly anyway, although she bitches about her to anyone who will listen. Francie takes a small sip of her smoothie. "Not exactly. I had an inkling."

Mama forks her beansprouts. "When?"

"After about a month. We exchanged a couple of poems and then I thought, this isn't a good idea."

"Why didn't you say anything?"

Francie presses her lips together. "At first, I didn't know if I was reading too much into things. Then when it became clearer, I didn't know what to say or who to talk to."

"You could have told me!"

No real response is possible without an assessment of who Mama is and why no one can tell her the truth. Francie knows this. I watch the circus version of her face in the sugar bowl blink solemnly. "I'm sorry. I just thought it might go away."

Mama scrapes her fork against the tablecloth as if she's sharpening a weapon. "You should have told me when this started."

"I didn't want to hurt anyone."

"Or, you had other reasons."

Francie stares at Mama. "Wait, you think I wanted this to happen?" A blush spreads over her body, coloring her arms, staining her cheeks. She's put in minimal effort for this dinner, just some mascara, a white T-shirt, a floral skirt—and even then, she exudes health, her arms are toned from Pilates, her stomach flat. Mama, by contrast, rushed back from work this afternoon to prepare for the dinner, insisting on wearing full body Spanx even though it's still twenty-six degrees Celsius.

"You tell me."

Francie makes her first mistake of the evening. She laughs. "You're not serious? Me and Charlie . . . that's ridiculous!"

"You think the idea of you and my husband is ridiculous?"

"It's ridiculous you think I had any part in this!"

"Because my husband isn't good enough for you?"

Francie puts her hands up and slides back from the table, but there is nowhere to go. Her head bounces against the mirror behind her. "You're twisting everything I'm saying."

"I'm just trying to get to the bottom of this."

"There is no bottom of this! Your husband might be in love with me, but I'm not in love with him." She immediately regrets her tone. Her face softens. "But I don't think he's a bad person. He's just lonely."

Mama goes in for the kill. She takes out her phone, opens a file entitled, "Charlie (bastard) pics," a prize from one of her fights with Daddy that contains all the photos he's taken. She flicks through until she finds what she's looking for. It's a close-up of Francie leaning over Albie, her cleavage magnified beyond recognition. "Still think he's not a bad person?"

Francie swallows. This is Mama's gift, turning everything to ash. Gently, she pushes Mama's hand down so the phone is flat on the table. "I'm sorry for you," she whispers.

My mother—who can out-scream, out-argue, out-hate anyone— falls to pieces. She covers her face with a white napkin and weeps. People are staring. Francie gets up to comfort her, but I shake my head.

"Come on, Mama."

When Mama doesn't stop, I tuck her hair behind her ear. "Don't let her see you cry. Come on. Sit up." I pull her face to look at me, and see the ruined downturn of her eyes, her puffy cheeks, and I think of the little girl trying so hard not to be frightened, in the kitchen, under her covers. She's not alone though, not anymore. She has me. A shred of *pak choi* dangles from her upper lip. I brush it off and take her hand to leave. Francie throws her credit card down and sighs. That sigh, as if she's so unbelievably tired of us, sets me ablaze.

I lead Mama to the entrance of the restaurant and then double back. "I've got a question. If you knew Daddy had feelings for you after the first few poems, why didn't you stop him from visiting? That was when, June? But he was coming over two to three times a week after that."

Francie starts to stutter. "I didn't know how to stop him."

"Did you try?"

"I didn't know what to do."

"I don't believe that. I don't believe that at all. You could have told Jacob, you could have told me or Julia. You didn't. I think you've been using Daddy for childcare so you can get a break, catch up with your friends, get in shape. You didn't care that he was in love with you as long as it was convenient. You would have let this go on as long as you could get exactly what you want. So don't play innocent. Just don't."

Francie is standing now, hands shaking. She throws down her napkin. "Your father's the sick bastard, not me. I didn't do anything!"

I think of sick bastards then, Mama's father, making her drink that spoilt juice, calling her those names, the terrible journey that little girl has made to become the grown, devastated woman behind me and I can't stand it anymore. I grab Francie's green juice and tip it over her shiny, dark hair.

20 / AMBUSH

ON THE WAY HOME, MAMA is ecstatic, whooping in the car, kissing me on the cheek, reaching over the handbrake to squeeze my shoulder. She's forgotten her humiliation and is savoring the details of Francie's. "Did you see her face? She was so shocked! That juice running over her—what did you say she ordered?"

"Green juice."

"Green juice! Soaked! If only your father had seen her. Did you see how she turned on him?"

"That snake."

"And you, you!"

She kisses me again and then parks outside our house, pulls the keys out of the ignition. The metal glimmers between her fingers. "I love you," she says.

"I love you too, Mama." I wait for the words to settle. "How was the food?"

She presses her hand to her abdomen. "Fine! The Vine must have sorted their problem with their cooking. About time, we've complained enough."

I've done it, I've actually *fixed* her.

Inside, Mama calls from the top of the stairs. "I have something for you." When I get to her bedroom, she's lying on her front, reaching under the bed. "There, do you see that? Can you reach?"

I pull it out. It's Mama's old jewelry box, large, with a floral print, the top furred with dust. She keeps costume jewelry in there. She takes out strings of pearls, huge earrings, silver bracelets like the one Jonathan bought her, and then gasps as she searches through the silk jewelry pouches. "Here it is." It's a polished oval stone set on a gold ring, the color of milk with a touch of amethyst, achingly beautiful.

"What is it?"

"Purple jade. My mother said the more you wear it, the darker it becomes."

I hold my breath. She never mentions her mother.

"It was her mother's before that, your great-grandmother."

"What was your mother like?"

"She wore this gold brooch—"

"Not what she wore," I interrupt as gently as I can. "Her personality."

Mama holds the ring in front of her like a rosary, and I think it is sacred—it can transport her to a place she rarely visits, to a woman she never talks about. "She wasn't a strong person, couldn't bear things well, but she loved me very much."

"What couldn't she bear?"

"My father, the war. War does things to a person, forces them into bad decisions, leaves them *hú li hútú*, confused."

"What happened to her?"

"She died in the fire." Mama tugs the bedsheet taut behind her.

My heart races. She's never told me there was a fire, although she's said that to everyone else. *Be calm*. "I thought it was a car accident."

Her pupils are wide and dark. "Did I say that to you, that she died in a car accident?"

I nod.

She pulls me to her, enfolding me in her arms, and I wait there, in the dark, sweet perfume of her skin. This is what the flashbacks have been leading to, this moment of *kairos* where Mama tells the truth and everything changes. But nothing does. "Take it," she says as she pulls away. She drops the jade ring into my palm, pushes a strand of hair back from my face, and I think *Now, now, Mama, say something true*. Instead, she says, "Lily, your roots are showing. Have you run out of dye? Should I order more? Let me order some more."

I break away quickly, step back through the doorway to hide my expression. I can't let her see the devastation. "Yes, please. Thanks, Mama."

JULIA VIDEO CALLS when I'm loading the dishwasher, except it isn't just her, it's Jacob too. They're in his flat, at the kitchen table. Anger flickers through me at the two of them preparing for this. "Ambush" from *embusche*, old French meaning "in the wood," except now, you don't have to spring out at people from behind a tree, you can do it from your Thames-view apartment with a hot drink in your hand and a blanket around your shoulders.

"What the fuck, Lil?" starts Julia.

I prop my phone up over the dishwasher so I can keep sliding in the cutlery and try to keep my voice level. "Francie deserved it."

"How did she deserve it?

"You should have seen her. She told Mama she was sorry for her. She called Daddy a sick bastard, that smug look on her face."

Jacob never lifts his eyes to the screen, to me, to anything. Julia blinks. By the imperfections of her makeup, I guess they've been ana-lyzing my misdemeanors for two hours, maybe three, because there's a sheen over her forehead that highlights a patch of bad skin, and her mascara has crumbled onto her cheeks.

"You were supposed to rein Mama's craziness in, not enable it."

"She was crying."

"So you defended her."

Mama's jade ring flashes under the kitchen spotlight. "Kind of."

Julia explodes. "She doesn't need you to defend her! We need defending from her! Why can't you see this? Why is everything so fucked up for you?"

I slam a plate into the rack. It cracks clean in two. "So either I agree with you, or I'm fucked up? Well, let's test that. If Mama's so bad and we all need defending from her, why do you always make it worse? If she's so awful, why have you left me with her?"

It's only then that Jacob reacts. His chin jerks up, his eyes dark on my sister. Something passes between them, a discussion they've had so many times they can have it now in front of me, without words, but I don't understand their secret language, not anymore. We used to be a three, in the summer we had a rhythm—TV in the morning, the beach, Greenwich Park or the museums in the afternoon, inventing improbable histories about falling masts, billowing sails, the ship figureheads. What happened? Where are those children? A rift has formed between us, but I can't explain when it happened or how to bridge it.

"If you knew what we knew, you'd agree with us."

We? Us? Well I'm not alone. I have something too. The flashbacks beat their wings inside me. "I know things. I know why Mama's the way she is, why our family's how it is, more than you. I'm making it better."

Julia withdraws suddenly, the chair legs scraping against the floor. "You know what, I can't do this." Her voice is cracking. "I've tried with you, no one can say I haven't." She covers her face with her hands. "But one day, when Mama freaks out at you, you'll know what she is."

Her rare tears, her dark prophecy, mix with a sickening memory— Julia on the ground grabbing her thigh, screaming—why was she grabbing it, what happened? Then, I don't care. "Mama loves me! Remember when I was sick for weeks and weeks and she took all that time off work to look after me? She did that because I'm her favorite, because she loves me the most. She's not the same with me. I'm not you!"

Julia looks so sad. "You're exactly like us. We're all Mama's boys, Mama's girls." She ends the call.

I want to smash every plate, my phone, her face, the jade ring on my finger. I pull it off, hurl it across the kitchen; it bounces off a kitchen cupboard before skittering back toward me. I peel my eyes away from it and stare out at the shadows in the back garden, the spectral outline of the shed. Daddy has lumped my bike in it, again, not properly, the door doesn't shut, the front tire is nosing out and I feel at once the creeping nausea that heralds another flashback.

The woman wore a flower-print dress and a headscarf. Her lipstick was a dark pink, and the polish on her fingers and toes was red. Her heels clacked all the way up to our front door. She reached up to stroke Sylvia, who squawked and made to bite her. She jerked her hand back and knocked.

She smiled when the girl opened it. She had perfect white teeth. "You must be Mei! Your Baba has told me so much about you!" She peered behind her. "Are your parents home?"

The girl closed the door and stepped out into the porch. "No."

"Oh." She paused for a few seconds and then pulled out a silk jewelry packet from her handbag. "Can you do me a favor, little Mei? Can you give this back to your Mama?" Her eyelashes fluttered. "Or tell your Baba he needs to buy me better jewelry than this if he wants to make it up to me."

The girl opened the packet. Inside was her mother's ring, the one her mother gave her. "Not worth much," her mother had said because the jade was small, but she loved it and when she was in a good mood, she'd let her try it on and they'd talk about what color it was. "Like clouded grapes," the girl would say. "Like the sky before a monsoon," her mother would reply. She'd worn it on her third finger every day until Baba took it from her. That time, her mother didn't lock her in her room so when it got very bad, the girl rushed in. He'd already stripped her mother naked by then and was saying all the bad words, threatening to throw her out. The girl begged her mother to give it to him, but she wouldn't, so he stepped forward and broke her mother's arm. Snap.

"Wait," the girl said to the woman who was already walking toward her car. She clacked back and crouched down in front of her. The girl cupped her hand around her ear: "You're worthless, you're nothing, you whore."

My mind is everywhere.

"Worthless," "nothing," "whore." I've heard Mama call Julia those names so many times, it barely registers, but hearing them on the lips of a child makes me keel over. She learned them from her father—the man who gave her mother's jewelry to his mistress, the man who stripped her mother naked, who broke her arm. She learned cruelty, she learned violence. I clutch the sides of the sink and retch, wanting to disappear down that perfect black plughole, to be wastewater draining away.

21 / SPLICE

MAMA'S WORKING FROM HOME TODAY so I can't go to the orchard. Just as well, I can't bear half an hour with Lewis. I told him about the flashback with Goldie but not about the teddies I laid out to celebrate Mama's return, and I don't want to tell him what I did to Francie or about the latest flashback. This is how it starts, secreting yourself away. This is how I end up like Mama.

In the hole, the dandelion is drooping, it needs more sun, but the ivy plants are faring well. Lewis said they're at their highest rate of growth, and I swear each one has put on a few centimeters. I check the soil. It's a little dry, crumbling between my fingers.

I'm climbing out of the hole to fetch my water bottle when Francie calls.

Her "hi" is nervous, guarded.

In the background, I can hear the boys whining in the heat—Leo asks if he can listen to nursery rhymes, and Albie begs for a snack. "What have I said about speaking to Mummy when she's talking on the phone?" Francie whispers. I hear her pad to another room, and then the click of a door closing. "Do you believe what you said? About me?"

I trace over a quote from Milton: *The mind is its own place, and in itself, can make a heaven of hell, a hell of heaven.* "I shouldn't have said it. There's more going on with Mama, with me . . . I'm sorry."

She is quiet for a few seconds. "I've been thinking about it all night, and I think you had a point. I didn't know for certain, but I suspected—and oh God." She's muffled, as if she's holding her hand over her mouth. "I let it go because he was so helpful, so great with the boys, and that's on me. I was wrong for doing that."

Her confession astounds me. Before this, I'd never given Francie a second thought, my focus solely on Jacob's frail happiness, the twins, when she might be the only adult in our family refusing to play games, bravely admitting blame.

"It's not an excuse, but it's just been hard. Some days, I just want to lock myself in a wardrobe. Other days, I see my friends doing the things I dreamed of, and I feel so resentful of the boys even though I love them." She sniffs. "Fucking LinkedIn."

We laugh a little. I water the ivy. "I'm really sorry about the juice. It was a horrid thing to do."

"No, I shouldn't have said that thing about your dad."

"That's OK."

"There's something else. Jacob said things last night, things he'd never said before. He was upset, ranting, Julia was in the background trying to get him off the phone. I wasn't sure afterward if it was true."

I pinch off a leaf. "What did he say?"

"It was about your mum, what she did to you all when you were children."

I jam my head between my knees, breathe slowly.

"Are you OK, Lily? I mean really?"

"Of course."

"You have friends to talk to, right? Friends you can trust?"

There's a man on a bench in a garden of curves. A seat beside him is empty. Lavender blooms. "Yes."

"Good. Because if you're not OK, you can tell me. I know things are difficult, maybe you can't get away, but if you need me, I'm here. Come round. You're family."

I let my mind dream about what staying with Francie might be like: shafts of sunlight dancing on the pull-out sofa bed; being awoken by my raucous, soft-cheeked nephews; herbal teas; yoga. I could do that. But then I think of Mama, arranging her teddies alone, pulling her Peranakan quilt over herself, staring into a carton of orange juice, the complex machinations of her mind that only I can unpick.

"Thanks, Francie. Speak soon." I get up, bring my dandelion to the sunlight, and do the small things to make my hole a home.

AT LUNCHTIME, MAMA asks me to go with her to Jonathan's—she hates going anywhere alone. She always thought Jonathan's flat was a steal; it's a five-minute walk away from the tube, but there's sweet justice to getting what you pay for. The building is ugly, "shit brick" Julia named the color, the communal hallways reeking of urine and weed. Mama convinced him to buy it, and usually, she can't resist making some comment about how incredible the place is, but today, she isn't drunk on the dulled gray of the Thames; she's high on my loyalty.

"That bitch!" she says, searching her handbag for Jonathan's keys. Of course he's given her a set. "She deserved it!" She says "deserved" with an emphasis on the second syllable, as if I serve revenge green and pulpy. I'm so ashamed.

"Lǎobǎn, boss?" she says, pushing the door open. No one should witness their mother flirting, the rare, gentle voice. The flat is hotter than it is outside; the closed windows, the drawn curtains, the news playing, all giving it a lair-like quality. Jonathan's boxers are on display on the drying rack, washed-out gray with gargantuan crotch pieces that would send Julia into hysterics. I wish I could tell her.

Jonathan appears from his bedroom, rubbing his eyes. I'm absurdly jealous. He doesn't have to drink spoilt juice. He doesn't have Mama's flashbacks.

Mama tells me to watch television on the sofa while she talks to Jonathan. I flick on an old movie, turn up the volume and prowl around. There's nothing much, a clutch of books on algorithms and coding, nothing that betrays who he is except for two laptops and three enormous computer screens. An imposing leather office chair is the only seating in the flat, it's the most money he's spent on anything save his computers. I fiddle with the headrest, tilt it back.

The murmur of conversation slows, so I tiptoe over. The door is ajar. Mama is crying against Jonathan's chest, a hand pressed against his checked shirt, and I have the sense that she is searching his body for comfort, a small animal nuzzling for warmth. He is completely unmoved. He absently pats the small of her back. His eyes drift to the time on the alarm clock, and then he shuffles with impatience. He is wondering when she'll leave, and then I'm so angry for my mother, for the layers of pretense and illusion she's desperate to be true. I don't care if he's gay or asexual or just plain not interested—how dare he not want her? I fetch a knife from the kitchen, slide under his precious chair and start slicing it in hidden places, first gashing through the base, and then I stand up to gouge the smooth leather under the flap of the headrest, all the while remembering a radio interview about a husband who beat his wife where bruises didn't show.

I leave the knife on the table and go back to the sofa. Mama comes out with a small smile. "Jonathan's given me a present. It'll help us find out if Francie seduced your father."

On the radio, the Met Office announces an extreme heat warning. While parents are informed of the weather's adverse effects on children and road crews spread grit on melting roads, my mother is gathering evidence of my father's adultery. Jonathan waves at me. I wave back.

AT HOME, MAMA is on the phone with Jonathan for hours. She's sitting in the kitchen with her laptop on the table while I cook around her. Daddy's told us he's at the lab. I suspect he's at The Sail Boat.

I signal to her that dinner's ready, and she says goodbye to Jonathan. She bristles with excitement. "Want to know what he gave me? It's software."

"What does it do?"

"It splices videos into photos."

"OK." I set down her food with a flourish—*laksa*, noodles with shrimp and fishcake in a spicy coconut broth. We'd eaten it in Katong, I thought she'd recognize it, but she just sucks a single noodle into her mouth and pushes the bowl away. "Look at this," she points to her laptop screen. "This is a video your father took of Francie last month, after she claimed she suspected. Look how relaxed she is."

Reluctantly, I leave my dinner and drag my stool next to hers. It's a classic Albie/Leo video—Albie is banging on a toy piano, Leo is singing. Francie is sitting on the sofa behind them, her slender legs pressed together, wearing a pair of green shorts and a white T-shirt. She crosses a long, bare leg; the video lingers on her for less than a second. But Mama has dissected that one lissome action into twenty-eight photos.

The steam disappears off the top of the *laksa*, I'm annoyed. It's taken me hours to prepare, and she isn't even eating it while she narrates the angles of Francie's crotch.

"Look at this one!" Mama clicks on the photo of Francie where the shadow between her legs is the largest. "It's like you said, exactly like you said."

"What?"

"You said she took advantage. You said she wasn't innocent."

I replay my conversation with Francie, her horror at the role she's played, the humdrum reasons why she let it happen. If she can own her part in this, so can I. "That isn't what I meant."

"What did you mean?"

"I meant she isn't as naive as she's making out."

"So she's part of it."

"She might have taken advantage of the situation, but it didn't start with her."

Mama's voice grows small and tremulous. She pushes the laptop away, draws her knees to her chin, a child's defense—although no one is attacking her. "You think it's me, don't you? You think it's my fault."

"No, Mama."

"I didn't want this to happen. I didn't want to be cheated on."

"Cheated on?" Does Mama think Francie is Daddy's mistress?

Mother, father, mistress.

Mama, Daddy, Francie.

Mama is drawing some association between her parents' marriage and her own, projecting a link that isn't there, and what have I done? I've blamed Francie. I've reinforced it. *I know things, I'm making it better*, I'd said to Julia and Jacob, but it's not true. I haven't made it better. I've made it more dangerous.

"Mama," I say gently. "Daddy didn't cheat on you. It was just a few poems."

A switch flips, child to adult. She slams her hands against the table. "That's how it starts," she roars. "Should I wait till the poems turn to lingerie, till the lingerie turns to jewelry?' She plucks viciously at the jade on my finger. "Will it be cheating then, when he gives her my things?'"

And I know what she's thinking of: her father giving her mother's jade ring to his mistress. "But he hasn't done that, Mama," I say carefully. He didn't give your jewelry away."

"He will! He will!' She jabs at an imaginary Daddy. "Then what will happen?"

Around her mouth, her fear is palpable. "What do you mean, Mama? What are you afraid of?"

"I won't let it. I won't, I won't!" Then I don't know who she's talking to—me, her mother, a teddy under the covers, but she pounds her chest with her fist, a move that is at once punishment, comfort, vow. The dull sound of bone absorbs everything in the room.

"Stop it, Mama. You're scaring me." But I can't reach where she's gone. I grab her wrists, shake them, but she doesn't stop, so I do the only thing I can, I cast Francie adrift, although it makes me sick to do it. "You're right, Mama, it's their fault. Daddy's and Francie's."

Their names pulse Mama back to life. Her fists unclench. She opens the laptop screen.

22 / GEOMETRY

HE SENDS ME A VIDEO midmorning of a Spit championship game in America, with the message, "We need to practice." The "we" cuts through the shame of what I did to Francie, how I gave in to Mama yesterday. *You have friends to talk to, right?* I speed through Mama's chore list.

London is the last to enjoy the weather before it breaks. Other areas have been devastated by flooding—banks have burst, roads have been cordoned off, gardens have disappeared under torrential rain—but here in Greenwich, the park is alive in the heat. A four-year-old's birthday party is being set up, enormous balloons signaling the exact location to guests, and games are underway—scooter races on the main avenue and catch under the horse chestnuts. Near the path, the air resounds with the thwack of tennis balls. Two parakeets dip low in front of me, swoop up into a chestnut tree.

> *A haze of green feathers*
> *Biting beaks*

I sink down against a tree trunk. A new memory is coming, something frightening, I can sense it, building inside. Birds, something to do with birds, Mama's always hated them, although she's never told me why. I bring my knees to my chin, cover my head with my hands, wait until I've calmed down.

Eventually, I make it to the orchard. I see Lewis through the gate. He's at a vegetable bed, the weight of his body pressing into the top of a pitchfork, and then he pulls up the bounty—a bunch of carrots. I want to be beside him, but the idea of harvesting, of answering his questions, seems impossible. I sit with my back against the park wall. My mind is awash with feathers.

I stay there the whole afternoon watching the sky pull down dark and low. Occasionally, the gate opens—a volunteer goes in or out—and my heart catches, waiting for something to take me in, but nothing does.

He comes out at four o'clock. He doesn't see me, his eyes are on his phone, but he swerves close and where nothing has roused me all afternoon, the scent of him does—clean cotton, earth. I trail after him. He takes the path along the east wall. I have no cover, but I don't care. Where the trees thicken out by the Maze Hill Gate, he picks up a fallen horse chestnut branch, and I pause while he brushes off the dirt and breaks off the twigs. Down the hill, a little girl riding on her father's shoulders shouts, "Hello!" He waves back, turns, sees me.

"Lily! I was hoping to see you at the orchard today. They're still harvesting, but I set aside some bits I thought you might like—ferns, some lavender—"

I cover my face with my hands.

"Come with me."

We go to a lookout point I've been to many times with my brother and sister; Julia found it a few months after we moved to Greenwich. The view down to the Queen's House isn't the clean, central view from the Observatory, but it is secluded, which counts for something, and I can see the boating lake, where one summer, Julia stole a boat and we played pirates.

"Have you had another one?" he asks gently.

"A short one just now, just a fragment, green feathers, beaks, some kind of bird maybe, and one longer one." I grip the railings. "She's getting worse."

"How do you mean?"

I rub my eyes. "My dad's been sending my ex-sister-in-law, Francie, these poems. Nothing sexual, white establishment stuff mostly, so cliché, doesn't matter—"

"It does matter," he says gently.

Above the Old Naval College, clouds are gathering, the densest part the color of a bruise. "I could have handled that if Mama hadn't found out, but it's made her crazy. She picks fights with Daddy all the time, and now she's decided it's Francie's fault. Mama went to The Vine, to confront her."

"And you were there?"

I nod. "Jacob asked me to manage Mama, but I made it worse. I felt so sorry for her, so protective after the flashback with Goldie—I don't know what came over me—I poured juice over Francie. Now Jacob and Julia aren't talking to me; they think I encouraged Mama, but I didn't mean to. Especially after the last flashback."

"What happened?"

"My grandfather . . . he was brutal, Lewis. He had a mistress, he broke my grandmother's arm, he would strip her naked . . ."

Lewis' eyes don't leave my face.

"And I think Mama's obsession with Francie is all to do with that. It feels like she's afraid of history repeating itself and I tried, yesterday, but I can't seem to stop her superimposing her past on our present."

We watch a skater do a heel flip on the path in front of the Queen's House. "A lot of blame falls on you, doesn't it?"

"It's not blame, more like responsibility. I manage Mama—"

"Why?"

"Why what?"

"Why do you manage her?"

No one has ever asked me that question before; it's terrifying being forced to answer. "Because I'm the only one who can."

"Just because you *can* doesn't mean you *should*. She's an adult, there are other adults. Where's your dad in all of this?"

I shake my head. "He can't . . . the family can't . . ."

"Function without you?" His voice is sharp; I've never seen him angry until now. "But at what cost?"

"What are you saying?"

"Everyone expects too much from you."

"But I can help her! I have the flashbacks."

He faces me suddenly. "Can you? The flashbacks are *her* memories. She has everything she needs to unpick this. She can help herself."

"You said they were important. You said they could change everything."

He presses his hand to his eyes. "But why, when you hear that, do you assume they're supposed to help her? What about you?"

"They're nothing to do with me."

"You're the person having them! She lies to you about her childhood, the flashbacks tell you the truth. You make her spoilt juice, the flashback is about spoilt juice. Maybe it isn't coincidence—"

"Stop!"

"Why do you think you're having her flashbacks?"

"I don't know! I thought if I could use them to help her, to make her better, I'd stop having them."

Lewis shakes his head.

"You think it's me, don't you? You think it's my fault I'm having her flashbacks. Because I'm the same as her in some weird, tangled way. Mama's girl, Mama's doll."

He puts his hand on my arm and shakes it a little, so I'm forced to look at him. "I've never said this is your fault, never even thought it. And if that's not obvious, let me make it clear: I do not think this is your fault."

An elderly couple approach the railings in raincoats, watching the storm come in. I break away and sit on a bench. It's a hexagon built around the trunk of an oak tree, the same bench Jacob jumped off to see if he could fly. He taped paper airplanes to his legs and arms and for the split second he soared, I believed he could do it, break the laws of gravity. Now, the bench will become part of another park, the park of Lewis and me, where he showed me the terrible economics of responsibility and blame.

"Can I ask you something?" He is sitting beside me now, his elbows on his knees, his trainers scraping the gravel. "Why do you follow me?"

I'm completely still, a thief caught in the act. I search for an acceptable explanation. There's none. "You knew?"

"I had a hunch."

"Why did you let me?"

He stretches his arms over his head, his neck exposed and long. "I thought it was something you needed to do."

Why is there so much latitude in this man, so much space? Anyone else would have freaked out, but he is only interested in why. "It's just a habit."

"Following people?"

"Men. When I was thirteen, this girl, Sloane, invited the whole class and guys from the boys' school to her house for a party. Everyone was drinking. We never drank at home, so the drinking hit me hard, I liked it, it made me feel distanced, layers inside myself. They were playing truth or dare; of course I chose *dare* each time.

"The boy I only vaguely remember, except his hand was dry and mine was sweating. When he let go to open the wardrobe door, I wiped my palms on my jeans. We giggled sitting down, there wasn't much space, our knees touched. 'Well then,' he said, 'shall we do this?' But as he came closer, I thought, 'How close the walls are, how dark,' and then I screamed, kicked the door open, ran. Since then, I'll only be with a man in the daylight, in my park, not in dark, small spaces."

Lewis is quiet for some time. "There are things we do as children to survive. Then, when we grow up, we can let go of them. Take you following me. You don't have to. I want to see you. If you want to see me too, you can just ask."

I don't tell him I'm ashamed of how much I need him, or the extravagant relief that he's here. I don't have to. He already knows.

EVENING, IN MAMA'S bedroom. Mama has got her laptop out again, still obsessing about the photos, that bloody software. Rain lashes against the window, we're supposed to get more in the next two days than usually falls in a month. "She's almost doing the splits. How high do you think she's lifting her legs? What degree?"

"I don't know."

Mama snaps up to examine my expression. That's all it takes for me to fall in line, no matter what Lewis said. I set down the tray of salmon and noodles and stare at the photo, pretending to calculate the angle, although we all know I'm not the family mathematician, but Mama's keeper, my greatest task to bring her back from the edge. "Almost a right angle."

"I agree." Mama gets out her phone, takes a screenshot, hits send.

"What are you doing?"

She smooths back a strand of her black hair. "Sending everyone the evidence."

The photo pops up in the "core family" WhatsApp group.

Jacob types *?*

Mama types with a smirk across her face. *Your ex-wife showing your father her vagina.*

Jacob replies, *When was this?*

Mama tells him it was a month ago, a month after Francie suspected. *Now do you believe that F SEDUCED your FATHER?*

On a call, replies Jacob instantly, his status changing to "Away."

I want to change my status.

Something hurtles through the air before smashing into the mirrored door of Mama's wardrobe. I crouch down, fling my hands over my head, emerge only when she starts crying. "No one believes me, no one does."

She's thrown her phone. The glass has splintered, a firework burst of mirror.

"She did it. She seduced him."

My phone pings again. It's Julia, replying with two photos. The first is of Francie in her green bikini, the exact one Daddy has in his porn collection. The second is of Mama in a fuchsia bikini, not the photo she sent us from Santorini, but one Julia had taken a few years back, of Mama's fleshy stomach spilling over the low band of the knickers. I clutch my phone to my chest.

Don't think F needs to seduce anyone do you?

"What is it? Who's replied?"

"Mama, I don't think you should—" but she snatches it from me. Her jaw quivers, she casts off the covers. Her dinner crashes to the floor, but that doesn't stop her; she's at her wardrobe flinging open the doors, scooping out armfuls of pink and purple swimsuits. The wind howls. Daddy appears at the doorway, we're both powerless watching her whimper: "Find it, find it, where is it?"

I shake my head at Daddy, a silent plea, relieved when he steps toward her, annihilated when he says, "Tell Lily what you're looking for, May. She'll help you." But she ignores us, crying and muttering to herself, flinging out swimsuits. When she locates the fuchsia bikini, her rage is physical. She falls on it, tries to tear it apart with her teeth, her bare hands. When she can't, she rips into it with a pair of scissors. The pieces flutter to the floor. A tremor of thunder brings a terrible privacy to her violence, as she turns from the bikini and attacks other items in her wardrobe—dresses, skirts, trousers.

"Stop, Mama!" I try to prize the scissors from her, but she twists them behind her back. "Please, it was a stupid thing she did, she didn't mean it—" and then, suddenly, the scissors are pointing at me.

"You're defending her?"

"No, Mama—"

"You're defending your sister to my face?"

"I'm sorry, Mama—"

"You better be clear where your loyalty is. Me or her, me or her?"

"You, you!"

"Then say it! Why did she send those photos?"

I know what she wants me to say, I've said the words hundreds of times before when I didn't know the brutal man who'd said them, or the child they infected. *They're words, just words*, but I'm in pieces saying them about my sister. When will I stop telling lies? In the distance, lightning strikes. "She's nothing, she's worthless, she's a whore."

Daddy's eyes slide away from me.

Mama steps back. "Clean this mess up."

I scoop up the salmon with my hands. The flakes slip between my fingers.

AFTERWARD, IN THE bathroom, I pick fish out of my fingernails. I can't stop seeing the glint of the scissors, her dead eyes behind them.

Mama loves me, I'd said to Julia and Jacob, *I'm her favorite, she loves me the most*, but even I can see that Mama is turning against me, and then I need stop the avalanche inside. I fill the bath with just the hot tap until it's about to overflow and then I plunge my left elbow straight down into the water, my hand hovering like a white sail, and think when Theseus sailed home from killing the minotaur, he forgot to change his sail from black to white and his father thought he was dead and killed himself.

My sails are white, Mama, live.

My sails are black, Mama, die.

23 / DATE

IT STORMS ALL NIGHT, WHISTLING between the houses, whipping against the windows, and at four in the morning, I let it in. Water rushes in from the deep, dark black, through the skylight onto my singed arm.

It isn't until the morning that I realize how protected we've been. The park gates have been bolted; a sign blows in the wind: "Greenwich Park is closed." I text Lewis to see if the orchard still needs volunteers. He replies, *Meet me at the main gate.*

Along the outside of the park, there is little sign of the storm except the fresh, loamed smell and the dull pearl of the sky. But once I pass through the gates, I see the park has been ravaged. The road down to the lookout is flooded, water pooling where the paths gutter into ditch. Bins have blown over, spilling bottles and juice cartons over the grass, and hundreds of branches have fallen, grasping at the air like spectral hands. Toward the Royal Observatory, two horse chestnut trees have been uprooted and are blocking the road.

"I didn't think it would be this bad."

"No one did. Otherwise, they would have secured the trees." Lewis isn't wearing his baseball cap today and his brown hair is almost black with rain. He holds out bin bags. "We've been redeployed."

All the volunteers from the orchard are along the main avenue; Lewis seems to know each of them. He's some sort of impromptu manager, directing some to pick up litter, others to take up the branches. I stay close to him, filling up bin bags, cowed by the damage. Just one fallen horse chestnut has pulled up writhing ecosystems of earthworms and centipedes. Near the base, the trunk is split; its pale heart giving me a sick feeling. I want to fling something over it, cover it up.

"Was she all right yesterday?"

I breathe in the last vestiges of the storm. "No."

"What happened?"

I sit on the fallen trunk. "Julia happened." I tell him about the photo Mama sent of Francie, the photo Julia sent in response.

It's raining a little now, but under the tree canopy, it's dry. He crouches next to me, tracing the ridges of the bark. A piece comes apart in his hands and he drops it, astonished that, however accidental, he's a part of the tree's destruction. "I've met your sister before, she's Chrissy's friend. I found her, on the surface, charming"—Lewis is exactly the kind of person she would flirt with—"but brittle. Is she cruel?"

"Cruel? No." A memory comes to me: Julia washing my hair in the bath when I was two or three years old. She would pull her knees up and tell me to lay my head against them, cupping her hand around my face so the water didn't splash into my eyes. She bathed me until I could wash myself. "She just goes on the offensive—that's how she protects herself."

"Protects herself from who?"

I shrug.

"Lily," he says, "what's your mother like with you?"

Outside the planetarium, men are busy tying up the other horse chestnut to haul onto a lorry. Our tree will be next. There's not much time.

"Lily?" He touches my arm and the sound I make surprises me, a gull's cry. I clutch my arm to my chest.

"What's wrong with your arm?" he asks quietly.

"Nothing."

"If it's nothing, show me."

"It's not what you think."

"What do I think?"

"I don't know, that I've hurt myself."

"Have you?"

It was an accident, I burned it in the oven, I burned it on the stove, there are thousands of things I could say, but his eyes blaze at me, and then there's only one thing to say: "It made me feel better."

There is a liquid quality to Lewis's face, a complete softening. "Drinking made me feel like that. On the streets, it kept me warm, but even when I reintegrated, well into my twenties, I still did it. I'd drink all Saturday until I blacked out, then spend most of Sunday sobering up." He is just beyond the shelter of the horse chestnuts. Rain trickles down his head, forms tributaries at his neck, but he doesn't notice. "I did it to stop thinking about my father, just for one day. I was the one who found his body," and I know what it has cost him to say that to me, that he is seeing, right now, the very image he fought to obliterate. Conkers fall around us. I pull him onto the trunk.

He stares at my hands on his jacket.

I unbutton my cuff and peel back my sleeve.

"You can tell me anything," he says.

We stay in the park for a while, the bright strawberry of my skin between us.

THE ACRIMONY BETWEEN my parents has bled out because of an inspired move by Daddy I could never have predicted. After Mama put her scissors down, Daddy wrapped his arms around her. She fought him for a few seconds before slumping against his chest. He rocked her like a child, buried his lips in her black hair. "You're beautiful, May, you are always so beautiful," he cooed.

Now, my parents have a date.

The message I've just received from Mama is very clear, *find my lingerie*. If Julia and I were talking, I'd message her, and we would have laughed. The three of us used to talk about it endlessly, our parents having sex. Saturday mornings, Daddy would make the climb from his easy chair, the fourth step creaking under his weight, and then he'd cross the landing and shut Mama's door behind him. Julia wanted to spy on them. "He's in!" she cried to wake us up, and we took turns staring into the keyhole, but we didn't see anything. Later, Julia sent me in to Mama's bedroom to determine what the obstruction had been. It was Mama's bra, slung over the handle.

I lay out some slimming lingerie that would cover the full spectrum of Mama's mood—a grapefruit pink slip she always felt comfortable in, a cranberry bra with high-waisted knickers, a yellow camisole with powder-blue appliqué in case she feels like branching out of pink. I stall over a bustier, sheer tulle embroidered with cherry red flowers with a matching suspender belt and stockings. Whose perspective should I be looking at this from, my mother's or my father's? I shove it into the back of the drawer.

"What did you pick out?" asks Mama, coming into the bedroom, and I'm so happy she isn't angry at me, I throw my arms around her. She pats me lightly on the back. "You're in a good mood."

Because you've forgiven me, right, Mama?

Over my shoulder, she glances at my selection. She steps away from me and slides her index finger under the strap of the sunny yellow camisole. "These aren't right." Her voice climbs the room. "Sexy, I need it sexy. Don't you know what sexy is?"

She takes in what I'm wearing, one of Jacob's old T-shirts—I haven't had time to change into pink.

"What are you going to do in Oxford if you don't know what sexy is?"

I blink like an idiot. My brain screams *say something*, but I'm bewildered at the myriad possible responses, aware that there is only one right answer, and if I were smart enough, clever enough, I would know what it was. Instead, I use that old familiar tool. "I'm sorry, Mama—"

"I don't have time for this." She sweeps the lingerie I laid out for her off the bed. "Take everything out of the drawer!" I obey. The cherry red set is the last to come out. She snatches it from me. "This. This is perfect." She undresses. I try and turn away, but she gestures impatiently to me, *tie the ribbon, fasten my stockings, fetch my lipstick.* When we're finished, she stands in front of her mirrored wardrobe. "What do you think?" she asks.

I think you look like a prostitute.

But she's not asking me. She's asking her reflection, which pouts and smiles.

I'M MAKING MAMA'S all-time favorite snack, *tu tu kueh*, a steamed, jasmine rice cake, but my mind is on what's happening upstairs. It's been ten minutes. I imagine Daddy's face when he sees Mama, how he'll have to reconfigure shock into a flawless pretense of pleasure. What are they going to do with that suspender belt? Mama can't unfasten the clips. Could Daddy employ his scalpel precision?

> *A haze of green feathers*
> *Biting beaks*
> *Black eyes*

Mama's screams call me out of the flashback quicker than it takes me to recover. There's a thud. I think she's hit him at first, but the sound is small and dull—it's the vase. Daddy came in with a bunch of roses, the expensive kind, twenty heads at least, the flowers on the edge of bloom. He presented it to her in her bedroom and asked me to fetch a vase. I put it on her bedside table.

I wash off the rice flour and rush upstairs, my heart still pounding from the flashes of beaks and feathers. Mama's bedroom door is open; Daddy is closest to it. He gives me a look of profound weariness and then tries to close the door on me. Mama stops him.

"Let her in! Let her see what you've done, how low you've brought me. Then she'll know what men will do to her. Are you watching, Lily? This is what men do."

Mama is not wearing the knickers or her bustier, just the suspender belt and stockings. She is slumped against the mirrored wardrobe, her misery multiplied to infinity—her smudged lipstick mouth, the hang of her breasts. Between my parents are the roses, some intact, the others missing petals. Did Mama advance on Daddy with the flowers or hurl the entire vase at him? Unclear. I press a towel against the darkening patch of water, fetch a dustpan and brush.

When I return, Daddy is heading across the landing. "Was she better than me, Charlie?" rasps Mama after him.

I catch his arm as he squeezes past. "Please, Daddy, don't leave me with her, don't go. Can you stay? Just this once?"

His face is savage. He wrenches his sleeve away. "I can't do this." He rushes downstairs. The front door bangs shut.

I half-lift, half-haul Mama onto the bed, unfasten the clips to her suspender belt, roll down her stockings. She says nothing, but she hates sleeping naked, so I get her a fresh pair of black hi-rise briefs and her nightie. She changes into them silently and lies down.

I tuck her under the Peranakan quilt, slip Sapphire between her arms. A single tear rolls over her cheekbones. "He doesn't want me. Not the same way he wants her."

"Did he say that?"

"Didn't have to. I could see it in his eyes, like he was making himself. I'm not beautiful like I once was, not compared to her. I tried to carry on, but I couldn't. I just kept thinking of him and her, him and her, those photos Julia sent." Her eyes are numb and unblinking.

"What can I do for you, Mama? What would make you feel better?"

She doesn't respond.

"Some juice? Some *tu tu kueh*? I made it exactly how you like with the coconut filling. Shall I get it for you?"

Mama sits up. The room is electric with threat. "You're plotting with her, aren't you?"

"What?"

"You want me to be fat. You want him to leave me."

"Mama, please—"

She pushes herself to the edge of the bed, holds out a finger at me. "Do you think I don't know? Do you think I don't see? I see. I see everything you're thinking. May's nothing, she's worthless." She leans toward me as she speaks, and in a very deliberate way, she rubs her thumb across my cheek, looks from the smear of makeup to the color of my skin, and then to my brown roots. A small, dangerous silence falls. "*Ang moh gui*, white devil. Get out."

I DO IT again when she's asleep, run the bath hot. The skin is peeling off my left arm in sheaves, the new skin bright underneath. My right then. I lower it into the water. The pain is white and complete, *Yes*. Beyond this, there is nothing.

Her father clawed at her mother, but she still managed to shove the girl into her bedroom and turn the key. Sylvia, the parrot, was in the girl's room. She glared at the girl, the stripes on her face vicious as a tiger's. The girl pounded against the door. She heard:

>*Her father shouting*
>>*Her mother begging*
>>>*All the bad words*
>>>>*A body slammed against a wall*
>>>>>*Trousers unzipping*
>>>>>>*Fabric tearing*

Her room was a haze of green feathers
Biting beaks
Black eyes
She didn't know
Who was squawking
Who was screaming
She couldn't remember
Her name.

Something is screeching, a bird being torn apart, a rabbit being slaughtered. A hand goes over my mouth. I bite down. My teeth sink into my own skin.

Not my memories, not mine. I'm fine in the attic, here is my skylight, here is Julia's bed, here is her dressing table, but then I'm frightened of my arms, the fraying edges of skin, the voice inside that says, *Scratch, peel.*

I change quickly, grab my rucksack, go. My skin prickles.

It's the middle of the day, I've overslept, and there are no messages. No one wants me, no one needs me. My hand trembles calling Lewis. I keep saying "please": *Please come, please meet me.*

He tells me he's already in the park. He says we can meet in the Royal Observatory Garden, another garden of my childhood, although I doubt I'll ever visit it after this.

My bicycle isn't outside the house, for fuck's sake, Daddy. Down the side passage, I glimpse the front wheel poking out of the shed. The sun illuminates the flaking white paint, the cobwebbed bolt, but not the ivy, it's so thick the pure citrine can't pierce it, and then my mind is blind with terror. I try to control it—the bike's just there—but it jerks and slithers and then I can't anymore. I don't stop running until I'm at the top of our road.

He's not there when I arrive, so I search for him up and down the length of the lawn, along the paths, my trainers smashing ferns, wild garlic. Two middle-aged women watch me over their picnic while their sons set up a badminton net, what is she doing, why is she running? The gate creaks, I see a familiar baseball cap. I sprint toward him. He puts out his hands, to hold me away from him, to settle me, I don't know—but he leads me to a bench set against the garden wall, sits me down. "Breathe, Lily, breathe."

I try to, I try, but there will be no calm until it comes out. I think I'm whispering but I could be shouting, my controls are shot, I can't make out volume or sound. "I had another flashback. My grandfather raped my grandmother."

A shuttlecock whips through the air, falls without being returned.

"My grandmother locked my mother in her bedroom, but she could hear everything through the walls and there was this bird, this parrot flying around the whole time. The beaks, the haze of green, it's all leading to this."

The air swoops, he's suddenly close, holding my hands back from myself because I'm beating them against my ears.

"Stop, Lily, stop."

"This is Mama's secret—her father. He's in almost every flashback, the spoilt juice, the visit to her aunt's, under the covers. Even when she was talking to his mistress, Mama remembered him stripping her mother naked, breaking her arm. I never saw it, not as clearly as this flashback. Why didn't I see it?"

"You're OK, Lily, you're OK."

I clutch the back of the bench, count *five, four, three, two, one*, but I can't stop shaking. "I'm not sure I am, I'm not sure I am. You know what I don't understand? Why she makes us so afraid. If your father was like that and you knew what that's like, why would you do that to your children? As a parent? As a mother?"

"She's hurting you, isn't she?"

The smirk on Julia's face when Mama slapped her.

How small Jacob looked when Mama pushed him out of the car.

The glint of a knife.

"Is she violent?"

Say it to the mossy wall, dark and soft and green, whisper it. No one is listening. "Not with me. She doesn't need to be. I do whatever she says."

"Lewis!"

A woman is approaching from the gate, dressed in a zebra-patterned wrap dress and black suede ballerinas, a professional, although it's hard to tell at what. Her hair is what Julia would call "distressing," carelessly fastened with a clip at the back of her neck so it bulges over her shoulders, but her mouth is full and beautiful. "I thought that was you. I was going to surprise you at the orchard."

Lewis makes a slight move toward her, a warning, but she doesn't see it. She is looking at me, extending an alabaster hand. "Hi, I'm Saskia, Lewis's girlfriend."

Saskia, meaning protector of mankind.

She smiles at me, a lovely smile. Her eyes are clear and green. "I know who you are, Lily, right? Lewis talks about you all the time."

I could have withstood everything, who she was, the shock of her beauty, if only he'd kept me a secret. I run.

HE MESSAGES ME over and over that evening. I delete them without reading.

In the hole, I type into Google as many variations of "Saskia" I can think of—"Saskia Blackheath," "Saskia Greenwich," and then the one that slays me, "Saskia Lewis Quinn." Too many hits, none of them relevant. Fucking common name.

Lewis's profile comes up from his university with a perfect photo, and the slithering part of me springs to life, the Mama's girl I'm always hiding. I take the lined pad of paper from my school file, and I write a letter. The nib pierces the sheet.

25 / SEQUIN DRESS

SATURDAY MORNING. I RUN A boiling bath and sear my right leg. Obliterate the baseball cap and the full-mouthed smile, mossy confessions. The pain makes me feel spry and alert. No mistakes. Perfect Mama's girl.

I steer clear of making her *kaya* toast; coconut jam will be on the new list of prohibited foods. I decide on half-boiled eggs, still Singaporean but healthy. Mama enters the kitchen in a pink velour hoodie and sweatpants just as I'm putting eggs into the water. She sits on the stool with her knees pulled up to her chin and looks at me like a beaten dog. I pour her some spoilt juice.

"Where is he?" asks Mama.

"In the garden." He's harvesting greengages, doing what I would do in the orchard, although in our garden, it's always felt sinister.

"He did something to me last night," says Mama idly.

"What?"

"Things." She draws circles on the kitchen table. "Bad things."

I bite my lip. Is this true or for show? Mama's bedroom is the only room with a lock, which means her door opens and closes loudly. I didn't hear it after I tucked her in.

In the garden, Daddy has fetched a ladder to reach the highest fruit. *Don't come in here, Daddy.* The timer goes off. I crack the eggs into three bowls. They're perfect, the yolks whole and luminous under the skin of white. I set them out on the table and turn to get the soy sauce.

"Why have you made so much?"

I nearly drop the bottle. It's her voice. She's trying to keep it level, as if she's asking an intelligent question, but underneath, there's a tremor of excitement. "You've used six."

I look stupidly at the cardboard egg carton, retracing what I've done through the arithmetic of broken shells, twelve halves, six eggs, two for each of us—Mama, me, and Daddy.

Her eyes are on my face like a slap. "You're making him breakfast."

"No."

"I thought you were on my side."

"I am!"

"Then why would you do that?" She grabs the bowl.

Until she does it, I don't really believe it. This happens to Julia and Jacob, and recently to Daddy, not me, I've done everything she said, given her everything she wanted. But where my mind fails, my body knows who I am, who Mama is, and I brace myself. The bowl slams into the top of my shoulder and shatters at my feet. Orange yolk runs down my arm like a drowned sun.

HALF AN HOUR later, we're in the car, Daddy, Mama, and I, off to Regent Street to buy toys for the boys. Daddy is driving. In the passenger seat, Mama is abnormally quiet. She's a talker, a mover—everything about her is energy, color, sound. She loses things with alarming frequency and on this kind of car journey, the passenger seat would usually vibrate with pink as she searches for the missing item in her bag or coat. A narrative, intended to draw us into her tight circle of drama, would accompany this, ranging from accusations ("You had it last!") to declarations that she is a victim of crime ("I've been robbed!"). Once the item is located, she'd share her grievances for the next forty minutes: the dirty look Jacob's new girlfriend gave her; why Julia never calls; whether Francie is taking good enough care of Albie and Leo. Instead, there's silence.

I do everything I can not to look at her. I tidy the back seat. I try to follow the Radio 4 program Daddy puts on. I cup the top of my shoulder where the bowl hit me. When I can't bear it anymore, I peer at her. Her head leans against the car window, and she presses a closed palm against her mouth. I watch her shoulders for the rise and fall that signals crying, but she isn't. She stares at the stream of cars and the pedestrians filling the pavements with blank fixity. I put my hand on her arm, more out of fright than anything else.

Daddy drops us near Hamleys just as Mama instructed, but when he goes to find parking, she walks straight past the store. There's no time to ask her where she's going; she's so fast, pushing angrily through chatting tourists and drifting window-shoppers, that anything less than a run will mean I'll lose her. She enters the Tudor revival front of her favorite department store, Liberty's, and makes straight for the lift. We get out at Level 2, Women's Clothing, and I follow her to lingerie. The pink walls and yellow lighting, the silk underwear form a startling backdrop to the shocking pink velour blaze, who starts pulling black bras, knickers, and suspenders roughly from their wooden hangers. Black instead of pink trips an alarm. Black isn't good. Not good at all.

She's finished in ten minutes. She doesn't try any on, just dumps her haul on the nearest till. It totals nearly a thousand pounds. I blink at the figure, but Mama doesn't bat an eyelid. The shop assistant smiles at how much Mama is buying, wraps the underwear in the finest tissue and hands it back to us in luxurious purple bags, as if it's not ammunition, as if it isn't purchased with the intent to harm. Mama shoves the bags at me and then, she's off. A runnel of sweat forms between my shoulder blades, it's too warm under my jumper, but there's no time to take it off. She slows down in the clothes section. She's looking at a black sequin dress.

She lifts the middle tenderly. I venture a comment. "Do you like that, Mama?" She smooths the sequins all in one direction. A shop assistant in a pristine silk blouse asks if she needs any help. Mama asks her the price even though she's seen the tag.

"Two thousand, five hundred, and forty pounds, madam." Her manners are impeccable, but the precise way she says those numbers will offend Mama. Mama slings the dress over her arm and says she'll think about it. A pool of sequins trails after her.

"Open the bag," she says dreamily when the shop assistant is serving another customer.

My mind is a wall of panic, she's never made me do this before, and then my brain floats away to acknowledge her inexorable logic. I was never really forgiven for the eggs. The slipup at breakfast was always going to lead to this. Still, I beg. "Please, Mama, no."

She drives her nails into my wrist. I open the bag. She tips the dress in. Sequins roar against the sides.

In the lift, I watch the floors descend, praying to whatever god will listen that the lift will go faster. Against the sleeve of my coat, Mama leans into my shoulder. She's gentler now, my loyalty has relaxed her. The lift doors open to makeup, the glass counters sparkling with gold compacts of pressed power and silver-lidded moisturizers. In front of us, a mother and daughter are trying perfume; the mother spritzing the air, the daughter lifting her wrist to her mother's nose.

"Don't look back," whispers Mama, heading casually to the exit. We join two couples leaving the shop. The sensors blare.

Two security guards stop us before we get outside and ask us to open our bags. They search my rucksack and the purple bags. Mama is silent. It's me that protests as the sequin dress is pulled out. *I don't know how that got in there. This is a mistake.* The guard shakes his head, gestures to the CCTV. They escort us back to Women's Clothing. The department manager, a tall woman with a sporty ponytail checks the underwear off against the receipt and looks confusedly at Mama. She says Mama needs to pay for the dress. Mama hands over her credit card. She tells her she could have reported her to the police.

Mama shrugs. She tells her never to come back. Mama blinks as if she can't speak English.

I think about what I said to the security guards as they escort us out. It was only a half-truth. The whole truth is this: *I don't know how I got here. This is a mistake.*

I HAVE TWENTY-TWO missed calls from Daddy. I ask Mama how she wants me to reply. She says we'll meet him at the car park. On the way, she spots a toilet and grabs the bags from me. I wait outside. When she emerges, she is wearing the black sequin dress over a black lace bustier. Her breasts have been pushed upwards by some feat of bra engineering into two enormous mounds, and she wears black stockings fastened to a black lace suspender belt that peek out from the slit of her dress. Her velour hoodie is draped over her shoulders.

"Mama?"

She looks at me like she's just remembered I'm with her. I take the bags from her. She leans against my arm as we walk.

Daddy asks us what we've bought, and I want to tell him "careful," but he knows, and we both sit there for a few seconds, waiting for what's about to happen. Mama takes off her hoodie.

"I bought this." She gestures to the dress and her ample bosom. "Do you like it?"

Daddy clears his throat, aware of the trap he's in. He just wants those few breaths before the axe falls. "Yes."

"You know Francie has no breasts, right? She couldn't fill an A cup, a double-A cup. I'm a D." She holds her hands below her breasts and thrusts them proudly at him. They are white and blank, like spilled milk. "You bastard. You pathetic bastard. How could you ever, ever think she was more attractive than me?" Her teeth are bared. "You don't like this? You want to fool around? I can do that too. I can pick up a man in a car park like this." She tries to click her fingers, but they're too damp. Furious, she pushes the door open and runs among the cars. Daddy goes after her.

I get out, clutching my rucksack, watch them disappear through double doors. I call their phones. Neither of them answers. I climb into the passenger seat, waiting for them to return.

She's back quicker than I can register; I see only gritted teeth, pale arms, the velour hoodie gripped in her hand. She pulls the door open and climbs in. The sequins at the bottom of the dress are sodden, she has to scoop them into the footwell. I scramble for my seat belt. She twists the key in the ignition, puts the car in reverse, and slams on the accelerator.

The crash takes a few seconds, yet time for me runs slow. The shriek of metal against metal explodes in my head and then I'm hurled forward toward the dashboard, wrenched back by the seat belt. My skull smashes against the headrest.

"Mama?"

When she turns to me, her eyes are an abandoned battlefield. She unbuckles my seat belt, reaches across me to open the door, and shoves me. "Get out!"

I feel nothing tumbling out.

The car roars away.

I believed once that my mother would never hurt me, that a line separated me from my brother and sister. They could be hurt, thrown out of cars, slapped, hit, not me, never me, I'm Mama's girl, Mama's doll. But that's not right, is it?

The tarmac is warm against my cheek, licorice dark, its voice half Lewis, half my tenderest self, *You're all right, you're all right, you're ready for this, remember? See what's in your hand, feel the strap, there it is, your rucksack, the zipped pocket of cash, phone charger, A–Z of London. Your anorak's in there too, trainers and snacks. You're ready. Get up. Five, four, three, two, one.*

I crawl into an empty parking space, haul myself up against a concrete pillar. Pain lights up my body—the pulpy back of my head, the seat belt strap across my chest, and less recent hurt, the dull ache of my shoulder, my seared arms and leg.

This is my body broken for her.

No more.

I will not put Mama together.

I will tear her apart.

26 / ICE

MY PHONE PINGS CONSTANTLY.

Where are you?

Where are you?

Get bk here

We're at the car park, where are you?

Your mother is very upset that you're not here.

Pick up.

Mum said you disappeared. Are you OK?

What happened?

U better be at home when I get bk

I can see Daddy's blame, Jacob and Julia's panic, the menace in Mama's commands, but they're messages to a person who doesn't exist anymore.

On the train home, I'm invincible, I'm a bird who's smashed its cage; I've uncovered my wings. I slough away the old me—rub off my makeup, tear out my contact lenses. No more evening appraisals. For the first time in more than ten years, I stare at my reflection in the day. My hazel eye is striking, gold-flecked amber fanning to agate. I do then what Mama said only whores do. I lift my eyes to every man in the carriage—a man in his forties, a group of young men coming back from a football match. One of the football supporters asks for my number. I've never felt more powerful.

I stand up as we come into the Blackheath Station, move to the doors and, as the train brakes, someone bumps into me, pushing me against the glass of the door as it swipes abruptly open. As I hurtle toward the platform, I remember the windscreen flying toward me, and then another flashback cuts into my thoughts.

"Where are we going? What are you going to do?" Her mother was driving very fast, and it was the girl's fault, all her fault, she shouldn't have told her about the woman with the lipstick, the woman who handed her the jade ring: Daddy's mistress. Her mother wasn't wearing a seat belt.

"I'm going to speak to her."

"She'll tell Baba."

But her mother was beyond caring about what her father would do to her. "She came to my house. She talked to my daughter!"

"What will you say?"

"I'm going to ask, 'Where is her shame?'"

The girl didn't see her mother run the lights. She only saw the glass shattering, as the car crumpled and her mother flew through the windscreen.

I'm exhilarated and dead, high and low. The tracks spark. I stumble toward them.

"You all right, love?"

It's a paramedic, a young woman in a green uniform, her hair tied back in a ponytail. Behind her, I see a woman being helped into a standing position by another paramedic.

"You're not trying to hurt yourself, are you?" She asks how old I am. I tell her. Unconvinced, she says. "Let me give you a lift home. What's your address?"

I tell her the address of the only home I know. "Thirty-nine Eliot Vale."

The journey to Lewis's is short, the village, the heath streaming by. My mind picks over the flashback, enumerating the facts: there was a car accident, my grandmother died, that's what Mama's so afraid of, but my own accident keeps cutting through. She did that to me, she did it, my own mother, to avoid the car crash of her past, she has car-crashed my present. I understand her. I hate her.

The paramedic accompanies me to the door. I tell her I've lost my key. She doesn't believe me. She knocks once, twice. She raises her fist to knock a final time. The door opens. Lewis blinks at the paramedic and then at me behind her.

"I tripped at the station," I say quickly.

"Ah." Lewis nods. "All OK?"

"Fine," I push past her into the house. "Thank you for the ride."

He shuts the door, waits two beats after she leaves. "What was that?"

The flashback, the train tracks have eroded my invulnerable edge. The back of my head is sore. "Can I get some ice?"

He gestures for me to follow him. The kitchen is white marble and gold taps, there's no getting away from the spotlights. I sit on a barstool. He gives me peas wrapped in a dishcloth. I press it to my head. It's almost as good as burning.

He's making dinner—tomatoes glow on the island—but he doesn't return to the chopping board. He pulls up the barstool next to mine, turns it to face me, and then he takes everything in, my mismatched eyes, my skin color. His eyes linger on my eyebrows, I touch them, find granules of asphalt. He signals at the bag of peas. "What happened?"

I look away, stare at the flecks in the marble kitchen top. "Accident."

"At the station?"

I shake my head and then wince. My neck hurts.

"Lily?"

"Car accident. Mama reversed into another car."

He presses his knuckles to his mouth.

"And it triggered another flashback—turns out my grandmother did die in a car accident after all."

"I don't care about her flashbacks. I care about you."

"You know I think I've always been ready for something like this, ready to be thrown out just like Julia and Jacob were. I carry my rucksack around just in case." I press down on the peas. "And now it's happened, it's made me see things more clearly. You were right at the lookout. Why am I using the flashbacks to help her? I should use them to help me."

"What do you mean?"

"I'm going to turn it all around on her, every last secret. It's my turn."

Lewis is silent.

I throw the bag of peas down on the counter. "After the accident, she pushed me out of the car. She made me steal a dress. She did this!" I pull down my jumper to show him where the bowl hit me. The bruise is the size of a coin, the blown blood vessels leaking plum under my skin.

Lewis is very still, and then slowly he puts his hand out, not touching me but trembling at some invisible boundary inches from my shoulder. "You said she wasn't hurting you."

My laugh makes my insides ache. "This is just physical. Every day, she hurts me, every day, I do exactly what she says. I put on brown contacts and makeup so I look like her. I make her spoilt juice. Jules calls me Mama's girl, Mama's doll. She says I've forgotten."

"I'm sorry."

"Don't." My forearms itch under my jumper. I rub them hard against each other so I don't peel off the skin. "Something needs to be done about her. She can't get away with this."

"Listen to me, Lily. Don't go home."

"Where would I go?"

"Stay here until Oxford."

"With you?" He's so close, I can smell the sweetness of his breath, and then I know how to stop the record playing—the bowl, the sequins, the crash. I lay my hand over his heart.

The way his body stiffens, I'll never forget.

"I'm sorry, Lily," he whispers gently, "I'm with Saskia. And even if I wasn't—" He leans back the smallest fraction so that I am no longer touching him. "I told you in the orchard I wasn't going to hurt you. I won't break that promise."

My mind is thick and viscous. I sling on my rucksack.

His barstool scrapes against the floor as he stands up. "Wait, please. I know it's not what you want, but don't go. There's still so much to figure out. We know there was a car accident, but what about the fire? Why are you having her flashbacks? Something else is going on. Let me help you."

I shut my eyes.

"It's really bad now, isn't it?"

I want to tell him it's so much worse, that I saw the ground fall away into sparked tracks and I wanted to fall away with it. But I've run out of grace.

27 / DESERT BEIGE

HE COMES AFTER ME, BUT the heath is mine. I know where to hide. I head to the pond among the willows, watching the hall of The Polar Explorer House flood with light before he slams the door behind him. My name on his lips brings me to my knees, but it's only my body that breaks, not my will, which watches him pass by—that's it, he's gone. My nails fill with tree bark as I pull myself up.

Eight in the evening—I can't go home. I get a black cab to Hammersmith, counting and recounting my emergency cash as the price on the meter goes up, playing word games so I don't stare at the missed calls from Lewis. "Emergency," from the Latin *emergere*, meaning to rise out or up, *this has arisen*. "Arisen," from the Old English *arisan*, meaning to get up from sitting, kneeling, lying, *I got up from the tarmac. I got up from the platform.*

> *Scissors.*
> *Open shut, open shut.*

I double over.

"What's going on back there?" The cab driver bangs on the plastic pane.

"Sorry, sorry."

"Have you taken something? Because if you're going to throw up, you can just get out."

Through the window, there are only unfamiliar roads, people eating at restaurants, homeless men slumped against walls. I clutch my rucksack. "Just a bad dream."

"Well, don't fall asleep then."

I don't close my eyes.

We turn into a quiet street lit by lampposts. I've only been here a handful of times with Mama, and even in the dark, it's pretty. Each Victorian terrace is exactly the same—three floors, expansive basements, pastel front doors. It could have been lifted straight out of Chelsea, but Goldhawk Road is cheaper, close to Shepherd's Bush Market where you can transfer money abroad or buy bales of fabric. The cab pulls over halfway down the road. I shove the bills at the driver and slam the door.

The curtains are drawn and dread seeps in; I've run out of money, I've nowhere else to go. I knock. No answer. I call. A phone buzzes inside. She picks up.

"Can you let me in?"

Julia says nothing when she opens the door, just stands there with her hand on her hips, as if she always knew I'd wash up on her doorstep. She leads me into the kitchen, and I sit at the dining table, surrounded by dirty plates and half-drunk wine glasses. She fills a glass of water at the tap. Before she hands it to me, she lifts my chin until my eyes are level with hers. I watch her read my naked face. "What did she do?"

"What has she said?"

"She said you ran away from the car park."

I wrench my chin away. This will become the truth, repeated over and over to Daddy, Jacob, Julia, and if I go back, I will have to say it, she will make me say it until what really happened is forgotten. "We were in a car accident. She backed into a parked car. I was lucky I was wearing a seat belt. Then . . ." I nearly don't say it, don't want to admit it to Julia that what she prophesied days ago has come true. "She threw me out of the car."

"Fuck." She sits down next to me, hands me the water. Her eyes are distant. She's been pushed out of the car so many times, I don't know which incident she's recalling. "Let me see."

I show her the back of my head, tell her of the pain across my chest. She looks up how to assess me for whiplash on her phone, feels the bump on my head, asks me question after question about what the car hit, whether I have neck pain, whether I have tingling in my fingers.

"You need to get this checked out."

I shrug. "It's fine."

Irritation flashes across her face. "I'm telling you—you need to get this checked out."

"I don't like doctors and hospitals. It's dirty."

Julia startles. "You don't believe that crap, do you? They never wanted us to go to the doctors, so the doctors wouldn't report."

"Report what?"

She stares at me, and then I know I'm finally joining the ranks of my brother and sister, the unwilling initiate of a club no one wants to be a member of. Slowly, I take off my jumper and show her the bruise on my shoulder. Her eyes darken, and then she pulls my right arm straight. "What's this?" She draws an imaginary line over the skin peeling on my arm. "Did she do this too?"

"No."

She unfurls my other arm. Her lips are pressed so hard together, they vanish completely. "You?"

I don't answer.

She doesn't call me fucked up or say, "I told you so." Practical as ever, she fumbles in the kitchen drawer for a tube of gel and signals for my hands.

"Don't tell me to ride this out until Oxford."

She squirts gel onto my arms. "I'm not."

"She won't stop, even if I'm miles away."

"I know."

"You don't understand." I think of the flashback I had in the taxi, what Lewis said at the lookout—what if I'm having the flashbacks because I'm too entangled with her? "I can't be with her anymore. I can't stand it."

"You can stay here with me." She rubs the gel in, circle after circle.

I shake my head. "It's not enough. She'll keep going."

"What do you want to do?"

"I know things about her, things she's lied about. I'm going to confront her. Make a break, once and for all."

"It's not as simple as that." She caps the gel and stands up, her hair falling over her face. "Let me show you something."

SHE LEADS ME to her living room at the back of the flat and flicks on the light. She hasn't unpacked all her things since Mama let her move back in, but the walls are full, different from how I've seen it before. Instead of framed posters, there are sketches in hard, carbon pencil and art postcards tacked in every space. I stand on the sofa to get a closer look. Some of the drawings are replicas of classic Madonna and child paintings, others are anatomical—babies inside the thick, fleshy wall of a womb, gaping holes for eyes.

"What are these?"

She sits down on the sofa. "I've quit."

I step down from the sofa. "Quit what?"

"Med school."

"What?"

She shrugs. "I don't think I really wanted to be a doctor. It doesn't help me explore what I want to."

My insides shrivel at the whole wall filled with mothers and babies, every part of me slipping into itself. "Which is what?"

"It's a project I'm working on. An investigation into motherhood." She points to a postcard of the Madonna and child. "Our entire visual history of motherhood is idealized. That chubby baby is God. He's perfect, so his mother can be perfect. But what about real children, real mothers? There are no paintings of mothers throwing things at their children or crashing cars with their children inside." She presses her finger into my bruise. I feel the ache through each layer of skin. "This is real motherhood, real daughterhood, this and this." She whips up her dressing gown to reveal the scar on the outside of her thigh, the clean width of the knife, and in that instant, I remember: Mama stabbed her. Daddy wouldn't take her to hospital. "When does a mother switch from protecting her baby to destroying it? In the womb? Or is it later?"

I look at Julia then, the devastation behind her unflinching exterior a mirror of my own. She will sketch these images forever, mother and child, mother and child, trying to solve the dark clot of a question we dare not utter even to ourselves: If our mother loves us, why does she hurt us?

She lets her dressing gown fall. "Anyway, I wanted to show you this because I submitted the best of them as part of my application to the Royal College of Art, and I got in." She smiles briefly. "But there's no way Mama's going to pay for this. I have to come up with the fees. So will you if you break away from her."

She watches the confusion on my face. "You haven't thought about it, have you? If you're not Mama's girl, things aren't going to get handed to you anymore. Your tuition fees, living at college, food in that fancy Harry Potter hall—do you even know how much that costs?"

I have spent so long thinking of Mama, pleasing Mama, being the girl she wants me to be that I am helpless outside her orbit. Isn't that what Tatum sensed? Real scholarship girls knew answers to those questions, thought about them, planned for them. How naive I've been.

"You're too late to apply for grants. Jacob will sub you some, I will too, but it won't be enough, not even if you get a job."

"I don't need fancy things, not as much as you. And surely Daddy . . ."

"You can't rely on him; it won't be consistent because his consultancy work isn't consistent. And he's careful, he won't want to undermine her, he won't give you enough to break free." She sweeps my hair back from my face gently. "Now might not be the right time. You still need her."

"How can you say that?" My jaws are clamped together, I slam my palm against the wall. Pictures fall. "After all this? After what she did to me? For years you've been trying to get me to realize how bad she is—why, if you didn't intend for me to do anything about it?"

Her lower lip trembles. "Do you think I want to be the one she hits? The one she hates? I don't want to be the only person angry. I wanted . . ." she wrings her wrist, a strangled gesture, ". . . not to feel so alone." She drops her hand like a stone. "But now, with the art stuff . . . it's going to be hard without her support. I've been working and working, and it still isn't enough."

I shake my head. I can't be with Mama anymore. I don't want to feel sorry for her, try to fix her, have her hurt me. The edges of Julia's face dissolve; I'm crying. She wipes away my tears and cups my face in her hands. "You know what, Lil? Forget about the money thing, I'll figure it out for us. It's your time. Do whatever you need."

I WAKE BEFORE Julia. She's in a vest top and shorts. In the shafted light, she has no dressing gown to hide the scooped-out hollows of her neck, the clavicles straining under her skin, although the beauty of her face is untouched. We're facing each other, my hand in hers, exactly how we used to sleep when I had bad dreams. Ten years later, my body still knows to cling to my sister; she will make me feel better. Now, in this nightmare, I am asking her to do the same thing. Her eyelids flutter open. "Can you teach me how to do my makeup?" I ask. "My real makeup?"

She sits up abruptly, takes charge. "Take a shower. Wash your face. I'll get ready."

When I come out, she sits me at her dressing table, which also serves as her desk. She is in the middle of a watercolor of mussels. The water for her paintbrushes is tinged with violet.

"Face me."

Slowly, I lift my eyes to meet hers.

"Wow," she says.

Brave on the train, I'm shy in front of my sister. I cover my face with my fingers. "Freakier than you thought?"

She recoils. "You don't believe that *ang moh gui*, white devil shit, do you?"

"You called them my freak eyes."

"Because I was jealous."

"How can you be jealous?"

Her eyes are suddenly fierce. "There's a lot to be jealous of." She soaks a pad and rubs my face in small circular motions. More makeup comes off—I mustn't have removed it all on the train—and the memory of Lewis seeing my bare, unseen face, my hand on his chest, fells me.

She grabs my chin. "Don't cry. She's not going to get away with it. If you're going to confront her, you need to be strong." She turns to four bottles of foundation on her dressing table, which she tests at the nape of my neck.

"Why do you have so much makeup?"

She smirks. "Do you think Mama pays for all my things? She just covers fees and rent. I work the makeup counter in Westfield. I've even started doing some freelance makeup on the side."

When we were at home, I could tell you where Julia was at any point in the day but since she's moved out, what she does, what she's thinking, her "investigation into motherhood" is lost to me. She—like Mama, like Daddy—inhabits a world inside herself that no one can ever truly know.

She turns my face this way and that, and then waves a bottle at me. "I was right. Recognize this?"

"No."

"It's the foundation I gave you for your birthday." She buffs it across my cheeks. "You're Desert Beige."

I try to look in the mirror, but she pushes me down.

"Not until I'm done. Pay attention. After the foundation, put this powder on. Then use this blush in coral. Now, what shall we do with your eyes? They're your best feature."

I shake my head. In primary school, I'd complained to Julia about the names people called me "freak," "weirdo," "walleyed." Mama overheard, nodding solemnly as if she anticipated all along the trouble my *ang moh gui*, white devil, eyes would cause me. The weekend after, she took me to the opticians and got me fitted for brown contact lenses. *This is love*, I thought.

"Don't think about her," says Julia. "Think about what you're going to do." She dabs on some eyeshadow, brushes on mascara. "There."

In the mirror, I touch my skin. It's the same color as Julia's, a golden milk, and now, there's no difference between the color of my cheek and my neck, the tideline I was always so conscious of, gone. My *ang moh gui,* white devil, eyes haven't been diminished but enhanced, my hazel eye, not freakish at all but striking. My undyed roots look more visible, an inch of light brown hair. *I don't know who you are*, but it is exactly the unfamiliarity of my reflection that holds out the possibility of being someone else. I watch Julia apply a nude lipstick. As my lips grow pulpy, I think, *This is war paint*. I think, *I'm not yours anymore.*

28 / LITTLE ACCIDENT

STAYED AT JULIA'S UNTIL she left for work, following her to West-field, watching her effortlessly lure customers in, wandering around shops I'll never buy anything from. Now it's seven in the evening, and I'm at my front door. I unlock it slowly, slowly. Mama grabs me by the scruff of the neck. "Get in."

The accident, my disappearance, has smashed something in her, all her inhibitions are gone. She shoves me into the hall. She is dressed in hi-rise white knickers and a nude vest top, which drains her of her usual color, the dull yellow making her top half look dead. Her lipstick has caked into the creases of her lips, her black hair, untethered by diamanté clips, springs from her shoulders. She takes in my jeans, the pink jumper I wore to Liberty yesterday, and then my face. When she speaks, she articulates every syllable. "You look like a whore. Your makeup, your roots. It's disgusting."

"This is my face, Mama. My real skin. My—"

Mama rushes to the kitchen. Daddy watches from the living-room doorway. I try to meet his eyes, gauge whether he will step in if this gets out of hand, but it has always been out of hand. He has never stepped in.

I hear the tap run and then a squirt. Mama returns with a sopping wet sponge covered with green washing-up liquid that spills off the edges in threads. She holds it out. "Take that makeup off."

The smile twitching at the edges of her mouth enrages me; does she think I'll fall back so easily? I'm Mama's girl, but not hers anymore, turned on the tarmac against her. I snatch up the sponge and rub it in exaggerated circular motions until my cheeks are slick with suds. "Watch me wash this makeup off, watch. I still won't be Chinese. I'm both." I throw the sponge at her feet, a poor shot, it lands inches from her. Water snakes toward her. When it touches her toes, she gasps.

Her next move I couldn't have predicted. She nods to Daddy, who takes a step into the hall. A bargain has been struck, a new allegiance has been forged—and then I remember what Julia said: "They never wanted us to go to the doctors." *They.* Including Daddy. His complicity isn't new. I've been Mama's lieutenant for so long I didn't realize the post was his before it was mine.

"Go upstairs," he says. "Clean yourself up. Don't come down until you're ready to listen to your mother."

I stand my ground. "This is what I want to look like." I look him straight in the eye. He quails.

Mama does not. "You've been going bad for a while—disloyal, two-faced, being on Francie's side, Julia's, making me fat."

I want to laugh, but there is nothing funny about the menacing way she is advancing on me.

"So now I'm asking you. Put on your lenses. Put on the makeup. Dye your hair."

"Or what? You're going to make me steal a dress? Leave me in the middle of London? You've done those things already. It hasn't stopped me."

Daddy steals an uncertain glance at her; he doesn't know what she's done. She's fed him the same story, *She ran away, I looked for her, crazy girl, making me worry.*

A weariness sets in between my eyes, her lies, the mechanical shifts in gear. "Why do you hate how I look, Mama? Why is it such a threat?"

"I'm not threatened. I want you to be good!"

"You don't want me to be good. You want me to be your doll, and I was, I did everything you wanted. Look where that got me." I turn to my father, pressed against the living-room door. "We were in a car accident, did she tell you that? She backed into another car. Feel it." I take his hand, lead it to the back of my head. "Can you tell she accelerated?"

Daddy walks his fingers under my hair. Tiny truths transmit from my scalp to him. Mama is incensed. She hacks at the bend of his elbow, her hand a machete. The connection broken, she slaps me again and again, roaring all the bad words.

I've been anticipating all day her lines of attack, practiced the grenades I'd detonate—you never got into Oxford, you never lived in an emerald house, you lied about how your mother died, your father was a rapist—but these are powerless against the force of her palm on my face. Thoughts flare, trail to nothing. That when your mother hits you, it feels like being torn. That I will never win. That Julia was right all along. *Don't feel sorry for her. This is who she is.*

THROUGH THE SKYLIGHT, I stare at the rooftops, the satellite dishes and chimneys, the thousands of houses, the cranes building more. A ginger cat pads carefully along a drainpipe, a child sings, someone is practicing the tuba. Daddy comes up the stairs. He is silent until he's crossed the attic floor and stands next to me.

"We've made a decision."

I twist the cuff of my pink jumper. It smells strange, it's been in too many places—Liberty, the car park, the station platform, The Polar Explorer House, Julia's.

"We should have kept a better eye on you, your mother and I."

We?

"So we've decided we're moving with you to Oxford. You won't need to stay in halls. You'll be staying with us."

The ground slips away, slowly at first, and then all my imaginings of what university would be like are swallowed in smoke. I'm desperate, catching his arm as he turns to leave, "Please, stop her."

He presses his fingers into his eye sockets. "You know I can't," he says. "We've taken the day off tomorrow. We're going to Oxford to look at houses."

A scream thrashes in my throat.

"I'm going to get some ice for your . . . little accident." He points to my face.

I lift my fingers to my cheeks. They're tender.

29 / OXFORD

THE NEXT DAY, EVERYTHING IS fine between Mama and Daddy. They're solicitous with each other, she even says "thank you" when he makes her a coffee, although no one makes me a coffee or says a single word to me. I watch my family reconfigure, wonder if it's as simple as Mama always needing a scapegoat. It's been Julia and sometimes Jacob, then briefly, Daddy. Now, it's me. Order is restored.

Mama prattles on about the different areas we need to scope out—Headington, Cowley, Park Town, setting out the advantages and disadvantages to each. Daddy goes out of his way to show he's listening, switching BBC Radio 4 off when normally he'd turn it up. The cock of his ear is so exaggerated, it's comical, but maybe that's how he really listens because he agrees with her at exactly the right moments, ascertaining from the notes of her voice whether to nod along or offer an opinion. He's better at this than I thought.

The estate agent, Angela, stands up from her desk to greet us in an office gray skirt and improbable heels. She hugs Mama as though she knows her, awkward because Mama is petite, and Angela is taller than Daddy. Daddy gives her a friendly wave. She shoots him a withering look but smiles at me, and then I know Mama has told her an overblown story about Daddy and Francie, but she hasn't updated her on the latest reshuffle: my demotion to black sheep.

"I've got some properties that tick all your boxes. Three beds, one for guests, and all within a half-hour bus journey to central Oxford. Where will you be working, May?"

"Oh," says Mama with a wave of her ruby fingernails, "I'm think-ing about setting up my own wealth management practice." She's leaving RPWM? I glance at Daddy for confirmation. He shrugs.

"You didn't tell me that! Impressive."

Mama smiles, a pretense at humility. "So, for the first year or so, I'll work from home, building up the business, and then I'll think about premises."

I dig my nails into the softs of my palms. There will be no letup if Mama works from home, no end to the spoilt juice I'll make, no trips to the park, no Lewis, not a second of relief.

"And Charlie, where will you be working? I'm sure there's lots of opportunities for someone with your . . . skill set."

Daddy, used to creeped-out reactions, is polite. "I'm thinking about going private. There are a few forensic pathology firms here."

Angela claps her hands together as if forensic pathology firms are a positive thing. "Where will Lily go to school? As you'd expect, there are some great schools in Oxford."

"Lily?" says Mama, leafing through Angela's printouts. "She's going to Oxford."

Angela startles. "Oh, I'm sorry, you look so young." She frowns. "Did you say you want three beds? Even with a guest room, you won't need three if Lily's at Oxford."

Mama doesn't look up. "Lily is staying with us."

I watch our family transform in Angela's eyes to something odd she can't quite put her finger on, a super religious family or a cult. She recovers quickly. "My mistake. Congrats for getting in. Right," she scoops up some keys, "shall we go? Follow my car if you get lost."

WHAT ABOUT THIS room for you, Lily? It has a view of the garden." Mama strokes the end of my hair. I flinch. She is taunting me, with this room, with her hand on my back, as if I haven't remembered that she slapped me, that she pushed me out of the car. "What's wrong? Don't you like it?" She looks quizzically at Daddy. I'm not sure if she can't feel the dissonance or if she's just pretending.

Please, please, someone help me. I walk around other people's homes, begging for flashbacks. Lewis was right, something else is off about Mama. Why has she lied about how her mother died, about the car accident? If I find out, it could protect me from her, I could use it against her. I bring to mind fragmentary images—*scissors, open shut, open shut*—but nothing comes, no one except Mama, who drags me constantly to her side. Who is this woman? Does anyone know?

Then a name jolts through me, electric—Rachel Tan. I lock myself in someone else's bathroom, hold my breath as I scroll through my inbox for an email from The Singapore Land Authority. That's her name, the current owner of the emerald house. She might know something I can use against Mama.

I research her in between the houses we visit, in the seconds Mama leaves me alone in an empty living room, in a dining room she imagines we'll eat in. Finally, I find an article that confirms it. Rachel Tan is an archivist, involved in an oral history project conducting interviews with prominent Singaporeans. There's even a photo of her outside her emerald-green Joo Chiat shophouse. All right, Rachel. Archive this.

> *Dear Ms Tan,*
> *I hope you are well. I'm doing some research on the shophouses*
> *of Joo Chiat for a project on Peranakan shophouses. Yours is*
> *particularly beautiful, and I wondered if you were available*
> *for a brief chat to discuss the history of your house? I'm eager*
> *to speak with you and can make myself available whenever*
> *you're free.*

I leave my number, wait for the satisfying sound of my email winging its way to her.

"What are you doing?" Daddy peers over my shoulder.

I lock my phone. "Just checking my messages."

We're in a living room next to a grand piano. Mama's talking to Angela on the patio beyond the double doors.

"You need to be more engaged. Your mother's trying to find us a house. Be helpful."

"I don't want to live here."

"Well," he says, patiently, "let's find somewhere you want to live."

I stare at the piano. "I don't want to live with you."

Daddy checks to see if Mama's heard me. He scowls. "Stop it. You need to stop."

"Why are you letting this happen?"

"Your mother wants to be a family, so we're going to be a family."

"How can we be family? After what you did? After what she did to you and to me?"

"She did nothing."

"She threw me out of the car! She crashed it!"

"Stop being dramatic."

My breath catches. How many times have I said that to Julia without realizing how silencing it is, how nothing I say matters? I push through my tears. "I found out about Mama. Her father . . ." I start, but I can't articulate what my grandfather was really like. "Her mother died in a car accident. There was no fire."

Daddy rolls his eyes. "Not this again!"

"But she's lying. Don't you want to know why? Don't you care?"

"I care about making her happy."

"How will you do that? You know you can't manage her, not the way I can. That's why you want me to stay, so I'll do it for you."

He grabs my wrist, twists, the reflection of his grip monstrous in the lacquer of the grand piano. "I told you, stop it," he snarls. "Get off your phone. Focus on this house."

"Everything all right, you two?" Mama asks with a wide smile.

Daddy lets go. "Lily was saying she wasn't sure about the size of the garden."

"The next house has a much bigger one," replies Mama. She stares at the bracelet of red thronging my wrist, then looks away.

MAMA WANTS TO visit my college before we leave, and there's no fight in me to stop her. She steps in through the door, which seems made for her petite stature, over the cobblestones and into the quad. "This is beautiful," she exclaims at the red brick, the chapel, the perfect symmetry of the windows overlooking the grass. "Let me just ask where the dining hall is, we liked that the last time we came."

She waves down a man in his twenties. "Excuse me, I'm looking for the dining room? My daughter is attending this college in October, and I just wanted to see it with her."

"Ah, a fresher," says the man, nodding at me. I look away.

"What year are you in?" asks Mama.

The man seems to grow two inches. He tucks his shirt into his jeans, adjusts his dark-framed glasses. "I'm doing a Masters. History."

"A Masters! You know, I was supposed to attend Oxford when I was eighteen."

"Really, why didn't you?"

"I was in an accident. A fire. If not, I would have studied here. This very college!"

The lie makes me swoon.

"That's why I'm so proud of Lily. She's fulfilling my dreams."

He smiles generously. "And what are you studying?" he asks me, although it is Mama who replies. "Law."

"Have your rooms been allocated? Are you quad-side or in the new building?"

Mama smiles. "She's not staying in college. She's staying with us. We're up looking for a house in Oxford."

He stares at me. "I've never heard of anyone not staying in college before, especially a fresher."

Mama puts her hand on his arm. "That's what she wants. She's a very quiet girl. Timid. She needs us close."

With that, Mama seals my fate. There will be no concealing my strangeness now, not even with a group of nerds. No one is living with their parents. I am completely alone.

The man points us to the dining hall, but the boarding-school beauty of it is lost to me. I will never eat at those three long tables, never sit under the portraits of old wardens. Mama studies my face to check if she's broken me.

Inside, steel glows red.

Throw me out of a car and you won't win.

Beat me and you won't win.

I'll find a way.

30 / SPOILT JUICE

ALL EVENING, I WATCH HER smirk at me, tell me how fun it's going to be just us three, about her plans to continue her search in Oxford tomorrow, and I think *no, no*. I set my alarm but don't go to sleep, don't even go to bed. I stay in the hole, surrounded by all my secret things. The dandelion is shriveled but the hole smells clean with lavender from the orchard, and the ivy plants are unbelievably long. I check for a reply from Rachel among their tendrils, but as the hours tick on, nothing happens. I'll have to take matters into my own hands.

When the alarm sounds the next morning, I start with my hair, the actions automatic—slipping on the gloves, mixing the bottles of dye, applying it along my roots, then running it through. I've done this so many times, the hair, the makeup, the brown contacts, but never as a disguise. Cover my tiger stripes, the rich gold, the black. She won't see me waiting to pounce.

Lewis has left me two voicemails, but I can't have his soft warnings circling in my head, not now. I delete them without listening and push a note under Mama's door, "Gone to get you a special breakfast." The promise of Gabrielle's croissants, the ones that give her only the mildest stomach ache, will buy me time. And the element of surprise.

I head to Gabrielle's first and then to the health shop. The last time I was here, there was a sale; Mama heaped bottle after bottle of vitamins into her basket. She appeared next to me when I was looking at some grapefruit-flavored gummies for hair and skin. "Get them if you want," she said, tucking a strand of dyed hair behind my ear. "Although, you don't need it. You're perfect."

But today, perfect me is going in to hurt Mama. From the spoilt juice flashback, it isn't clear what she's allergic to, it could be a milk allergy or lactose intolerance. The shop assistant shows me bottles of enzyme tablets to digest lactose. That's the opposite of what I want. I find the milk powder on my own, whole milk, 500 grams, baking ready.

At home, I work quickly. I have steady hands. If Daddy got a splinter, he'd call for me, hold out his enormous palm. "You should be a plastic surgeon," he'd say, watching me ease out the sharp fragment. Now, the same calmness floods through me, my mind blank except for this precise task. I pour a glass of spoilt orange juice, a day more rancid than I'd normally give her but that will balance out the milk. I test it after I mix in each quarter teaspoon of milk powder. My tongue, trained to discern her tastes, my mind, so attuned to her flashbacks, are weaponized against her.

Beyond two teaspoons, the juice turns pale, that kick of acid neutralized by cream. I make up a fresh glass, put the croissant on a pink Peranakan bowl and take it upstairs.

She is sitting up, her hair spread out upon the pillows, whispering to Sapphire. She is so like a child, dwarfed by the enormity of her bed, her billowing nightie, that I feel muddled, *why am I punishing her again?* But then she gestures impatiently at me, and I remember.

"So?" She tucks Sapphire under the silk quilt next to her and sets the tray across her thighs. "What do you have to say for yourself?"

"I'm sorry, Mama." I sit on the edge of her bed.

She inches the end of the croissant into her mouth. Croissants were the invention of local bakers to celebrate Vienna's victory over invading Turks, to eat one was to devour enemy forces (the Turkish flag still has a crescent moon). I watch her take bite after bite, each one, a declaration of future victory. But I will not be devoured.

Her lips are powdered with sugar as she picks at stray almond flakes. When her plate is clear, she pulls my hair, not hard, but enough to force me to bend my head toward her. "You've dyed your roots. Finally."

Not a child, I think. *Not a child at all.*

She squeezes my chin, checks my lenses in the low, curtained light. "Good, good." She gives me a little push. "You need to apologize to your father for what you said about the car accident. He was very worried."

"Yes, Mama." My face is stone.

"It's a good plan, don't you think, moving to Oxford? Good for a fresh start. Your father came up with it."

Inside me, mines explode. Was it really his idea? He wants to keep me a child, forever preserved as Mama's girl, Mama's doll, while he hunts out new vistas to enjoy his Peronis. Or is this another tactic to divide us, keep us doubting one another, hating one another? My heart says *fight*, but my mind says *wait, watch*. Her fingers are curled around the glass. My voice is an automaton's. "I think it's a great idea. Give us time to mend relationships. Be a family again."

She drinks the juice like she always does, gulping it down, so thirsty, then hands me the empty tray. "Right, up, up, up. We don't want to miss our appointments."

OUTSIDE THE BATHROOM, I wait for the low groan—there it is. She calls to me quietly, the pain stealing the pitch of her voice—but I don't go to her, I let her say my name for five glorious minutes, a wild, reckless joy trilling through me. Only when she's given up, do I compose myself and knock on the door. "Mama?"

She doesn't reply.

"I'm coming in."

The smell is overpowering. I hold the inside of my elbow over my nose. She's on the toilet, but she's slumped backward, her head lolling against the cistern, her skin grayed and clammy. I blink my eyes to take this photo. *Click.*

"Are you all right, Mama?"

No response. *Click.*

"You don't look well." I flush the toilet. The sound rouses her, her eyes flutter open, but her gaze is bleary and unfocused.

"Can you stand?"

She puts her hand against the sorbet pink wall, her other hand reaches for me. "Help me back to bed."

I put her nightie back on and lead her under the covers.

"Cancel the viewings," she whispers.

I've won.

I want to run around in loops, howl, telegraph my triumph to the world. Nothing beats the brokenness of an enemy, the sweet twist of everything suddenly going your way.

IT'S LATE IN the afternoon. Mama's been asleep for hours. I'm still jubilant at purchasing this entire afternoon of peace. This is more reliable than making Peranakan food, much less effort than retelling invented childhood stories. I could titrate the dose, sprinkle a little more when she's being annoying, constantly adjusting and readjusting the quantity of that precious powder in spoilt juice, snacks, dinners. Her turn to be Lily's girl, Lily's doll.

"Her stomach's playing up. She can't go," I announced to Daddy earlier.

"Oh." He didn't bother to mask his relief, and I wonder if it was really his idea to move to Oxford or if that was just another one of Mama's lies. "I did need to check on something in the lab," and that was him gone too. I spent the day on the sofa reading *The Wonders of Language*, gorging on all the things she can't eat—a cheese platter, triple-chocolate ice cream, slices of coffee cake.

I get a message from Francie, *Are you OK? Jay told me you were in a fight with your mother*, and one from Julia, *How's it going?*

I ignore Francie and give Julia a thumbs-up emoji and a high five.

Daddy slams the door when he comes home. My fault. I should have told him to come in quietly. I hear her voice. "Lily?" She's stronger now, there's only a wisped undertow of weakness.

I roll my eyes at him and head up the stairs.

Her room glows a little with the sun setting behind the shut curtains. "Did you cancel the estate agents?"

I shake my head. "I couldn't get into your emails, and I didn't want to wake you." I stroke her hair. "How are you feeling?"

Mama tuts, annoyed at herself. "Fine, fine, what was going on with that croissant? From Gabrielle's, right? They're usually a little painful, but not like that."

"Must be something wrong with the recipe. Was it really bad this time?"

She hugs her stomach protectively. "Very bad, much worse than I've had it before."

I ache to smile.

"Can you reply to those estate agents and apologize about missing those appointments? Ask if they can rearrange for the weekend."

"The weekend?"

She props Sapphire up against the pillows. "We have to view quickly if everything's going to be ready before your term starts. First week of October, right?" She types her password into her laptop and passes it to me. "Email them while I take a bath."

This isn't going to end, is it? I can't poison her every time she tries to visit Oxford. She'll find out.

I stare at Angela's confirmation of the appointments, scrolling numbly up and down the email chain when something catches my eye. Mama's original email to Angela is dated the day after she got back from Santorini.

Moving to Oxford was never a punishment for running away or the scene yesterday. This was always the plan. My rebellion is merely an excuse to tighten the reins, to explain the inexplicable: Mama was never going to let me go.

My phone rings, a foreign number.

"Hello?"

"Hello, is that Lily?" The voice on the other end is confident, a little gruff.

"Speaking."

"This is Rachel, Rachel Tan, calling about your email."

I go to Julia's bedroom, shut the door, recall my Singaporean manners—treat everyone older than you like they're part of your family, call older women "Auntie." "Hello Auntie, thank you for calling back."

"No problem, no problem."

I haven't heard the lilted Singaporean accent for months. I press my phone to my ear to make sure I catch everything she's saying.

"Are you at the National University of Singapore?"

I consider saying "yes" to make my questions more legitimate, but I don't want to be caught out, she might know someone there. "No, Auntie. I'm at school."

"I thought so, you sound young. You're not Singaporean though?"

My accent has already marked me out as someone different. I need to feed her the right mix of truth and lies. "No, I'm from London."

"London, huh. And your school is making you do a project?"

This woman is sharp—I'm not going to pull the wool easily over her eyes. I need something else in my arsenal, something to help me get past her walls. The deception comes to me easily, after all, I have a lot of material for a convincing story. Here you go, Auntie, this is a Mama's girl special, half-truth, half-lie. "Auntie," I make sure my voice breaks a little, "my mother is . . . was Singaporean, she was Peranakan. Before she died, she took me to Singapore, showed me Joo Chiat. Your house was our favorite. After she died, I wanted to do my own project on your house, to honor her, our Peranakan heritage. If you cannot help me, it's OK, I understand, but if you could, I'd be so grateful."

She interrogates me a little more on how I found her details, why I like Peranakan shophouses, but the gruffness is gone, she'll answer my questions.

"Well, the house has been in my family for generations. It's been through fire, it's been through war, do they teach you about the Japanese occupation of Singapore or just the Nazis?"

The fire. I am so close. Slowly, go slowly. "Just the Nazis, Auntie, but my mother told me about it. But the house was set on fire?"

"Oh yes, when I was only a girl."

"How did it start?"

"No one knows. My mother thought my uncle started it; he was staying with us for a while after his wife died. He started drinking a lot."

Mama's Baba drank a lot before that too.

"My father thought it was thieves because things were missing. Not a lot, a small amount of money, one of my grandmother's *tingkats*."

"A *tingkat*?" I slip out of Julia's room, pad down the stairs and into the kitchen.

"Yes, a *tingkat*, very rare, an antique. My grandmother collected them, she had maybe twenty, thirty. She displayed them behind glass cabinets in the dining room."

Clutching the phone between my ear and shoulder, I haul myself up onto the kitchen counter and reach for my mother's most precious possession.

"I don't think they really knew what they were taking, maybe just snatched one as they went past, but the one they took was priceless. Blue flowers on white porcelain with gold handles shaped like bamboo."

I trace the blue flowers.

". . . and the house, it was made of wood, the furniture was made of wood, the back burned quickly."

"Was anyone hurt?"

"My Uncle Jimmy died. His daughter also, my cousin. They never found her body. She was only eight. Tragedy after tragedy, my uncle's side of the family."

My voice is the smallest whisper. "What was your cousin's name?"

"Meilin Tan."

Meilin.

Mei.

May.

Mama.

I drop the *tingkat*. The bottom layer smashes first as it hits the kitchen counter and then the top two layers slide off, splintering against the floor tiles. All that is whole among the blue-patterned shards is the gold, bamboo handle, and then the reel of Mama's past shudders into motion.

After he cut her, there was stuffing all over the floor. Goldie lay facedown. The girl couldn't see how bad it was until she turned the teddy over. She made sure she looked straight at Goldie's glass eyes not at the hole where her nose used to be.

"It looks fine," she told her.

Goldie didn't believe the girl. She buried her head in her arms, frightened of scissors, of open shut, open shut, of him.

The girl picked up the nose her father had cut off. "I'll get him back."

"How?" Goldie asked.

The girl stroked the teddy's face, her fingers slipping into the cigarette burns he'd bored into her fur. His gold lighter, flicking, always flicking, she hated it. "With his lighter."

"When?"

The girl knew what he was doing, it hadn't changed now that they had been staying at her uncle's, because he always did the same thing after he finished with her mother, and now, after he finished with her: he'd be napping in his bedroom, cradling a bottle of whiskey. It was a good time. Everyone was out. "I want to get something from downstairs, and then I'll do it. Now."

There was a fire.

My grandfather died.

But it wasn't an accident.

My mother started it.

My phone is in the *tingkat* smithereens, I can hear Rachel on the line, she asks if I can hear her, if I'm there, and then the dial tone. I don't pick it up.

I know two things.

I know my mother is insane, that she has been for a very long time.

And I know how to break her.

31 / SAPPHIRE

CREEP BACK TO MAMA'S room. The bath has stopped running, the air filled with the citrus notes of her bath oil. My mother is soaking all her aches and pains away. I hear the slow splashes of her arms moving, the shower gel squirting out, and then the low, insistent scrape of a loofah against her back, *scritch, scratch, scritch, scratch*. My mind scratches. I have dressed, fed, loved a murderer for such a long time.

I peer through the doorway to glance at her. She stares at her left foot as she scrubs, the pink pedicured toenails turning the hot water tap absently on and off, on and off. She is humming, not a song, just a sound, an expression of contentment, like a daydreaming child, but that doesn't steer me from my course. Children can kill.

I step back and search the room until I find what I'm looking for. The scissors Mama used to cut her swimsuit are on the shelf of her bedside table, stuffed into a roll of shredded nylon. I pull it out like a sword from a scabbard and take the scissors on the slow walk around the bed to the window seat of teddies, those rows of mini Goldies. The blades sound clean against their noses. Destruction is astonishing, the flashing beauty of open-shut.

"What are you doing?" Behind me, Mama stands up in the bath. Water runs off her. She screams at the rows of faceless teddies, a primitive cry, the sound of a mother coming upon the rending of her cubs.

I grab Sapphire, hold the scissors to her neck. "Don't come any closer."

Daddy rushes in, torn between Mama's shouting and the teddy dangling from my fist. "Give me the scissors, Lily."

His intervention decides it. I drive the blades into Sapphire's back, slice her from arse to throat, and then I'm at her face, ripping through her snout. Mama hurls herself at me, wet towel, wet skin, snarling, biting, trying to wrest my fingers off, but I don't loosen my grip with one hand, the other snatching out handfuls of stuffing from paws, stomach, brain. My head is exploding, I love it. She'll never be able to repair her. No more comfort for you, Mama, no more.

Mama rears back and then keels over.

"What's wrong with you?" roars Daddy. "Are you crazy?"

"Not as crazy as she is!" I try to push past him to get to her, but he grabs my arms so hard I think he'll break it, but that doesn't matter. I have my tongue—that's still a blade. "I know all her mixed-up lies. I know what she did!"

Daddy shakes me. "What are you talking about?"

Tears stream hotly down my face. "Her family never owned the emerald house. And her mother did die in a car accident, but that wasn't the end of it, was it, Mama?"

Mama covers her mouth with her hand, a desperate attempt to stop the spill of secrets, but they aren't spilling out from her, they're spilling out from me, and I will say all of them, every last one. "There was a fire. The one her father died in. You think she was such a clever child, right Daddy, smart little girl, running away instead of hiding, but it wasn't because she was clever. She ran away because she started it. She murdered her father."

The light in my mother's eyes dies.

I've broken her.

I wait for a beat of triumph, but it doesn't come. I summon it, *I wanted this, I wanted this,* but something is very wrong, not with Mama, but with me, with the way I am strangling Sapphire's neck, the way her black eyes bulge out of the empty carcass of her head. There was another bear whose eyes bulged out. *No, no, stop, I don't want to know,* but I am powerless to stop another flashback.

"I like you in a sarong kebaya," her father said, opening the door. "It suits you, little nonya. But such an ugly face." He set down his lighter and his whiskey bottle, but the cigarette still burned in his mouth and then, in two strides, he was standing in front of the girl.

"Always with that stupid bear," he mumbled, and then he grabbed Goldie. "What is it about this bear that you like so much? This face?"

He turned Goldie toward the girl and she didn't like it, how Goldie's eyes bulged because he squeezed her head so tight. "Want a cigarette, bear? Here, here." He took out his cigarette and pressed the lit end against her mouth, against her head. The girl screamed, jumped up to wrench her back. Her father laughed. "You love this bear more than me? More than your Baba?"

The girl doesn't remember what she said. Only that it wasn't enough to make him stop.

"You'll learn." He took a pair of scissors and cut the teddy bear's nose off, open shut, open shut. The stuffing came out of her like a blizzard.

"Come here."

The girl wet herself.

"Take off your clothes."

The girl didn't fight him like her mother used to. She lay still, reaching, reaching until she found Goldie's paw. Hand in hand, they went through the rooms of herself turning everything off.

Wait, wait, he raped Mama too?

My Mama?

"Mama?"

She is curled against the wardrobe, her fists balled up in front of her face.

"Did he hurt you?"

She makes the sound of a frightened animal.

Words dribble out of my mouth. "I didn't know, I didn't know he did that to you. I didn't know what Goldie meant, I wouldn't have done that if I'd known!" but rows of holed faces condemn me, the glimmering, bulging eyes of Sapphire.

"What shall I do with her?" Daddy asks Mama.

Mama's voice is thin and strange. "Take off her clothes."

There is a moment of confusion when Daddy thinks he's misheard. He glances at Mama for confirmation, she gives him a small nod, and then there's a pause, he won't do it, no way; he hasn't helped her like this before, why would he do it now, and then things happen very quickly. He pulls my jumper over my head with one arm, the other, a vice across my ribs. The shock of his hands on me makes me freeze. I cannot comprehend it, but he is stripping off my T-shirt. I kick out at him, at Mama, my feet trampling air. I fight, scream, scratch, twist to be free, clutching at fleeting triumphs—his skin under my nails, his feet squirming under my stamps, but they're millimeter gains, he's got it off. He falters at the clasp of my bra, shame perhaps, his fingers thick and clumsy, but after excruciating seconds, it springs open and then he wrenches my sweatpants and knickers down together. All my fight goes to covering the dark triangle of hair between my legs, my breasts.

"Push her outside."

I beg. For my mother, for my father, for mercy. Daddy drags me across the landing and down the stairs, levering open the front door while I struggle against him. I shout back at Mama, "After everything I've done for you, save me, just this once," but she doesn't reply. His breath warms the back of my neck before he shoves me out of the door.

32 / OUBLIETTE

NSTINCT TAKES OVER, NO LOGIC or thought, just synapses twitching into action. *Crouch down, don't look up, now go.* I half lurch, half crawl past the front of the car, push the gate open, then run down the side passage shadowy with moss.

My mind doesn't kick in until I've pulled back an iron bolt, shut a door behind me, curled myself into a ball. A deck chair thrusts itself between my shoulder blades, dirt scrapes against my skin. I taste soil.

I'm in the shed.

I'm never in the shed.

It's because of Jacob. He told us he'd seen a snake in here eat a rat alive, and even though Julia and I said we didn't believe him, the snake slithered so deeply among the weeds of our memory that neither of us would go in the shed again.

Now, as I start to shiver, I think that snake was something else. Something my brother, so young when he went out there, couldn't verbalize except through a fear of shadowed corners and things that scuttled. Maybe there wasn't anything that scuttled. Maybe it was just his mind that scuttled as the cold descended over him and his eyes adjusted to the dark. Did he know that if he hid in that shed, a part of him wouldn't come out? How does a ten-year-old express to his sisters over cereal and cartoons that he has been devoured?

He says, *I saw a snake eat a rat alive.*

I scream.

Oubliette, *oublier*, to forget, except that it's me who's forgotten.

I know why I'm having Mama's flashbacks.

And then I'm retching with fear because I remember the deck chair against my shoulder, my nails scraping against this uneven wall, this intensifying darkness.

I pull back tennis rackets and camping equipment, watering cans and fertilizer until I locate what I'm looking for, a rucksack. I fumble at the zip, shut my mind down to *scissors, open shut open shut, take off your clothes*, pull out what I know is in there—a sweatshirt, T-shirt, sweatpants, trainers. I choke on the terrible smell of seasons after seasons of mold, comforting myself with the tender practicalities of escape, *put your T-shirt on, that's it, nearly there, don't forget your laces*, then I kick the door open and run. Past the outdoor tap dripping black pools of water, past the house where my mother is spinning another tale and my father is settling down on his easy chair. Out, out, and away.

33 / THE FLOWER GARDEN

WHEN THE OLD CIRCUITRY BLOWS, a new one takes its place. An unconscious map unfolds, and it is of one place, a place where there are other places to hide, a place I know better than my own home—Greenwich Park.

I keep stumbling. Twice, I'm sent sprawling on my hands and knees, my palms bloodied, my nails broken. Twigs scratch my face; my tongue pushes out wet leaves. The park is shut, of course it is. I can see the lock from across the road, but that doesn't make a difference. I watch for the road to empty before climbing over the gate. A nail catches on my sweatpants, tearing across my knee.

The park is frightening at night. There are no lampposts, just moonlight on the avenue, and around me are monstrous shadows of horse chestnuts, rustlings, cracklings, long-murmured syllables of animals. I go to the Flower Garden, climbing over the gate, searching for cover. Everything is in shades of navy except masses of bushes pale with flowers. I cup my hand under one, draw it close. It isn't one flower but a ball of nine, each one bell-shaped, their stamens spilling out in curls. Rhododendrons, from the Greek *rhodon*, meaning rose.

I crawl underneath the bush, stopping when the branches open to a small space. Very, very slowly, I lie facedown into fallen petals and let it all come.

> *They're not Mama's memories.*
> *They're mine.*

She called them "stories."

She'd come back from work around eight, past my bedtime but I'd wait for her, listening for the sound of tires against the gravel, the front door slamming, her tread on the stairs. "Still awake, Lily?" she'd whisper at my and Julia's bedroom, and I'd open my eyes and follow her to her room, under her Peranakan quilt. She'd put her arm around me, and I'd inhale the scent of her, feel the white silk of her shirt against my cheek. "What story would you like?"

"One about you, when you were little," and she'd tell me about the tea parties she'd play with her teddy, Goldie, and her pet parrot, Sylvia.

"What does Mama tell you when you go to her room?" Julia had asked.

"Nothing."

"You're in there for ten minutes at least. I've been timing her." I shrugged. "Just stories."

"Why doesn't she tell me stories?"

"You wouldn't care." But I knew that wasn't true. It was because I was special. That was why I could talk Mama out of punishing Jacob and Julia, why she never punished me. I was her favorite girl, her best girl.

Someone help me, someone save me.

How long had Mama been telling me these stories? When did they start to change? I don't have answers, time runs slow and then quick for a child, and then differently again when it's forgotten and remembered.

She told me about the emerald house, her Uncle Henry's house. She'd never seen anything so beautiful, her grandmother's collection of tingkats, the sarong kebayas her cousins wore, the maids bringing Peranakan food. She told me about her mother. Slowly, the images changed, a kaleidoscope of color twisting to storm. A woman crumpling against the wall. A haze of green feathers. All the bad words. A woman flying through the windscreen. I started having nightmares. Julia would pull me into her bed. "Hold my hand, shush, shush, you're all right."

Stop. I don't want to remember.

By the time she told me the final story, I was a wreck. She called me to her bedroom. I went but I said, "Please, Mama, no more, no more."

Her voice went very flat. "You think it's so easy, 'no more, no more,' and it will stop? It doesn't stop for me. It goes round and round every day." Her finger drew circles in the air. "All you hear are stories. You'll never know what it was really like."

I begged her not to be angry. I grabbed her arm and put it around me again, but she shrugged me off. "Nothing, worthless. I thought you were better than the others, but you're not. Get up."

Did I resist or go limp? I don't remember except the feel of her hand dragging me by the collar of my pajama top, the slaughter of the words: "Nothing, worthless, whore!"

She dumped me in the hall downstairs. "Take off your clothes."

I was wearing Julia's old pajamas, the Little Mermaid on the front, the bright green trousers a tail.

"Are you deaf? Take off your clothes."

Daddy approached from the back of the living room, I called to him. He gripped the handle of the living-room door and shut it. The world opened up under me.

I felt heavy taking off my clothes, like a building had fallen on top of me, all that rubble on my arms, my legs, my toes. Julia

hurled herself against Mama over and over, Jacob cried behind
the banister, I cried for both of them when Mama opened the front
door and pushed me out.

Stop, Mama, stop.

> *I was in the shed.*
> *I was never in the shed.*
> *A spider crawled up the rim of the window, the deck chair*
> *shoved against my shoulder. I bit down on my knee. Someone will*
> *come for me, someone will come, by the time I've finished counting*
> *they will come.*
> *Five, four, three, two, one.*
> *Five, four, three, two, one.*

THERE ARE SO many unanswered questions. What happened afterward? Why did I forgot the stories she told me as a child? Why have I remembered them now? The questions carve ravines into me that I can't cross, no matter how much I try, and yet tremoring deeper, and then deeper still, is something so obscure it can't be framed into a question because it's not a question but a person. Mother. Child. Victim. Murderer. A woman who's loved me and destroyed me, as I've loved and destroyed her.

Petals fall on me like snow. Let them fall. Let them fall.

THERE'S BEAUTY TO falling off the edge. Certain things become brighter; others fade in lavish lengths of time. The rhododendrons of the bush I sleep under are snow white, with a flush of green at their throats. Others are trumpet shaped and speckled inside, near invisible hairs growing on their stems. People disappear into the background— they're too busy for me, unobservable over long periods, rushing across my vision, talking into their headsets, training for marathons, although I like watching the park gardeners tending the circular flower beds, and wondering, dreamy children no parent can hurry.

I am prepared for this. Living with Mama, while ruining me for normal life, has granted me certain talents. I'm rarely hungry, accustomed to interrupted, half meals, and not picky after spoilt juice—I eat leftover picnic lunches without recoiling from the taste. The winding branches of rhododendrons cover me like hands, flowers color my waking. I'm frightened of nothing but myself.

In the public toilet mirror, I watch myself disappear. The makeup has long rubbed off; my face is covered in a thin sheen of grease, and there are petals in my hair. I run my tongue along my teeth, the enamel furred and rough. In one ear, there is the diamond stud Mama gave me for my sixteenth birthday, but its matching earring is gone.

On the slope down to Greenwich, I tap on the shoulder of a woman. She shrinks back—is it my uncovered eyes or the dirt under my fingernails? Her friend, taller, with dyed red hair, steps forward. She asks me what I want.

"What's the date?"

"Thirty-first August," she says, her aggression fading.

The last day of August, my second day in the park, but in those forty-eight hours, I've achieved a kind of suicide. The girl turns to walk away. She is wearing exactly the same sweatshirt as the one Jacob gave me, the familiar university insignia emblazoned over the breast. I sink to my knees.

I've been everywhere now, each bench under the horse chestnut trees, the bandstand, the Rose Garden, although there are areas in the park I will not visit—the orchard, the east lookout point, the Royal Observatory Garden; they belong to another girl and a man. But the Astronomers' Garden tempts me.

I want to relive how I saw it then, but as it opens before me, I know that's impossible. It isn't raining. The sky isn't gray but a cloudless blue, and there are too many people—tourists with enormous cameras around their necks, school children in purple jumpers. The image in my mind has shifted from the reality of it, so overlaid with myth and meaning, I might never see it as I once did.

I wander through anyway, drifting past telescopes and sundials, reading the signs. All these astronomers competing to tell the time by the sun, the moon, the stars, when time is the very thing lost to me. The sun warms my face. I close my eyes and wish myself back to a garden silver with rain, where a man says, "You've got me, I'm watching."

"Lily?"

I won't open my eyes. I will listen to his voice in my head.

"Lily."

I blink. It's him. I reach out and touch his arm. His skin is so warm.

He holds his hand over my fingers. His hands are shaking.

"I've been looking for you, for days. Are you hurt?" I flinch under his gaze, but he doesn't care, searching my clothes, my face for clues. He winces at the rip over my knee. "I've been calling you again and again. And then I asked Chrissy, and she said you'd run away."

He was too close, much too close. What if he'd got my address and witnessed my run for the shed, my naked back, the knobs of my spine, my hair undone like an animal? If he could step away from me in The Polar Explorer House, what would he do if he'd seen me like that? "I don't want to see you."

But he catches my arm. "Don't, Lily."

"Everything all right?" A man detaches himself from his girlfriend and straightens up behind Lewis, his silver necklace catching the sun. I know the type, macho, eager to prove, and I laugh because it's a joke, right? That I need rescuing from Lewis is insane.

When Lewis doesn't release me, the man rolls his sleeves up.

He's going to deck you, I think, but Lewis surprises me. He doesn't let go of my arm but stretches his other hand out to stay the man and says in a voice like splintering ice: "Please."

The man steps back, reclaims his girlfriend. "Is she OK?' he asks.

"She will be," says Lewis. "She's going to be. Come on, let's go."

I shake my head. I'm so tired then, I want to go back to my rhodo-dendron bush and sleep.

"Listen to me, Lily, I know what it looks like when a teenager falls off the edge. I thought something was wrong at the engagement party. I saw your mother pouring out that champagne and you running away. Why else do you think I gave you my number?"

The past reconfigures itself right before my eyes. I've understood nothing.

"I'm not perfect," he says, his voice catching. "But I'm not going to hurt you, I promised you that. You trusted me once on the heath. Trust me now."

He reaches out his hand to me, the same hand that reached out four weeks ago on the hottest day of the year.

I take it.

34 / HANDS

HE DOESN'T SAY ANYTHING WHEN we get to The Polar Explorer House. He sits me on the sofa and disappears. I listen to him padding from one place to another, the kettle boiling, the water gushing, and then he shows me upstairs to a full bath, tea balanced on the edge. It's the most beautiful bathroom I've ever seen, sparkling taps, walls tiled with bright, white hexagons. I take off my clothes and lie on the floor, imagining paths up to the ceiling. When I'm older, I'll have a bathroom just like this and I'll do exactly what I'm doing now, lie naked, admiring hexagons.

No, not naked, never naked.

I tear down a towel from the rack and wrap it around myself. Then I lie back down.

When Lewis finds me, he says my name three different ways—mumbles it, shouts it over the percussion of his palm on the door, and then, after he breaks the lock, as if he's exhaling, as if his heart is breaking. I imagine him glancing at the bath, the clean water, the untouched mug, and then following a trail from my toes to the edge of my towel, but I don't really know, I'm staring at the walls.

"Lily? Can you hear me?"

His breath is on my face.

"I'm calling a doctor."

I'm frightened he'll leave, but he stays in the bathroom, heaping more towels over me in case I get cold, having conversations I can't follow except through single, snatched words—*emergency, park, shock.*

He talks to me while we wait, mostly about the orchard—the bumper crop of tomatoes, the caterpillars on the radishes, the ribbed skins of the squashes and marrows. My mind, porous to Lewis, fills with pumpkins, their flat teardrop seeds, their slippery orange fibers.

The doctor who comes doesn't need him to open the front door—she has her own keys. It's Saskia. She's dressed in jeans and a cream T-shirt, her chestnut hair pulled back into a ponytail. Lewis explains she's an A&E doctor, but she doesn't acknowledge him, she's appraising me from the doorway all the way until she's close. She asks me to sit up, I've forgotten how. She asks me questions—*are you in pain, has anyone hurt you, does this hurt, does this*—but I don't know what she's talking about. When? Now doesn't matter, nor what happened a few days ago. Find the child in the shed.

She takes my blood pressure, her eyes drifting down my peeling arms. The roar of my blood astounds me with a strength I don't feel. She asks me when I last ate. I shrug. She takes out her stethoscope. The metal circle, the taut gray of the diaphragm approaching my chest ignites something in me, and suddenly, I know how to get up, how to crawl away. I haul myself up on the side of the bath, pound my feet against the tiles until I'm flat against the wall.

She puts the stethoscope down. *Has anyone touched you in a way you didn't want to be touched?*

I start crying.

Lewis tells me it's all right, everything's going to be all right.

Outside, they whisper, and then return together, Saskia behind Lewis, Lewis on the edge of the bath. His eyes on me are unbelievably sad. "Listen, Lily, if something's happened to you that you want to report, or you think you might want to report, we can take you to a specialist center. They're very good there, they can take a statement, run medical checks. Is that something you want to do? We can go with you. You won't be alone."

I shake my head. Lewis glances at Saskia; he thinks I should go, but Saskia takes a step toward me. "You're not going to do anything you don't want to, Lily, do you hear me? That isn't going to happen anymore." It's the first hint of her anger. She crouches down in front of me. "You're afraid of being naked, aren't you? That's why you can't wash."

I cover my face with my hands.

"How about you keep the towel on and wash underneath? That way, the towel stays on."

She's kind, why didn't I realize she's kind? She reminds me of Francie—observant, considered, practical. I nod. She fetches a facecloth. "We'll wait for you outside," she says, as Lewis slips out.

"Stay?" It's the first word I say to her. "Please."

She closes the door behind her and fills the basin, dipping a facecloth in, holding it out to me. I struggle to follow her instructions—*lift your arm, the left one, that's it, now the right*—she has to repeat herself over and over because it's so hard to understand her, as though I'm listening underwater, as though I've been in an accident and can only hear sirens. She turns away when I reach under the towel.

When my body's clean, she asks if I want her to wash my hair. I say "yes." She sits me on a stool, lifts my hair into the basin. I close my eyes.

I think of hands. One used his to tear my clothes from me, another to make me clean. God, let me think of these people, only these.

35 / SWEATSHIRT

HOW DO YOU COME BACK to yourself when you're not there? It happens quietly, slowly, like sunlight stealing under the curtains. I start to notice things. The ocher of the guest room I'm staying in that deepens in the sunlight. A sculptural lamp over a mirrored dressing table. A bookcase illuminated with spotlights. Lewis keeps apologizing for the room, but I don't know why—it's perfect. Nothing reminds me of home, no unfinished floorboards, no ceramics, no teddies.

Sleep is strange and fitful, the honey walls melding into the Flower Garden, the shed, a bedroom in the emerald house, Goldie's fur. If I scream, one, sometimes both, will materialize. They let me sleep as much as I want in the first few days, and then gently start waking me up for mealtimes, a game of Spit, a walk around the room until I'm awake at normal hours, though still not out of bed.

Saskia is living with Lewis at The Polar Explorer House, but her hours at hospital are odd, her schedule impossible to follow. Lewis is a constant. He's stopped going to the orchard, pretending he needs to prepare for lectures, although he's just worried about leaving me alone. He works at the dressing table, testing his tutorial questions on me: *who am I, what is consciousness, am I the same person I was in the past?* He says I'm helping, but I know what he's doing. He's calling me back. Each thought he pulls from my sluggish mind, each word on the tip of my tongue bids me away from the mute girl in his bathroom.

That isn't his only strategy. He remembers the book I was reading, *The Wonders of Language,* and borrows it from his university library, together with other books: *Historical Linguistics; An Introduction to*

Language; *Linguistics as Cognitive Science*. The words, the concepts flow into me. Slowly, my edges start to sharpen.

In the evenings, one of them cooks, Boy Scout food when it's Lewis—fish fingers and chips, sausages and peas—more put-together meals when it's Saskia—sea bass, tuna salad, pasta with roasted vegetables. Some evenings, we watch prerecorded episodes of *University Challenge* on the small guest-room television, but my attention is too frayed to form answers before the buzzer. Instead, I observe them, the strain in his neck when he rages against the contestants, the quiet way she responds to the science questions. Other nights, Saskia regales us with stories from the ward—a ninety-year-old man who accidentally took too much blood thinner, a ruptured appendix, an absconding patient. Listening to her reminds me a little of Daddy. When that happens, I pretend to need the toilet and press my forehead against the hexagons.

There are still moments when I shut down. When the animal in me that has learned only danger, flies away.

Can I be sure that other people's sensations are like mine?

I pull the covers over my head.

They invite me to the supermarket, to the farmer's market, on an expedition to find a new armchair. I shake my head. I can only hold myself together between these sunny walls. But while I refuse to go out, I can't refuse the gifts they bring back—a purple cauliflower, two types of ferns, doughnuts from a pop-up stall outside Saskia's hospital. One day, Lewis hauls a plastic bag onto the bed. The contents are separated into three brown paper bags, a scented mango in one, some greengages in another. What's in the final bag makes my hands tremble. "Do you know what these are?"

Lewis is collecting up my breakfast things. He glances up. "No idea, just thought they looked interesting."

My heart beats very fast. "They're mangosteens." I take one out. It's the size of a mandarin, with a mottled purple skin, four succulent leaves at the stalk.

Lewis puts the tray down and comes up to the bed. "How do you eat them?"

I turn the fruit on its side, squashing it between my palms. The thick rind bursts open to reveal six snow-white segments, and then I'm in Tiong Bahru market with Mama last year, picking up a golden starfruit, a handful of longan, watching Mama in her element—testing the firmness of the fruit, squabbling over a few cents. At the bus stop, she opened a mangosteen and held it out to me. I shook my head, the color of the skin unfamiliar, a dusty aubergine. "Be brave, you'll like it." I did—the crisp, sweet taste filling my mouth.

Am I allowed to miss her? She's the only person who'd feel the same about this fruit in a London farmer's market.

You're nothing.

You're worthless.

Whore.

Take off her clothes.

Lewis asks me if I'm going to finish the fruit. I drop it into the bin.

SIX DAYS AFTER I arrive at The Polar Explorer House, I decide to go downstairs. Perhaps it's the gifts that remind me of the outside world, the Sicilian purple cauliflower, the Indonesian mangosteens, or maybe it's as simple as not wanting to miss the last day of summer. I can hear a lawnmower on the heath. I push back the curtains. The sky is a cloudless azure.

Saskia doesn't blink at me being out of bed. "Coming down for lunch?"

I nod. She offers me her arm as I go down, the gleaming white of the stairwell disorientating after living in yellow.

She releases me when we get to the kitchen, gestures to the barstool next to the island. "Lewis is making onion soup. You can help if you feel up to it."

Brown papery skin slides off his fingers, the onion a bright globe in his hands. He glances at the recipe on his phone. "I need four cloves of garlic thinly sliced. Could you do that?" He nods at the shopping on the kitchen floor. "Just bought some."

I search the bag closest to me. Under the bulb of garlic, there's new clothes—an anorak, two packets of black cotton knickers, T-shirts, leggings.

Saskia stops pulling dry laundry out of the tumble dryer. "I picked those up for you. I hope they fit."

I smooth out the packaging.

"I bought you a few things when you first came, but I thought you could do with some more." She pauses, and I know something is coming. "You didn't come with any underwear."

My fingers throng my waistband. I'm wearing supermarket knickers and a pair of Lewis's pajama bottoms.

Lewis puts down his knife. "Lily, what happened?"

The lawnmower is still humming outside, the sun streams through the window. The world is carrying on even though the three of us are absolutely still.

I go back upstairs.

WE DON'T TALK about what happened, but it circles around in my head hundreds of times, an endless laundry cycle.

The next day, I see the clothes.

Saskia is in the guest room, the laundry basket tucked under her arm. She sets it on the dresser. I get up to put them away. I want to do more around the house. She smiles.

They're in the lowest drawer, the three pieces of clothing I wore when I arrived—a sweatshirt, sweatpants, a T-shirt. I pull out the sweatshirt. My voice is shaky. "This isn't mine."

She frowns. "It's definitely what you came in."

"It's not mine."

"I don't understand."

I stare at the clothes.

"Let me get Lewis."

I lay the sweatshirt over the dresser. It's black, with a Star Wars logo, the yellow words faded, the right toggle is chewed, and I know why. Jacob chewed it when he got nervous. The sweatpants are his too, an old school pair. I unfold the T-shirt like the secret it is. It's Julia's, gray with a purple stain from when she spilled black currant squash on it. When they come, I tell them: "It happened to all of us."

Lewis's hand is on the doorframe. "I'm not following."

I pull the toggle taut. "We were all thrown out naked."

He holds his breath. "What?"

My breathing is shallow. "I'll tell you, but I want you to make me a promise. After I finish, don't say anything, I can't bear it. Just leave and shut the door."

They nod.

I tell them about Goldie and the fire and the rape. I tell them what I realized in the Flower Garden, how the flashbacks are the bedtime stories that Mama told me long ago. I tell them that Daddy threw me out naked, that I knew to go to the shed and where to find the clothes. "But they're not mine. They're Jacob and Julia's. Which means, even though I don't remember Mama doing it, she must have thrown them out too. My brother and sister put them there because they knew she'd do that to them."

I wait for the click of the door. Lewis and Saskia keep their word, as I knew they would. But on the other side of the door, I hear Saskia crying.

36 / LETTER

AFTER THAT, THE FLOODGATES OPEN. It's all we talk about at mealtimes, during the day, in the evenings where once we watched *University Challenge*. Lewis and Saskia are hesitant, anxious of my fragility, but I persuade them that it helps, like dissecting a word, finding its constituent parts, its hidden meaning.

"How did you know I was missing?" I ask Lewis, putting down *The Wonders of Language*.

He looks up from his laptop, rubs his eyes. "After you left that night, I called and called."

"I know," I say, flushed at the memory of my hand on his chest, but he isn't thinking about that. He bites his lip. "I told myself it was fine, your phone was on at least. But when it started going straight to voicemail, I panicked. I visited Chrissy."

I prop myself higher up against the pillows. "Did you see Julia?"

"No. But Chrissy told me you'd run away, and the family was frantic."

Frantic? How long did Mama and Daddy leave it until they raised the alarm? Not until morning, I bet. Not less than the time they left me when I was a child.

"I searched the park after that. All the places we'd been. The time I found you was actually the fourth time I'd tried the Astronomers' Garden."

"I'm sorry."

Lewis shuts his laptop and fixes me a navy stare. "Don't say sorry. I should've found you earlier, searched harder. I couldn't decide—should I stay in one place for longer or hit as many locations as quickly as possible? Saskia thought I was cracking up."

Guilt is liquid, poured out by the person to whom it belongs, taken up by someone entirely different. "Lewis, none of this is your fault."

He slumps in his chair. "There were moments when I could've intervened—at the party, when I saw you asleep on the bench, when you told me about the flashbacks . . . the violence in them . . . I should've asked you what was going on. I should've pushed harder."

"If you'd pushed any harder, I would've shattered."

Mama is a constant topic of conversation—did she stay with Aunt Liling after the fire, how much of her behavior is driven by her past, how much is she responsible for? And then, the most frightening question of all: "Did she kill her father?"

We're eating dinner in the guest room, but this evening I've flung the windows open. Lewis and Saskia exchange a glance, they're on the lookout for signs of progress. I wish I could give them that, but all I want is the balmy dusk on my skin, the final shafts of sunset. It's not just me. The neighbors to the right are having a BBQ, and the smell of burgers sizzling on the grill and charred corncobs wafts up over the salad Saskia's prepared.

"It would explain the intricacy of the lies she told, her complete reinvention of her father," says Lewis, taking a sip of water. Neither of them drinks or even talks about drinking. They've agreed long before I arrived that this is an alcohol-free house.

"That's not definitive, though," says Saskia. "The lies could equally be a product of the abuse. Your mother never told you she actually killed him."

"It's implied though, isn't it? She told me about wanting to do it with the lighter." Below us, children have been excused and are racing up and down the garden, shrieking in delight when some imaginary finish line is crossed.

"Does it matter?" She offers me another helping of salad. I decline. "She was raped, probably more than once. So what if she killed him? He deserved it."

Lewis clears his throat. "That's pretty flippant for a doctor."

She puts down the salad bowl. "And that's pretty bold for a philosopher who's never once had to examine a child-abuse case. Do you know there's a special dye we use in sexual assault to improve the visibility of lacerations? It's called toluidine blue. The last time I used it was on a two-year-old boy who was abducted for nine hours and then dumped on a motorway." Her hands make a faltering gesture. "So please don't lecture me on what I should or shouldn't be flippant about. I'm not flippant about a child who's been raped. That's evil beyond anything a child can do. Even murder."

The sky has deepened to a cloudless cobalt. "And after that?" says Lewis gently.

"After what?" she speaks, as if to her plate.

"After the child becomes an adult, and she has a child, is she responsible for what she does then? For forcing her children out of the house naked? How much of a pass does May get?"

Saskia doesn't respond. Even in theory, Mama is divisive.

SASKIA ASKS ME in that quiet, practical way of hers, for permission to look into some of the questions I had—why I'd forgotten, why I'd suddenly remembered. She took seriously the vow she'd made me in the bathroom—I wouldn't have to do anything I didn't want to, "and that includes accepting my help." Of course, I accepted. She worried that it was too soon, that I might be upset, that I might be disappointed if she didn't find anything for weeks.

It didn't take her weeks. It took her one day. She came straight in from work and sat next to me on a picnic blanket. Lewis had lured me into the garden, and I'd agreed to stay for a bit on one condition—no deck chairs.

"I've had a chat with a colleague from psych." She reaches out and squeezes my hand. "What you experienced, memory loss, is completely normal. It's a symptom of trauma. There's a study of young girls interviewed in a hospital right after they've been admitted for sexual abuse, and then interviewed twenty years later. One third didn't recall the abuse."

Lewis, weeding in the beds, pulls off his gardening gloves and sits down.

"I wanted to show you something." She takes a printout from her bag. It looks like a pencil outline of a brain on graph paper on which ink has been splashed. Julia would enjoy the art of this. "It's a scan of a brain in trauma. Gray or dark is blood flow or neural activity. But see how these parts are white? When a person is traumatized, certain parts of the brain are disconnected." She points to two blanked-out sections near the front. "This part gives you a sense of time, and the thalamus here integrates sensations into autobiographical memory. You can see that there's no activity there."

"So, during a traumatic event, the brain doesn't store memories like it normally would?" I ask.

"Exactly. Forgetting is normal. It's called traumatic amnesia."

"And remembering?" I imagine dark swells of ink inside the outline of my brain. "If my brain didn't store what happened in a normal way, how have I remembered?"

"Generally, recall is triggered by something that matches with an element of the trauma. With the first flashback, was there something that jolted your memory? A phrase? An object?"

Mama and I were making Peranakan tarts. We were looking out over the garden, I hate the garden, mostly because of the oubliette . . . *oublier*, *oblitare*, "to forget," it's there, in the very nickname I gave it, folded in its etymology. I've always known that I've forgotten. "The shed."

"I guess that's why so much of your memory returned when you were actually in the shed."

I smooth down the corners of the scan, trace the blanked-out whites. The forgetting was instinctive, an inbuilt obliterating mechanism. *Obliteratus*, *obliterare*, "to cause to disappear." "My body protected me."

Lewis finally speaks. "It stepped in when no one else would."

I HEAR HER before I see her—the creak of the low iron gate, the doorbell. Lewis opens the door. There are raised voices before he slams it shut. He bounds up the stairs. "It's your sister."

I've called her to me, staring at that stain on her T-shirt, the empty spaces of brain scans, the obverse of prayer, and she has answered.

Lewis's cheeks are flushed. "Do you want to see her? Because I'm very happy to tell her to go away." He's bristling. He shoves his hands into his pockets as if, otherwise, he might punch her, and then I know she's said something to him, used that clean, flay of the knife.

I put down *The Wonders of Language*, meet Saskia and Lewis's eyes. "Do you think I shouldn't?" The three of us have gone round and round about what I don't know, what I can't remember. How often were Jacob and Julia thrown out? How old was I when it happened to me? Did anyone come? Guesswork, speculation, grasping at the fragments, still no closer.

He sighs. "I'll let her in."

Saskia looks up from her laptop—she is writing a paper on broad spectrum antibiotics to treat severe sepsis. "Do you want to speak to her in private? We can go."

"Please, stay," I say. The memory of me saying those same words in the bathroom when I first arrived passes between us. She grasps my hand.

Julia flings open the door. She's in full battle gear—high-waisted jeans and a cropped T-shirt that shows off her painfully narrow midriff, her eyes rimmed with kohl. She hurtles toward the bed and flings her arms around me. She's crying so hard, her words slur into one another. "Has he hurt you? Are you hurt?"

"I'm fine, Jules."

Her brown eyes pierce mine. Even through her tears, she's weighing every movement for lies, truth. She pushes my head this way and that and then she flings the covers back and runs her hands down my arms and legs.

I shrink back.

Saskia stands up from the desk.

Julia turns and screams, "Don't come any closer, bitch—I'm talking to my sister!"

"Are you serious?" snarls Lewis.

Julia points a ruby-nailed finger at me. "What's wrong with her? Why is she in bed in the middle of the afternoon? What have you done to her? Have you fucked her?"

"Stop it, stop." I close my hands on hers. "They're my friends. They're helping me."

Julia's eyes are still fixed on him. "With what?"

"With Mama."

That gets her attention. She holds my face between her hands. "I will help you with Mama, not them. Don't know who the fuck she is, but he's dangerous, a complete psycho. Did you know he was a beggar? Just lived on the streets after his father killed himself. He's insane. Just like his father."

I don't need to look at Lewis. I can sift the truth from the lies, I know who he is. "What did she say?" I whisper.

She peels her hands from my face. Her nose is dripping. She rubs it briskly against her sleeve. "She said you ran away. She called the police. I had to go with her to fill out a missing person's report."

"Did she say anything else?"

She is silent.

But the truth, once unthinkable to say, has been spoken so often between these sunny walls, it slips out easily. "She threw me outside naked. I went to the shed."

Julia grasps the base of her throat, like she's feeling for a noose. She steals a glance at Saskia. "Let's not talk about this here."

"I want to talk about it here." I climb out of bed. My legs are unsteady. I pull open the dresser, hold out her T-shirt. "Is this yours?"

Julia takes it from me as though she's in a trance. I watch her register the color, the stain on the front. "What's this doing here?"

"It was in the shed."

She lowers it onto the bed, puts her hand softly on the stain and turns it over. Her voice sounds very distant. "You need to come home now. Mama knows you're here."

"Is that why you've come, to take her back?" says Saskia. "She doesn't have to go anywhere she doesn't want to."

Julia looks slowly from Saskia, to Lewis, to me—a look that takes in everything between us. She draws me slowly to her and says, very clearly, "Listen to me, Lil. People like them don't love us like they love normal people. They love us like broken things. Do you understand?"

"I'm not broken. I'm getting better."

"You'll never be better. We're all like Mama."

"That's a lie," Lewis says.

Julia pulls out an envelope from her handbag, lays it on the T-shirt and leaves.

Nobody moves. This is new to them, although it is familiar to me, the preciousness of time before everything explodes.

Saskia, the bravest of us, moves first, stepping forward and breaking the seal. Inside is a single sheaf of paper. Halfway through reading it, she holds it away from her, afraid of it touching her. When she finishes, she hands it over without looking at me. It's a photocopy of a letter on lined paper in my handwriting:

Dear Faculty of Philosophy,
I write with respect to one of your lecturers, Mr. Lewis Quinn.
This summer, Lewis struck up a conversation with me at an

engagement party, offering to tutor me. I agreed and we started meeting in Greenwich Park and at his house in Blackheath. I had just turned eighteen.

We met up three to four times a week. Lewis encouraged me to tell him intimate details of my life, and he told me about his life too—his troubled childhood, his broken home, his period of homelessness. Looking back, I think he was grooming me, fostering a relationship quickly that felt deep and profound.

Our relationship took a different turn a few weeks ago. He kissed me as soon as I walked through the doorway, he pulled down my jeans. I told him to stop a number of times, but he wouldn't.

I've been deeply scarred by this. I'm afraid of leaving the house. I worry that what he did will affect me for the rest of my life.

I'm in the process of reporting this to the police, but I wanted to let you know the situation, as he will soon return to teaching, for the sake of your students.

Please contact me if you have any questions.

Lily Clarke

No, no, no, the letter is in my school pad of paper, I never even tore it out.

Lewis takes it. I watch it devastate his face. "Did your sister write this? Or your mother? Whose handwriting is this?" He squeezes his temples between his fingers. His eyes are obsidian. "Tell me it wasn't you."

Once, I'd have thought nothing of lying. But not anymore. "I can't."

He grimaces.

"It's not true, is it?" Saskia wrings the envelope as if it's cloth. "Tell me it isn't true."

He staggers away from her, collapses into a chair, a windup doll wound down. "The fact that you could even ask . . ."

He lifts his head only to regard her with the wreckage of his eyes. Saskia's hand flies to her mouth.

"It's not true!" I shout. "I made it up! I was angry he had a girlfriend. I just wrote it to make myself feel better."

Saskia blinks at me uncomprehendingly. "You used what Lewis told you to make yourself feel better?"

"I didn't think anyone would read it."

Lewis's head is between his knees. "It's happening to me, what happened to my father, it's happening to me."

Saskia is immediately by his side, her hand on his back. "Listen to me, listen. It's not happening to you. It's a mistake, a teenage mistake. Everything is fine. If anyone sends it to the university, Lily will just deny it."

Lewis smirks, the first time I've seen him ugly with her. "Do you know what it's like out there, what the climate is like for this kind of thing? Even you believed it, just for a second." His laughter is terrible. "There's an old Jewish teaching about how rumor is like a feather pillow split open to the wind. You can never get back all the feathers."

Images flash before me—playing Spit with him in the library, an orchard raised with dandelion stars, Saskia washing my hair—they can't amount to this, I won't let them. I take the T-shirt, pull the sweatshirt and sweatpants from the dresser. "I'll get the letter back. I'll fix this."

Lewis catches my sleeve, and I feel, in the material between his thumb and forefinger, what I've done to him, the shape of my harm—ragged breath, lungs that aren't filling with air. *Say it*, I think, *I deserve it, say you're nothing, you're worthless, Mama's girl, Mama's doll.*

But he doesn't.

He speaks only to save me. "It's a trap. This is what she wants. She's dangerous."

I take his hand briefly. *So is this. So is this.*

THE SKY IS mauve and opaque with clouds, the rain coming down in sheets. Through the water, my house looks unreal, a mirage of a doll's house, every light on—the living room, the dining room, Jacob and Julia's bedroom, Mama's. Only the attic is dark.

My mind is clear, I know what I have to do. I wish there was another way but there isn't, and it is strange and beautiful that this is the only course. I don't knock on the front door. I go to the side gate. It isn't locked, I push it open, the deluge of rain concealing the sound of the hinge.

The shed still frightens me, the overhanging ivy, the grimy window, but I don't run. I let the images detonate in my head—the spider, *Take off your clothes, five, four, three, two, one*, feel my heart explode. *I know, I know. It's not a secret anymore.*

I slide open the bolt and step in. It's quiet inside, like it's been waiting for me. I'm still as my eyes pick out the shapes, and then I take everything out—the deck chairs, the shears, Daddy's gardening tools, the rucksack that held my brother and sister's clothing. Shed emptied, I walk its length—three steps long, two steps deep, the measure of my fear no bigger than that.

A hand reaches in and touches my shoulder. "You're back."

37 / BAD FRUIT

S IT THE RAIN OR being away that makes Mama seem so much smaller? She's holding one of Daddy's forensic pathology journals over her head, but she's completely soaked—rain runs down her face, over her wrists, into her sleeves. Part of me is anxious that she's out here in this weather. I shove my fists deep into the anorak Saskia bought me to resist fetching her an umbrella.

Mama glances at the contents of the emptied shed without a hint of recognition. "Doesn't matter about this. Come inside."

I follow her numbly. Like the front, the house is lit up at the back, the warm light of the kitchen spilling out into the garden. Mama opens the patio door and goes into the living room.

Nothing has changed in the past two weeks. The Peranakan urn is still there, to the side of the sofa, Daddy's journals are stacked into towers, the low coffee table stretches out before me. Daddy gets up from the easy chair, holds me awkwardly against his chest. "There you are," he says.

Jacob throws his laptop off his knees, takes in my mismatched eyes before flinging his arms around me. "Lil." He hugs me for a very long time, until Mama pulls us apart. "Let her see Julia."

It's the kitchen that shows my absence most starkly. The *tingkats*, once jewel bright, are covered by a layer of dust, and the table is a mess of ingredients: a rolling pin, a slumped bag of flour, an unwashed chopping board, a bowl of meat mixture. A pan of dumplings spits oil on the stove, and there's a distinct smell under the frying that I cannot place. It's the fruit bowl. A cantaloupe is rotting, its gray-green skin mottled with mold. I walk my fingers over it, ease it up. Underneath, the clementines are white and furred, the bananas are black. Why haven't Mama and Daddy noticed? Not thrown out bad fruit?

Julia doesn't look at me as she pushes past. Gone is the heavy eye makeup, the clothes that cling to her body. An apron is tied around her waist and under that, she wears black leggings and a pink long-sleeved T-shirt. Her forehead gleams with sweat as she scoops dumplings onto a plate, and then I know what I'm looking at. It's the new me, the new Mama's girl, Mama's doll.

Mama leads me out of the kitchen and into the dining room. It's set for a celebration, exactly how I would do it, the table laid with cut crystal glasses and Peranakan china, and not for the first time, I think how efficient Mama's machinations are, how effective—the issue of a threat, the preparations for my return. Did she watch my arrival from her bedroom window?

She's wearing clothes I don't recognize—a mulberry crew-neck jumper and a matching pencil skirt, nothing bosomy, nothing over-flowing, and I remember her buying all that new lingerie for Daddy; she's done the same for me. I sit down and take off my anorak. She pulls up a dining chair and pats my arm. "Don't mind your sister," she whispers. Then, slowly, she looks straight into my *ang moh gui,* white devil, eyes. "You know I love you, right? Forget about what happened, it's over." She strokes my hair back from my face. "We don't need to talk about it. We can be a family again."

Inside, all the walls crumble. This is all I wanted, for my mother to look at me without flinching, without wanting me to be anything else. Her eyes fill with tears. The shed, her father, the car accident vanish. She pulls me into her arms. I'm speechless with the relief her body offers.

Julia comes in with the dumplings and we take our usual seats—Mama at the head with Daddy on her left, me on her right, Julia next to me, and Jacob next to Daddy. Mama reaches out and squeezes my hand. "Tonight, we're celebrating Lily's return. Lily"—she looks at me and smiles—"we're so glad you're home."

She asks for my plate. I give it to her.

"What are you wearing?" Julia grabs my shoulder so we're facing each other. The second she sees the Star Wars logo of Jacob's sweatshirt, she flings me from her and backs up against the window.

Mama's voice flips to sharp. "Stop your theatrics, Julia." She scans my clothes, but she doesn't understand, glancing at Daddy, who doesn't know either. But Jacob's hand flies over his mouth, and it's terrifying witnessing his transformation to child. He draws his knees to his chin and whimpers.

"Stop it, both of you, let's eat," Mama says, filling my plate.

I could have gone along with her. I could have eaten dinner at that beautifully laid table, drunk deeply the easy draught of our collective amnesia. But Jacob curled up in the dining chair and Julia plastered against the window superimpose themselves on a different image, three children, no four, Jacob, Julia, me, and Mama, clutching our meager belongings: sweatshirt; T-shirt; rucksack; teddy. How can we stand being near one another?

We don't.

We hide under duvets.

We humiliate.

We hit and poison and cut each other to shreds.

"Lily, take your plate."

"No."

"What?"

Julia gasps.

"You can't throw me outside naked and then expect me to have dinner. Because I haven't forgotten. I remember."

"Stop! He can't hear this right now!" Julia drags Jacob into a standing position, shoving him around the end of the table and out of the dining room. She shuts him out and slumps against the wall.

"What are you talking about?" asks Daddy, rubbing the side of his temples. He pushes his chair back and stands up, leaning on his palms, his head reaching across the table. "Is that what you've been doing at that man's house? Brewing some made-up story about how awful we are, lying about what we're like?" He points a trembling finger at me.

"I didn't make up an awful story." My voice is quiet. "I told him what happened."

He jerks away as if I've slapped him. "I didn't do anything to you."

"You took my clothes off, Daddy. First my jumper, then my bra, then my knickers."

He stares at Julia and Mama for support, for validation, for some idea of how to respond, but Mama is staring into a vanishing point in the distance, and Julia is making a soft, keening noise. So he lies. "I didn't do that."

"You did. That's how I found these." I tug at Jacob's sweatshirt, lift it up to show him Julia's T-shirt.

"I don't know what that is.'

"This is Jacob's sweatshirt. This is Julia's T-shirt. They were so scared Mama would throw them out of the house naked, they put clothes in the shed. It happened to me too when I was little, I remembered when you threw me out."

He blinks at me, and I recall the living-room door closing, the extinction of my hope. "Where were you when Mama threw us out? Were you on your easy chair?" I glance at it in the living room behind us. Enormous in my memory, it's so small now, another distortion of time and truth. "It's right beside the patio doors. Did you hear us calling for you in the garden? Did you hear us run to the shed?"

"I don't know what you're talking about." Flecks of spit land on my cheek. "Do you know what she's talking about?" He addresses Mama, but she's retreated so far into herself, she's rocking. "Look what you've done to your mother. To your sister."

"I haven't done this," I say. "I was a child."

How extraordinary that it ends like this, him coming for me instead of Mama. Except, in a way, it is the Mama in him, Mama and my grandfather and whoever showed my grandfather how to hit and hurt, and the person before that. Their violence is contaminating, and my father—with his profound understanding of disease—can't recognize when he's been infected. Or perhaps it wasn't from Mama at all. Perhaps it was in him all along, until seeing what he's allowed to happen awoke a long, dark anger. *Violentia, violentus, violare,* I am so lonely in this moment.

He slaps me just like he'd punch, with his whole body, his shoulder, his arm, straight across the jaw. The sound of it reverberating through my skull is so loud I can't hear anything except one long crack. My head hangs off my neck like a broken doll.

"You're nothing, worthless!"

Nothing, worthless, whore.

"Tell your mother and your sister you're a liar!"

Julia hauls herself up.

"Tell them!"

She thrusts herself between us. "Stop it, Daddy!"

"Tell them, or you can pack your things and get out!"

"For God's sake, she's lying, she made it all up!"

"I need her to say it." He raises his hand again.

"Just tell him what he wants to hear!" she screams.

I turn my aching face to look at my father so he can truly see me, the tears rolling down my cheeks, the tender swell of my jaw, and close my hand over his raised palm. "I haven't made it up. This"—I shake his hand—"this is what you're really like. And you don't even know why." He stares at my hand over his. "I'll get my things."

38 / COLLATERAL DAUGHTER

THE ATTIC IS A WRECK. Clothes have been wrenched off hangers, bags and shoes spilling out like the aftermath of a fox raid. Photos, drawings, my old school books are scattered over the rug, and my folders are open. I feel sick crossing the attic. At the hole, the floorboards are up.

The damage is the most savage here. The fairy lights have been ripped off the walls, the bulbs smashed. There are no towers of books anymore, just rubble; *Anne of Green Gables* and my etymology dictionary look as though they've been bludgeoned. The drift glass in my beach jar has been pulverized to smithereens. Sheets of paper have been torn out of my writing pad, that's how Mama found the letter about Lewis. The worst is Lewis's ivy. Each beautiful length has been ripped into smaller pieces, the leaves rotting, the stems already brown.

There is no time, though, to linger over this exhibition of rage. Anything could happen, Daddy could start again, Mama, even Julia. My jaw throbs. I drag over an old bag, drop in my etymology dictionary and a handful of drift glass. The jar of Japanese paper stars is smashed at the bottom, leaking promise into the shadows. Jacob said the number of stars meant different things: 99 meant limitless love; 129 meant everlasting love; 365 meant a whole year of blessings. He'd bought me 365. I fumble for them between shards.

"I'll start on your clothes." It's Julia. Her eyes are raw, her nose is running a little. "If you just take those things, you'll have nothing to wear."

"Did you do this?"

She shakes her head. "Mama. She found it two days after you disappeared." She stifles a sob. "I've been in there though, every day . . . just to be close to you."

"It's true, isn't it?" I step out of the hole, pick my way over the debris. "She threw us all out."

She takes a jumper from the wardrobe, plucks a bobble off, drops it with a flick. "Why does it matter?"

I think of the letter I wrote, the powder I poured into Mama's juice, scissors snipping through fur, the rage coursing through my veins. I need to trace its source, understand its tributaries, or it will burst again. "It matters to me. Help me, Jules. There are things I don't remember, blanks in my memory . . . I'm trying to piece them together, but I can't. How did I know there were clothes in the shed? How many times did it happen to you? How many times did it happen to me?"

She keeps plucking at the material, the movement mesmeric. "Do you know when Jay's freaking out, this is all he talks about? What Mama did to us?"

I drop to the rug in front of her, our knees touching. "No. Why didn't you tell me?"

"Jay always wanted to, but I made him promise." Her voice shakes. "Sometimes I wanted to. But most of the time, I thought it was better you didn't remember. You wouldn't be like us, rotting from the inside."

She stares at the corner of the dressing table. "Do you remember Mama throwing Jacob and me out?"

"I remember she left you and Jacob in the hall downstairs, and I would creep down to get you—"

"—No, that's not right," she interrupts loudly. She composes herself and traces the outline of the jumper. "She never threw us into the hall. She threw us outside. You would calm her down, and then, when she was asleep, you'd let us back in through the kitchen."

"I don't remember."

She reaches out and strokes my cheek. "I think it's because you were very small—six, maybe seven. You were letting us into the house a long time before it happened to you. The shed was your idea, you know. You said Mama couldn't see it from the back."

"See if he's there."

I climbed on top of the radiator in my bedroom, opened the window and stuck my head out. Mama held me around the waist in case I fell. I scanned the garden. Jay's pale arm waved at me in the moonlight. I nodded to Mama.

She went to her bedroom and shut the door. In her mind, they were safe.

But that was one night.

The next, she insisted that Julia and Jacob leave her property. She paced the windows of the back rooms searching for them in the garden, running a torch along the flower beds, each bush, every tree. If she saw them, she'd march downstairs and pull them from their hiding place, through the side passage and into the front garden. They'd curl under the fir tree or crouch behind the hedge. They were more afraid of Mama than the cold.

The next day, when Mama and Daddy went out, I searched for a better hiding place, one that Mama couldn't see out of any window.

"The shed is too far to the left," I speak slowly, as if recounting a dream. "You can only see it from the bathroom if you push your head out of the frosted window above the toilet, and no one was small enough to crawl into the alcove—"

"—except you. You remember?" She presses her knuckles against her mouth. "She only threw you out once, but something was wrong ages before then. She kept calling you to her bedroom, telling you these stories, but there was something off about them because you started having nightmares. Do you remember me telling you to say 'no' to her, 'no more stories'?"

I shake my head.

"The night she threw you out, we tried to get to you. We knew she locked all the doors and took the keys upstairs with her—you told us that—but she'd never done it to you before. We didn't know where you'd hidden the spare key."

Under the sink. Behind the dishwasher tablets.

"I threw clothes down for you, and blankets," her voice is straining, pushing through tears, "but in the morning, they were still on the patio. When we finally got to you, you wouldn't speak. Mama was so frightened, she wanted to take you to hospital, but Daddy refused. He forged a signature, got you signed off for weeks. Mama nursed you back to health."

"I thought I had a virus."

"You had a breakdown. Do you remember begging me to tell Mama I didn't want to share a room with you anymore?"

I shake my head.

"You wanted to move to the attic. You couldn't stay in our room, couldn't look out the window without screaming." Her left hand grasps her right hand. "After you moved out, you disappeared. You didn't seem real, not like how you used to be. I'd call you names to get you to react, but you'd just look through me."

Mama's girl. Mama's doll.

"She changed too. She didn't tell you any more stories. I guess she was worried about breaking you again. And you . . . you did everything she said, anything she wanted. You started making her spoilt juice and tidying her room, all those Peranakan snacks. You let her change how you looked—your hair first, and then when you started secondary school, the contacts, the makeup. Eight years old and suddenly you were completely different."

Eight.

I want to shrink into myself, vanish into a single speck where there's no hurt, no pain, no past. I press my forehead to the rug.

She holds me, shushing me, telling me I'm going to be all right, but it's such a slip of a whisper against my loud, faltering heart, and then I don't know if it's my fault when she starts saying dangerous, deranged things, or if this was part of her plan all along. "Listen to me, listen, I know you're upset right now, but you knowing, you remembering is a good thing. It solves our problem."

"What?"

"Mama called me after you disappeared. She's going to pay for art school, my rent, everything, she didn't even ask what the art was about, and that was just when you'd run away. Don't you see? We've got her where we want her. We can use this."

I untangle myself from her. "Use what?"

"What happened to us." Her face is impassive. "What's the point in truth unless you can use it?" She smooths down her pink T-shirt. "The things she did to us are like bank deposits, and now it's time to withdraw. We can have anything we want, study what we want. Just stay. She won't forget what you think about her, but now you're in control, you have the power."

"That's your solution? To stay? For money?"

She shakes her head, as if I don't understand. "It's not just the money. What you said is protection; she can never hurt us again. Any time she tries to piss us off, sublet our flats, refuse to pay our tuition fees, we just mention the shed." Her eyes are luminous. "Don't you see? This is our inheritance."

I'm so frightened then—for Mama, for Julia, for her children and my own—the relentless line of mothers and daughters hurting and inflicting hurt. If I stay, will I have to lie to my own daughter, ashamed of what I've endured and what I've done? Our inheritance isn't a degree or rent. It's a fire. It's a shed.

I circle my fingers around her wrist, push back her sleeve. Her arm is shockingly light, just bone, no flesh. "Once you blackmail her into giving you what you want, will you stop starving yourself?"

She is ferocious, flinging me away. "You don't understand anything!"

A memory comes to me, the dance of moonlight on Julia's back as Mama pushed her outside, the sound she made, like a dying animal. I know the topography of her rage, the contours of her vengeance. But it isn't a place to stay. I hold my hand out to her, as she once did in this attic, as Lewis has done, in an astronomer's garden. "Come with me."

She doesn't move.

I put my arms around her. For throwing clothes down for me, for standing between me and my father's fist, for trying to find me in the soil and broken glass, I will always try to free her from this. But she won't come today.

39 / FIRE AND SHED

WITHOUT MAMA'S TEDDIES, HER BUBBLEGUM pink room is empty and strange, as if she's in the process of moving out. Clothes litter the floor, the silk embroidered quilt is bunched at the end of the bed, and the window seat is patchy in places where the color has leached out.

Mama is sitting on her bed, her heel bouncing to the side, murmuring to a teddy. It's not hers—I made sure of that—it's one of Jacob's, Brody the Beaver, its tail trailing between her fingers. There was no discernment in her choice, just desperation. He'd sat on Jacob's bookcase by the door—it was the first teddy she could find. She looks up when I come in. "You're going?"

I drop my bag down at the doorway and nod.

She wipes her eyes. "I can talk to Daddy if you want. He'll let you stay."

I shake my head.

"Because you remember."

It takes everything in me not to cry.

She combs through Brody's fur with her fingers. "I worried you might. Sometimes, I was glad I told you, even though you'd forgotten. Other times," she pulls Brody's tail hard, "I knew I shouldn't have." She hits the side of her head with her palm. "Nothing, stupid, worthless mother. Too much for a little girl, even as a story. I spent years trying to correct it, telling you different things about my childhood, taking you to nice places in Singapore."

My heart is in my throat. "You lied for me?"

She moistens her thumb and starts shining Brody's nose. "I thought if I told you better stories, nicer stories, they'd cancel out the bad things, just blot them out." She makes a rubbing motion with her hands. "Sometimes I came close. So many times, I wanted to take you to see my aunt—"

"—Wait a minute, your aunt? She's still alive?"

Mama bites her lower lip, nods. "That's why I go to Singapore every year, to visit her. She's very old, in her nineties, but she only has me to give her the best, the best care, the best nursing home, and still, it is nothing compared to what she did for me."

The money, that's where all Mama's money has gone. That's the reason she fights Daddy and Julia, why she's lied to get us scholarships. The kindest part of my mother has been hidden under so many lies.

". . . and I tried once to tell you the truth. I told you about the car accident."

Sweat prickles my back, I'm struggling to keep everything straight. "You told me your parents died in a car accident, but only your mother died."

She waves at me impatiently. "Because that's what it felt like when she died, that we'd all died, we'd all been in a car accident. After that, everything changed. There was no one to protect me anymore, no one to lock me in my bedroom, nothing to stop him coming, coming, coming." And then I realize lying doesn't mean to Mama what it does to other people. In the shocking place of open shut, open shut, lies are comfort, lies are salvation, lies are truth.

I sit on the bed, reach out for her. She stares at my fingertips, and then slowly, lays Brody down and clutches them. She knows what's coming. She knows what I'm going to ask. "Did you kill him, Mama?"

She is very still. "I was eight," she whispers.

"I know you were a child," I say gently. "But did you?"

She bites her lip. "Do you think I did?"

"I wouldn't blame you. What he did was very wrong—"

"—Was it? I'm not so sure. Maybe at that exact moment, it was, but if you take my life as a whole, I think I deserved it. A punishment upfront for the things I'd do. That makes sense, doesn't it?"

I can't keep hold of what she's talking about—killing her father, how she treated us, her looping, merciless logic. I want to pin her down, stop her chimeric flutters of confession, but what would be the point? Her refusal to answer that one question betrays her answer to larger ones—will she let me know her or just a version of her? I let go of her hand.

She grabs it, suddenly a child. "Wait, you're really going? Please don't leave. Everything is fine now, don't you see? I've learned my lesson—I won't be bad anymore. The dress, the car accident, nothing like that will happen again. I won't move to Oxford; it was a silly idea. I'll be good, I promise, even with Charlie and Francie. Here's the letter you wrote. That's what you came for, isn't it? Take it, I didn't make any copies." She hands it to me from under her pillow. It is rumpled a little and smells of her, that warm hint of sandalwood, and I look back on the two of us together—in this bedroom after she came back from Santorini, in Liberty's, in the silence after the car accident. In any of those moments, I'd have jumped at this offer. But now, when my mother puts everything on the table, it isn't enough. I don't want good behavior. I want a real me, a real her. I shake her gently off.

Her gaze falls over Jacob's sweatshirt. "I don't know what those clothes are."

"Let's not, Mama." I stand up to go.

"I really don't know."

"Mama," I say slowly, "you stripped me naked. Just like your father did to your mother, just like you did to Julia and Jacob. You did it again a few weeks ago."

"That wasn't me, that was your father!"

"Because you told him to!"

She shuts her eyes and shakes her head frantically. "After I told you about the fire, you got sick, you couldn't go to school, that's all, I swear. I didn't do anything to you. Maybe you misremembered. Your memory . . . it isn't the greatest."

I've spent so long trying to remember. Now I want to forget this moment when my mother turns the obliteration she inflicted against me. But I don't think I ever will. Her eyes shut in denial, the dark spray of her lashes are vulcanized in my memory.

The urge to punish is pure and beautiful. I could let it all burn. I could tell Mama how I counted down again and again, waiting for someone to come. I could drag Julia and Jacob in here and damn her with their testimony. I could tell her that Jonathan isn't interested in her, show her Daddy's porn collection. I could pour out every last horrifying secret.

But I know better. I've seen a way out of wounded and wounding, in a sunny yellow room where a man I've betrayed tries to save me, and now, I feel for it as I would a lost thing.

I draw my mother to me. Her skin against my skin, I find her ear. "It's not happening to you again, Mama, do you know that? Daddy and the poems and Francie—it's not going to lead to the car accident, what your father did, the fire."

She gasps against me.

"And those words you always said to us—'you're nothing, you're worthless, you're a whore'—he said them to you, didn't he, and you believed him. You believed all the bad things."

Her heart stammers.

"Listen to me, Mama, it's very important. I love you, I love you, I love you."

I pick up my bag and leave.

EPILOGUE

I N THE ROYAL OBSERVATORY, THERE is a dome that houses the Great Equatorial Telescope. Around the dome, there's a balcony. From here, you can see the entrance to the Astronomers' Garden where Lewis found me, and the avenue of horse chestnuts, where on a storm-felled trunk, I showed Lewis my arm. Still, there's no view where everything is visible. The rhododendron bush I slept under and the orchard, once filled with dandelion seeds, are masked by sycamores.

He's coming. I watch him cross the courtyard, that familiar gait, the tilt of his cap. He stops at the remains of a telescope, turns and raises his hand, half a wave, half a salute. I wave back and wait for him to climb the stairs.

After I left Mama, I walked straight to The Polar Explorer House. I hadn't seen it for so long from the outside—the small, manicured front garden, the rose light from the library, my room above it on the first floor. The curtains were drawn, but the yellow walls were dark, no one was there. I took it in before pushing the letter through the door. I meant to slip away—to Jacob's perhaps, or even Francie's, lay low until I'd formed a plan—but Lewis opened the door. His eyes were wet. "Come here," he said, and then I was engulfed by his arms, by Saskia's, drawn again into the civilizing circle of love.

"Finished the reading list?" he asks, a little breathless.

"All done."

Lewis has only pushed me about a single thing since I left Mama— what I'm going to study at Oxford. "You're not even interested in Law," he'd said. "You can't just drift into the next stage of your life, I won't let you," and Saskia backed him up. I told them drifting was exactly what I wanted. I wasn't going to Oxford anyway; I had no money for the fees. I reminded them of Saskia's promise: no one would make me do anything I didn't want to. Saskia said she wasn't making me—she was just expressing her opinion. Lewis said he was absolutely making me, and he didn't care because he hadn't promised. He was tricky that way.

That wasn't the only thing he'd been tricky about. *The Wonders of Language* and the other books he took out during my yellow convalescence were on Oxford University's Linguistics reading list, and he wrangled me an interview with an old friend of his, Dr. Dan Watson, an associate professor in psycholinguistics. I wasn't sure. The subject was fascinating, but the thought of traveling to Oxford, interviewing, applying for emergency grants, seemed overwhelming when all I wanted was to play out the rest of the holiday in a sunny yellow room.

"Speak to him," Lewis insisted. "Just see if you like it."

He drove me to the interview himself. Dr. Watson was nothing like Lewis, but his questions lit a spark of possibility.

What is language?

How do you think the English language has changed over time?

What happens to language when the brain is damaged?

So now I'm going to study linguistics. Tomorrow, I leave for Oxford.

I gather up my books. Around us, sycamore seeds fall, the autumn air alive with delicate wings.

He takes a thermos flask from his rucksack, pours hot tea into the cap, and hands it to me. "What was in the package this morning?"

There've been a lot of boxes addressed to The Polar Explorer House since I left. The smell of them panicked me at first; Lewis had to carry them into the dining room. But a few weekends ago, Saskia and I went in together, slowly knifing through the tape, pulling out the contents. Dangerous items were mixed with safe ones—bottles of black hair dye lumped in with my clothes, a pair of Peranakan cookbooks with my old textbooks. My rucksack, still full of emergency things, brought on a crushing feeling that didn't leave me for days.

There was no malice in it. The boxes were packed by Jacob; he'd slipped in photos of the boys and notes asking me how I was, although he never called. None of them did.

Two boxes weren't from him. Inside was everything I didn't take from the hole, including three pots of ivy, all the books Daddy bought me, a little cloth bag holding the missing origami stars, and something wound tightly in bubble wrap—a beach jar. I poured it out on the library rug. It's my drift glass salvaged from Mama's violence, the poison bottle fragment, and the frosted marble, but also things from Julia's collection. She has made up the jar with her prized shells.

"Just this." I hold out my hand. The package that came today wasn't from my brother or sister. It was a brown envelope, hastily taped. Inside was a red, silk jewelry pouch. My heart caught, watching the jade tumble into my palm; I could send it back, I could stuff it in the rucksack with all the things I can't bear to see. But two voices came to me: a small child's and a mother's: "Like clouded grape." "Like the sky before a monsoon." I put it on.

He takes a swallow from the flask. "I have something for you too." He reaches into his pocket and pulls out the playing cards. They're soft and battered; we've played them almost every day, sometimes with Saskia, sometimes with Noah next door.

"Thank you."

He stands up and brushes down his trousers. Later, we'll have a small celebration, Saskia, Lewis, and me at The Polar Explorer House, not in the guest room with trays on our laps, but in the dining room, emptied of my boxes.

"Ready to go?"

I've been watching the park transform, the new honey of the trees, the infinite browns of fallen things shrinking into the earth. Now, I take it in for the last time, all the seen and unseen gardens, the places where I've forgotten and remembered, loved, and been torn apart. I've been waiting for this moment, day after day. I've been gathering strength for it.

"Ready."

ACKNOWLEDGMENTS

To Hellie, who believed in this novel when it was just a handful of words, your passion, confidence, and fabulous style have carried this novel through to the finish line. Thank you for being such an extraordinary agent, person, friend. Thanks also to Marya. Style icon, wordsmith, earliest US fan, your astute editorial eye and profound understanding have been utterly indispensable. Thanks too to Ma'suma, Emma, Mackenzie, and the whole team at Janklow & Nesbit for your creativity and support.

To Alessandra at Astra House, thank you for being so fierce and dedicated and thoughtful. I've loved every minute of speaking with and learning from you. To Charlotte at HarperFiction, your brilliant vision, insight, and talent have made this book the best it could possibly be. I couldn't have done it without you. Thanks also to Rola, Tiffany, Rachael, Susanna, Emma, and the rest of the teams at Astra House and HarperFiction who've championed this book.

Thank you to my Faber Academy 2016 writing group, especially Ania, Charlotte, Alice, Natalie, Emily, Laura, and Chris. Early readers, critics, friends, what a precious gift it is to talk to you every week about people who don't exist. And then there's the inimitable Sarah. Without you, how would I have known what this story is about?

Thank you to my wonderful family and friends, especially my parents, who filled our house with stories and gave me confidence to pursue my dreams; Dave and Sue for their wise counsel; Hannah G and Hannah C for answering obscure medical questions; Frances for talking with me for the last twenty-five years about the books we've read and then the book I wrote; my American family for going on journeys with me into Peranakan culture and family history; and the Philip-Howells and the Makonis for making me brave.

To a very special person, Patrick. My ally before I knew I needed one, you taught me about God and love, forgiveness and redemption, and in doing that, changed the course of my life. Thank you for being the real Lewis.

To my father. Way-maker, promise-keeper, light in the darkness, only you know how long this has been on the cards. Thank you for calling me out beyond the shore.

Finally, to my husband. This book is more than my words on a page. It is your pea and bacon risotto, homemade iced lattes, your track changes, the hours you spend listening to me read out passages, the games you play with our daughter—in short, everything you do every day. This book wouldn't be here without you. I wouldn't be here without you. And to my daughter, who teaches me how to be freer and happier than I ever thought possible, I live, breathe, and write for you.

PHOTO BY GEMMA DAY

ABOUT THE AUTHOR

Ella King is a Singaporean novelist who lives in London. A graduate of Faber Academy's novel-writing program, she is an award-winning writer who has worked as a corporate lawyer and for anti–human trafficking and domestic violence prevention charities.